Praise for the work of Graciela Limón:

"Graciela Limón's first novel, *In Search of Bernabé*, leaves the reader with that special hunger that can be created only by a newly discovered writer. Ms. Limón's prose is self-assured and engrossing . . . deserves a large audience."
—*The New York Times Book Review* on *In Search of Bernabé*

"Downright hypnotic."
—*The Washington Post Book World* on *Song of the Hummingbird*

"[This novel] should awaken the conscience and compassion that drive and haunt every reader . . . a novel of absolute stylistic and social integrity."
—*Booklist* on *The Memories of Ana Calderón*

"She is as sure-footed in the terrain of compelling storytelling as her indigenous Mexican Indian characters are in their huaraches."
—*The Washington Post Book World* on *Erased Faces*

"In her absorbing, politically engaged work, Limón restores dignity and identity to the inhabitants of a violent land, sketching tangled landscapes where faces are constantly erased and swept into anonymity."
—*Publishers Weekly* on *Erased Faces*

"Murder. Madness. Execution. Suicide . . . all of the plot workings of an exciting modern take on Euripides' Medea and the Mexican legend of La Llorona . . . Limón hits all of the right notes."
—*Los Angeles Times* on *Left Alive*

"A sort of *Canterbury Tales* . . . as [immigrant travelers] come together in sorrow, tragedy and impending death. Thoughtful reading for anyone who wants socially engaged fiction."
—*Library Journal* on *The River Flows North*

THE MADNESS OF
Mamá Carlota

Graciela Limón

Arte Público Press
Houston, Texas

The Madness of Mamá Carlota is made possible through a grant from the City of Houston through the Houston Arts Alliance.

Recovering the past, creating the future

Arte Público Press
University of Houston
4902 Gulf Fwy, Bldg 19, Rm 100
Houston, Texas 77204-2004

Cover design by Pilar Espino
Cover painting Charlotte of Belgium by Albert Graefle, c.1860.

Limón, Graciela
    The Madness of Mamá Carlota: A Novel / by Graciela Limón.
    p. cm.
    ISBN 978-1-55885-742-1 (alk. paper)
    1. Sisters—Fiction. 2. Carlota, Empress, consort of Maximilian, Emperor of Mexico, 1840-1927—Fiction. 3. Mexico—History—European intervention, 1861-1867—Fiction. 4. Mexico—Social life and customs—19th century—Fiction. I. Title.
    PS3562.I464M33 2012
    813'.54—dc23
                                    2012003146
                                    CIP

♾ The paper used in this publication meets the requirements of the American National Standard for Information Sciences—Permanence of Paper for Printed Library Materials, ANSI Z39.48-1984.

12 13 14 15 16 17 18   10 9 8 7 6 5 4 3 2 1

In loving memory of

Polly Robles
(1932-2011)

AND

Katie Grace
(1922-2009)

This novel is dedicated to the memory of two extraordinary women who have played a powerful role in my life:

To Polly, whose strength, sense of humor and honesty inspired me to be true to myself. It was Polly who had just enough time to read the first draft of this novel before passing, and who took the time, despite her ordeal, to call me to say that she was sorry that the read was over. She wanted more of it.

To Katie, whose great faith carried me through a period of crisis and profound sadness by helping me to see that everything in life has its purpose.

Here's to both of you remarkable women who will be forever in my life.

Acknowledgments

I'm particularly grateful to the administrators of Bouchout Castle, site of the sixty year confinement of Empress Carlota. The castle, located outside of Brussels, Belgium, is not open to the public but it was Dr. Paul Borremans, docent, who in the Spring of 2010 took time to give me a two-hour tour of its interior. His knowledge of every chamber and anteroom of the castle, including its medieval dungeon, was a huge inspiration. So, too, were his lively and detailed descriptions that brought to life the old empress as she must have walked the corridors of Bouchout Castle during her captivity. For his generosity and time, I sincerely thank Dr. Borremans.

I'm indebted to Diana González Lemere, my dear cousin, whose encouragement led to our trip to Brussels that didn't end until we reached Bouchout Castle.

I'm profoundly grateful for the insightful editing on the part of Dr. Nicolás Kanellos, as well as that of Dr. Gabriela Baeza Ventura. Their views and ideas put the right touch on my novel.

I'm also indebted to all my friends and family whose interest and enthusiasm for the novel was a true inspiration. I thank all of you most sincerely.

"Qué lejos estoy del suelo donde he nacido . . . "
(Canción Mixteca)

It was a turbulent time. Mexico was again hit with war, shifting governments, foreign invasion and indescribable upheaval. It was a time of huge displacement and mass migrations of Mexico's countless tribes: Zapotecas, Mixtecas, Cora, Chontal—too many to here list.

The tale you are about to read tells of the sad and tragic Empress Carlota of Mexico who, although here fictionalized, was real. On the other hand, her beloved companions, the Chontal sisters, are my creation; every part of them is a figment of my imagination.

Although the sisters first appear in and around the sacred grounds of Cholula, they consider themselves part of the Chontal tribe, a people traditionally rooted in Oaxaca. Why do they appear so far from their land, as if out of nowhere? No one knows. Perhaps they are among the many of Mexico's indigenous children that are displaced and lost. What is known is, like Mexico itself, the sisters become an integral part of Empress Carlota's life, destined to walk by her side as her companions, even as that path leads them to a foreign world where, as the Mixteca song tells, they find themselves far from the land of their birth.

MEXICO

1852-1866

Chapter One

*I*t began when *i* was a child, when the dream first came to me, when I dreamed of the empire. Then, on a certain day, the dream came to my doorstep. It took shape when I was a young woman at Miramar Castle where Maximilian and I resided. On that day the Mexican emissaries approached him to become emperor of their country. They came dressed in fine clothing. They were stiff, awkward men obviously made nervous by surroundings none of them had ever experienced. Nonetheless, it was they who came to offer us a Mexican empire.

In the beginning I feared the undertaking because I had doubts about Maximilian's weak nature, but then it became clear to me that those emissaries had brought the seduction of the empire for my taking, not his, that I had come face-to-face with my destiny. I was incapable of turning my back on that allure. What my enemies later called inordinate ambition was instead my dream, one that turned dark and fatal. It was the force that drove me. It was the aspiration that compelled me to embrace the illusory Mexican throne.

Chapter Two

CHOLULA, MEXICO, 1852

Hacienda La Perla

The three little girls had no recollection of when they were indentured as maids into the hacienda known as La Perla. They didn't remember their mother or father, nor did they have memory of brothers or sisters to call family. Their first recollections began when they were already living on that hacienda, where they were attached first to one maid and then to another so they might learn the ways of a good servant.

La Perla was so vast that its master needed a week each year to make his way on horseback to the far corners of his holdings of herds of cattle and horses. His spread covered hundreds of hectares of rich land that stretched from the fringes of Cholula, westward to Tochimilco. From there, any traveler would need to head north all the way to La Posta, and then south to Teyuca, just to cover the surface of the hacienda. Only when that traveler approached el Gran Teocalli did he know that he had gone beyond la Perla's holdings and that he had wandered onto the sacred ground of Cholula.

La Perla had been in the possession of the Acuña family since the days of the Spanish Viceroyalty, and, during those centuries, patriarch followed patriarch, each man passing ownership of the hacienda onto the oldest son. That son had, among other demanding duties, the obligation to provide the clan with sons to inherit the family patrimony. Like other families, the Acuñas had their secrets, but those were closely guarded; hardly anyone was aware of them. Publicly, the family fabricated an image of themselves as upstanding and honorable. The men were portrayed as brave, hardworking, faithful to their wives and staunchly Catholic. At least, that was their public image. The women were beautiful, modest, also faithful to their husbands, models for their daughters and always fertile. This also was the public image.

Above all, the family took particular pride in their purebred ancestry, one that the family tree traced directly to Spanish nobility. Over time it became an unwritten family rule that its children intermarry only with those of equally pure lineage in order to preserve those roots. There were, however, whispers that somewhere along the line there must have been at least one ancestor of Indian blood. This was evident, judging from the brown complexions of some of the Acuña children born over the years. But as expected, it was forbidden to repeat this rumor, although the kitchen help liked gossiping about it, regardless of that rule.

When this story begins, the head of that hacienda was Don Melchor Acuña, master of countless peons dedicated to tending fields and livestock. Inside the rambling buildings, almost as many maids served the patriarch's large family that consisted of his wife Doña Herminia, and numerous sons and daughters. As the years passed, the Acuña children grew, married and lived on the hacienda along with wives, husbands, children and personal servants.

It was at this hacienda that, on a certain day, three little girls of the Chontal people appeared at the kitchen door. No one saw them approach nor knew how they had made their way from the neighboring hacienda or village. They had come from out of nowhere. When one of the scullery maids on her way back from fetching water saw them, she was startled because she had not seen them on her way out of the kitchen. The young woman looked around, trying to locate how the girls had come, but when she didn't see signs of a cart or a wagon that might have brought them, she stared down at the girls. Taking her time, she examined them from head to foot and saw that they were dressed like the Chontal women of distant lands. The little things were pretty and, she guessed, they must have been around ten years old.

"¡Hola, niñas!"

"¡Hola!"

The maid was taken by the way the girls spoke, with one voice it seemed. They didn't say more than hello, but only smiled, not seeming afraid or nervous. At a loss for what to say or do, the maid made a move to go around them into the kitchen, but then stopped to look at them again.

"What are your names?"

"I'm Tila." The girl that appeared to be the oldest was the first to respond. Then the middle one piped in, "My name's Chelo, and this is my little sister Lula." With that introduction, the girls made a little curtsey and smiled again.

"Where are you from?"

"From over there." The girls pointed toward Cholula, but said no more about a village or mother or father or even brothers or sisters.

"What are you looking for?"

"A place to live." Tila spoke for her sisters, who didn't lose their smiles or their calm way.

Not knowing what to do next, the maid opened the narrow door that led into the kitchen, and the girls followed her in. Once inside they waited for their eyes to get used to the dim light, and then they were able to make out servants at work over large stoves and cutting boards. Everyone was busy stirring, mixing, chopping, peeling and patting dough into balls that would soon be slapped on the grill for the evening dinner's supply of tortillas.

The girls had never seen such a large kitchen with so many people busy at work, and they stood very still, all the time staring. The maid went to the woman in charge, exchanged a few words with her, causing her to look over at the girls. She wrinkled her brow and interrupted what she was doing. She seemed at a loss as to what to do or say, but in a few moments she wiped her hands on her apron, came over to the girls and stooped lower to look each one closely in the face.

"Niñas, are you good workers?"

"Sí, señora."

"Bien. Go to that table over there. Eat and drink what is brought to you, and when I'm finished here, I'll tell you what to do."

The woman watched the girls make their way through the traffic that was at its pitch just before the family's dinner, and she was pleased by how they walked with small, dainty steps. She liked their smiles and bright eyes, and something told her that they would be a fine addition to her cooking staff. There would be no need to ask permission of Don Melchor; after all, the girls would require only a place to sleep and food to eat and that was hardly a reason to ask permission right away. Maybe that would come later on.

This was how the Chontal sisters became part of La Perla, where they would remain for ten years, all the time moving upward in that intricate world of peones and patrones. The first thing the cook did was to take the girls under her guidance, making sure that the room attached to the kitchen, usually used for grain storage, was cleared and that a bed wide enough for the three to sleep on was moved in. Along with the bed, a small stand with a basin and a jug were brought in as well. The maid could see, from the expression on the sisters' faces, they were happy and grateful.

In the beginning, the sisters washed dishes and pots, and then, when the cook saw how quickly and efficiently they worked, she brought them closer to her, where they learned her recipes. When they mastered those, the sisters were moved up to places inside the household, prime places where they tended to the needs of the family members. No matter where they worked, the sisters were liked and even sought after.

As time passed, the girls became acquainted with the house, as well as with the servants that worked alongside them. For their part, they grew to like what they did, so much so that people knew where to find them because the sisters always sang while at work, their voices blending so beautifully that most people called them las canarias. When it was their task to dust furniture and polish the long, tiled corridors, they sang with even more spirit because they enjoyed walking through the house's vaulted chambers, patios and terraces that led to fountains and birdcages; some small, but some big enough for them to fit into. Whenever the girls interrupted a song, it was to gaze at the faded portrait of a long-ago Acuña patriarch, side by side with one or two viceroys. The sisters found those wigged and bearded men so imposing that it almost took away their breath.

One year followed the other as the sisters developed into beautiful Chontal women. Tila grew into a thoughtful, practical young woman. Chelo was gifted with the ability to make people laugh, and Lula's talent was a beautiful singing voice. Although she was the youngest sister, Lula grew slightly taller than Tila and Chelo, but the three shared a lovely complexion, almond-shaped eyes and lustrous black hair. Early on, the sisters' looks became so striking that young men often stopped what they were doing just to gaze at them when they happened to pass by. Naturally, there were those young indios who approached one or the other sister with warm smiles and soft words, and the girls responded happily because that was their nature. But none of those suitors was in a position to offer anything in return for marriage, so everyone understood that the time for the sisters to take that step had yet to come. Besides, who would give them away? There was not a father or even a godfather to speak up for them. In time, the sisters contented themselves to be smiled at and to smile in return.

Chapter Three

Arcides Acuña was the youngest of eight children. In all, the Acuñas were a brood of five boys and three girls. The oldest was Baltazar, the future patriarch of the family. The youngest was Arcides, who was born late in Doña Herminia's childbearing years. He was conceived when changes had begun to afflict her body; it was a period when she struggled with waves of heat that swept over her, and her menstrual cycles were fading. When she became pregnant, Doña Herminia felt a mix of surprise and joy as well as fear—she didn't know what the child would be like. But her apprehensions disappeared the moment she held the infant in her arms and she saw that Arcides would be the most beautiful of all her children.

From that instant the boy became his mother's favorite child, perhaps because the other sons had by then grown and left her to form their own families, or perhaps it was that Doña Herminia felt lonely, or even forgotten. Whatever the reason, the child brought her profound consolation and satisfaction, and she took full possession of the boy. It had been different with his older brothers, whose father had overseen their training, the same father who now seemed to have forgotten about his youngest son.

Doña Herminia didn't resent her husband neglecting Arcides, because the truth was that she welcomed the blessing of keeping the new child to herself. Arcides quickly became his mother's only joy, the center of her attention, and she coddled and pampered him, hardly ever allowing him out of her sight. In the beginning, when she breastfed the child, it was taken as natural, but when the boy grew out of infancy, when he became a toddler and then turned four and five, matters changed. Doña Herminia still allowed the child to suck her breast. People gossiped, but there was nothing to be done because not only was she the mother of the future patrón, she was also a stubborn and willful woman.

Tongues wagged for years until Doña Herminia became so fed up with the whispering that swirled beyond her bedroom door that she responded first with anger, then with furtiveness, and then she gave strict orders that no one was to enter her bedroom while she and her son were in it. But her prohibition only inflamed curiosity. Because gossip is like dampness or mold that creeps from under doorways, around hinges and even through keyholes, and because rumors will not be contained, word got out that the boy still slept with his mother, although he was older than twelve years of age. Eventually the murmuring became so loud and widespread that it soon reached the ears of Don Baltazar, now the new patrón. No one was surprised when he responded with shock and then outrage at his mother's treatment of Arcides. As soon as he became aware of what was happening, he barged into her bedroom and confronted her in a bitter face-to-face quarrel.

Baltazar shouted and raged. Doña Herminia screamed and wept. In the end Arcides was dragged away from his mother's breast, and he was forbidden to go near her. Doña Herminia secluded herself after that confrontation and abandoned herself to what others saw as morbid, unrestrained grief. She died a few months later. Her passing was dutifully marked by the required thirty days of masses, novenas and rosaries, but thereafter the maids and peons of La Perla hardly spoke of the old woman who had loved her little son too much.

With his mother's death, Don Baltazar took the reins of his brother's training, but it came too late because Doña Herminia's obsession for Arcides had rooted an irreversible corruption in him. As the boy developed into adolescence, he manifested a disdain and disrespect for others, especially for women, and nothing that Baltazar or the other brothers did or counseled took him off the pathway of self-indulgence that was rooted in him.

The worst began when Arcides was no more than fifteen, when he took to prowling neighboring villages and haciendas in search of whatever girl he thought beautiful. At first the outings happened occasionally, but as he grew older the habit became a routine that took him out every night. He had a favorite horse that people swore was a part of him. They said that the brute sensed when the boy was ready to go and in what direction they would be riding. After a while, he and the horse became a terror to the neighboring lands as what Arcides did on those prowls became widely known. Villagers openly talked about how he targeted a girl, dismounted, said flattering words to his victim and, because he was so handsome, he easily seduced her. Soon word made its way throughout those places that the Acuña son was ravishing their girls and that something had to be done.

Confronting a scion of a powerful hacienda with such an allegation was dangerous; however, it was not long before a band of outraged fathers worked up the courage to approach Don Baltazar with their complaint.

"Don Baltazar, we have a grievous issue to discuss with you." One of the villagers had volunteered to be spokesman for the group, and it was he who stepped up to the patrón.

Don Baltazar, sensing that something was wrong, went on the defensive. "Speak, but before you do, be certain that what you say is true and important and that you can prove it."

The villagers, hats in hand, flinched at those words and moved back slightly, but the spokesman didn't lose his nerve.

"Patrón, it's about your youngest brother, Don Arcides."

"What about him?"

"He has violated several of our daughters, and we demand that he be punished."

Don Baltazar was expecting a complaint about overwork, about too little grain, about bad soil, but he didn't expect what he was hearing, and it caught him off guard. After a moment's reflection, he admitted to himself that the grievance was undoubtedly true, but Arcides was his brother and Baltazar had no choice; he had to be loyal to him. Without asking for details or proof or any more talk, he shut down the discussion.

"You're lying, and you're the one that's going to be punished. If someone else has the same complaint, he, too, will be punished. Now's the time to step forward with whatever you have to say."

He waited for his words to sink in, but when no one moved, Don Baltazar signaled his peons to take the man who had faced him with the accusation, strip him and punish him in the usual manner: The peon was flogged until he lost consciousness. This was done in the presence of maids and workers standing around as witnesses. The man's punishment was meant to teach them what happens when the patrón is challenged.

Tila, Chelo and Lula stood alongside the other horrified maids and peons. Like everyone else, the sisters felt each lash almost as if it were ripping into their own flesh. Soon they found the ordeal too much, so they quietly moved away, slowly at first so as not to be noticed, and then at an open trot until they reached their room. Once inside they cried for the man who endured the lashes that should have instead landed on Arcides Acuña's back.

As for the offended fathers, they faded away without a word, never again to protest what the youngest Acuña was doing to their girls. After that, the only recourse left to those peasant families was to hide their daughters whenever the hooves of the terrifying horse echoed through village streets and other surrounding spreads. And it was from that time that Arcides Acuña became known as El Centauro.

Chapter Four

W hat happened next was inevitable, not even surprising. What was unexpected, however, was that it occurred not at night, but in plain daylight, not in a village or an empty field, but close to where the Chontal sisters worked day in and day out. Unexpected also was how little time it took for Arcides to rape Lula, the youngest of the sisters.

It happened when she went out to the shed for firewood; the predator caught a glimpse of her as she slipped into the dim hut. It took very little effort for him to slide in behind her, close the door and throw himself on top of her. Although older than Arcides by some two years, Lula was slight of build, small-boned and, more importantly, caught by surprise. As for him he had the advantage of being experienced in how to maneuver himself in such encounters.

Lula tried to scream for help, but he slapped a cupped hand over her mouth while he pulled and tore away her garments with the other hand. Lula was not altogether at his mercy, for she was strong, her hands used for wringing out wet sheets, lifting crates and chopping wood. Once she overcame the initial surprise of the attack, she put up a ferocious fight, all the time scratching and kicking Arcides until one of her knees landed on his groin, forcing him to crumple back in pain. Despite losing his breath, he recuperated almost instantly, more than ever intent on getting in between her legs.

He got what he wanted when he ripped her undergarment away and thrust a hand deep between her thighs. All the time Arcides, in lustful frenzy, scratched, slapped, twisted and bit whatever part of Lula's body he could reach. When she was finally subdued, he pulled down his trousers. It was a struggle, but when his member was free, he thrust himself into her with such force that she yelped in pain.

Lula was a virgin. When he penetrated her, his stiffened penis was like an iron nail that tore at her as it plunged in and out, causing her indescribable injury. Her whimpering only inflamed him more, urging him to lunge up and down, faster and harder, until he reached a climax. Moments afterward he calmed down but stayed on top of her, satiated and panting, waiting to regain his normal breathing. When that happened, he got to his feet, buttoned up his trousers, smoothed his rumpled shirt and then he let himself out of the shed. Lula's ordeal had not taken more than a few minutes.

When her sisters found her lying on their bed doubled over with her knees held against her chest, they knew why she had disappeared that afternoon. Without asking or probing, Tila and Chelo straightened their sister's wounded body, stripped away her soiled, tattered clothes and bathed her, all the while weeping bitterly.

In the beginning the sisters were overwhelmed with alarm and distress, but their emotions shifted to rage with the discovery of each new bruise, then indelible hatred for Arcides Acuña. When Tila and Chelo saw the wounds on Lula's thighs, belly and breasts, they ground their teeth in outrage, but even more when they saw the savage bite marks on her neck.

After tending to their sister, Tila and Chelo decided what to do. They saw it with the clarity of a vision that might have appeared right there in the dim room. They had to make Arcides Acuña suffer the same pain he had inflicted on Lula, but going to Don Baltazar with their grievance was out of the question. They had witnessed his past responses. Keeping silent was equally impossible. It was against their nature to allow such an offense to go unanswered. They had to kill Arcides Acuña but they didn't yet know how or when. Lula fell into a fitful sleep, but Tila and Chelo went sleepless that night planning their revenge.

"We must kill him." Tila was the first to put into words what her other sister was thinking.

"Yes, but how? How can we manage to even get near him? And what about after we kill him? We will be caught and punished."

"No, not if we make a plan."

Chelo had never before heard Tila speak with such calm. She wondered if Tila might be feeling the same fear as she was experiencing, but at that moment something told Chelo that her older sister had a strength that perhaps neither she nor Lula had. She made up her mind. She would follow Tila in whatever steps she took.

"Very well, Tila. Let's do it with poison. It's easy to put in his morning chocolate."

"I don't think so. It would be hard to get near his food. Besides, poison is too fast, too easy. No. Whatever we choose must hurt him and he must realize why he's dying and who's responsible."

"Well then, if not poison, we can slip into his bedroom after he's asleep and smother him with a pillow."

"Chelo, once again, it would be very difficult to get that close to him. Also, that might give him an opportunity to overcome us."

"Tila, you put too many obstacles in our way. I still say that poison is the surest way. It would also make it more difficult for the worm's family to know who did it."

At this moment Lula startled her sisters when she suddenly snapped out of her feverish sleep and lifted herself on an elbow. "With a knife! That will cause him great pain!"

A knife! Tila and Chelo looked at one another knowing that a blade, if worked skillfully, is painful and slow and effective, like disemboweling a pig. It would give Arcides time to see that it was the Chontal sisters that had taken revenge. After a few moments, Chelo spoke up.

"But once again, hermanas, killing him that way means getting close to him at an unguarded, unexpected moment. How can that happen?"

After some thought Tila nodded in agreement, but showed that she was not willing to change the plan.

"Then we must be patient and wait for that moment. It will come. Of that we must not have any doubts. And when the time comes, we will be ready."

The sisters fell silent as they pondered what those next steps meant to their lives. All the while each woman understood the gravity of her intentions.

"We will be hunted." Chelo spoke those words slowly, almost forming a question.

"Yes! Nothing will stop el patrón until he captures his brother's murderer." Tila's voice didn't betray a trace of doubt; rather she spoke with a steely conviction that made her sisters turn to look at her for assurance that she had really spoken those words.

"Our plan must include what steps we will take to escape Don Baltazar's anger." This time Chelo's voice reflected her sister's resolve.

"We cannot be afraid, hermanas." Lula's voice was strangely flat but it also carried resolve.

Tila and Chelo turned to look at their youngest sister and saw that she was not showing anxiety despite her unspeakable ordeal. Lula's sisters kept silent, but with that silence they agreed with her that fear should not intimidate them nor make them change their minds.

And that's how the plan began. From that moment on, the sisters dedicated their every thought to devising a strategy detail by detail, step-by-step. They pictured over and again where and how they would put the plan to work. Part of their strategy included conjuring unforeseen obstacles, even the unlikeliest. That way they would not be caught unprepared. They took their time, always careful to reject whatever rash thought crept into their scheming.

In the meantime, their personalities changed. Gone was the singing and laughter and joking that had been their way. Chelo and Tila shared this change, but the severest transformation was the one that invaded Lula's soul: she became gloomy and ill-tempered; she hardly spoke to anyone, not even to her sisters. Most distressing of all was that her eyes, once bright and filled with joy, now darted around with distrust.

"Our sister's spirit is losing its way. What can we do?"

"We must give her time to find peace, hermana. It will happen. We must not doubt that, and, in the meantime, we cannot let her feel that she's alone."

It was not only Tila and Chelo who felt anxiety because of their youngest sister's drifting spirit. The day came when Lula's transformation became so evident that women who toiled with the Chontal sisters quietly murmured about it, and they took it to their husbands and companions who worked the fields. Talk became widespread until it spilled out beyond the boundaries of La Perla and even to the most removed villages. Everyone concluded that the sisters had changed because the youngest Acuña had again committed the unforgivable. The women saw that Lula was behaving just like those of their daughters who had endured the same evil. The word passed from mouth to mouth that if the sisters were planning vengeance, well then, it was the right thing for them to do.

In the meantime, the sisters went on planning. Yet, one piece of their scheme eluded them, the hardest and most important part: where to track down Arcides. Everyone knew that he was cagey and secretive, that he prevented anyone from getting close to him, and this posed the greatest obstacle for the sisters. One day when the sisters were walking toward the laundry shed, having just emerged from the inner arches, arms loaded with sheets, they heard a whisper.

"¡Pssst! ¡Epa, hermanas!"

The women were about to turn in the direction of the whisper, when they heard, "No! Don't look. Just act like you're talking to one another and hearing what I have to tell you. I know that you'll be interested to know that every day Don Arcides rides out to Los Nogales. After he finishes dinner with his family, he goes out to spend the afternoon hours sleeping under the trees. He stays there until sunset, when he and his devil horse ride away for the night. He comes back late, sometimes at dawn. That's all I have to say, hermanas."

The sisters, still motionless, stared at one another. When the voice faded away, their faces snapped to look in the forbidden direction, but there was nothing except the archway and its column

with potted geraniums at the base. It didn't matter, because someone had taken the trouble to give the information they needed, and
they were grateful.

The place known as Los Nogales was a secluded spot along the
fringes of the hacienda. It was known by that name because large
walnut trees grew profusely there. They were so dense that sunlight
barely made its way through to the damp earth. It was a beautiful
spot, shrouded in shadows and lush with greenery. An arroyo
rimmed the grove and at certain times of the year it swelled, trap-
ping water into deep pools that reflected silvery images of swaying
branches and puffy clouds. Hardly anyone went to Los Nogales
because it was far away from the main flow of the hacienda's everyday comings-and-goings. Now and then, someone ventured out to
that place, but usually that didn't happen because most people
found the place too remote or too lonely, maybe even a bit scary.

There was one exception: Arcides Acuña preferred Los
Nogales because it gave him the seclusion he loved. He made it an
everyday routine to gallop out on his horse after the family's dinner hour, when everyone broke up for the siesta. Early on, Arcides
got to love the cool shade under the trees, and when the day was
excessively hot, he stripped naked and waded into the arroyo
where he floated, arms outstretched, all the time taking in the view
of treetops and patches of blue sky. Afterward, he lay under the
trees where he napped until dusk. When he awoke, he dressed,
mounted his horse and went on the hunt for what he and the beast
enjoyed.

Now the sisters were finally prepared to set their plan in
motion. The following day, after joining the other maids in the
kitchen to have a taco and a glass of fruit juice, they slipped away
and headed for Los Nogales. On the way, they retrieved the necessary knives and packed knapsacks they had hidden with food to
keep them on the road.

By the time they got to Los Nogales, the sun was beginning to
decline, which made it better for them because the grove was now
shrouded in deep shade. They had agreed that once they were close
to the trees, there would be no talking, not even one word. The sis-

ters kept to the plan, moving silently as they skirted Arcides' teth-
ered horse. Slowly, with stealth, they slid in closer and closer until
they sighted the man asleep and naked.

As planned, the women stripped off their clothes until they,
too, were naked. They folded each garment carefully by their sacks,
took hold of the knives and approached their target from behind.
On a signal from Tila, the sisters surrounded Arcides, knelt beside
him and then raised their knives high with both hands clenched on
the hilts. As if jerked by an invisible puppeteer, all at once three
blades plunged into Arcides' vulnerable belly.

When the first blows penetrated him, Arcides let out an ago-
nized groan, his eyes snapped open in terror and he raised his arms
in an attempt to defend himself. It was too late, as the next volley
of stabs came down on him, this time deep into his groin. It was
just a flash, but in that instant Arcides recognized Lula, and he
realized what was happening to him.

Except for the squishing and sucking sounds of blades on flesh,
the stabbing went on in silence until the youngest Acuña brother
was dismembered. Only then did the sisters stop the onslaught.
Their hair was matted with gore as were their faces, necks and
breasts; they were covered in blood down to their bellies and
thighs.

Struggling to catch their breath, they looked at one another for
long moments until they took hold of each other's hands and muttered prayers in their mother tongue. Then they dragged Arcides'
remains into the deepest part of the arroyo and waited until the
corpse rolled over several times and sank out of sight.

The sisters bathed carefully, helping each other wash away the
last of the detested Acuña. It took time, but they were calm and
deliberate all the while, and they were glad when the moon began
to rise above the tops of the walnut trees because they could see
everything as if it were daylight. When they were sure that the last
trace of blood had disappeared, they emerged from the water.
Then they dressed, secured their knapsacks onto their backs and
headed toward the road leading to Cholula. From there they would

go on to the city of Puebla, where rumor had it that the bishop had enlarged his mansion and was hiring maids.

On that trek, the sisters began to experience a change in the satisfaction they had experienced when they killed Arcides Acuña. During the first hours of the journey, each of them felt a strange emotion creeping up on her, one that each hesitated to divulge to the others. At one point Chelo spoke in a voice so low that she seemed to be talking to herself.

"I didn't understand until that moment how quickly a person dies. I saw that even the evil ones die from one instant to the other. There was just a little gasp and then he was gone."

Tila and Lula abruptly stopped where they were because their sister's words had cut deep. When Chelo saw that her sisters had come to a standstill, she, too, halted.

"Aren't you thinking the same thing, hermanas?"

Lula answered. Her voice sounded older, like that of a woman twice her age, and it trembled slightly.

"No, I don't feel regret, if that's what you mean. I'm glad he's dead, but I'm afraid now that we have done it."

"I didn't mean that I regret my actions. I'm only saying that I didn't understand how easy it is to die. What about you, Tila? What are you thinking? Do you regret it?"

"No, I don't regret any part of what I've done. Arcides Acuña was evil and he caused too much shame and hurt. But like you, I'm thinking about what I've done and I'm afraid of what our punishment will be if we're caught by Don Baltazar's spies."

"Do you think that it could happen?"

"I *know* that it will happen unless we make it impossible for him to discover us. It means that we will always have to be in hiding, perhaps all of our lives. This is the thought that most troubles me. Ours will be a life of always looking over our shoulder to make sure those sniffing dogs are not close. That's why we must make our way to the city and lose ourselves in the multitude."

Without another word, the sisters resumed their journey toward Puebla, walking at a slow pace, and blending in with the other migrants fleeing toward the city. News had broken that

French invaders were prowling those parts, that the city would be the safest place, so people were running for shelter. In the beginning, those travelers moved in small clusters but soon they became throngs, their huarache-clad feet pounding the earth into swirls of transparent yellow dust that rose high above them. Hidden deep in the heart of that river of refugees, the sisters felt safe despite their fear of being discovered and captured.

Chapter Five

The Battle, 1862

Cinco de Mayo

"¡Alto!"

Certain that they had been caught, the sisters dropped their knapsacks and froze, one foot in midair, about to take the next step. On the verge of daybreak, the waning night gave off little visibility, so the young women were hard-pressed to detect who had ordered them to halt. Each sister swiveled her head at the same time, first to the right of where she stood, then to the left, but impenetrable blackness prevented them from locating the voice they heard.

"¿Quién es?" It was Tila who challenged the voice, but no one answered. They waited motionless, hardly breathing and sensing the presence of someone close by. They didn't move for fear of what might happen if they disobeyed. The darkness was wrapped in silence except for the whisper of a breeze filtering through thick tree branches. Aside from that sound, nothing else disturbed the calm of the ridge overlooking the sleeping city of Puebla.

"Where are you women going?"

The face of a young soldier suddenly appeared. It happened so quickly that the sisters didn't know where he had come from. Soon they realized that he was like them, un indio, and that he was still a boy. He was armed with a machete so long that it almost matched his height. With a quick glance, the women took in the soldier's white cotton pants and shirt, and, although the oversized brim of his straw sombrero darkened his face, his eyes shone bright even in the gloom.

Chelo responded, "We're going to work in the city. We're the bishop's new maids, and we must get there before sunrise; otherwise, there's the risk that he will change his mind."

Tila and Lula gawked at her, surprised that she had so easily fabricated such a story. All the while the boy soldier stared at them with friendly eyes as he took in the rebozos covering the young women's shoulders and the long colorful skirts that told him they were from nearby Cholula. They were obviously Chontal women. He moved closer to make out their faces, and he saw that they were beautiful and so much alike that he could not distinguish one from the other. Each india wore her hair pulled back tightly in braids coiled around her head like a crown, and below that was a flat smooth forehead made beautiful by delicate eyebrows that spread out like the wings of a black heron. Their eyes were narrow slits emphasized by high cheekbones, and their mouths were wide and rimmed by thin lips.

After a few moments he whispered, "Hermanas, if you want to make it into the city on time, you must be on your way immediately. Head for Calle del Mercado without wasting a moment."

"Why that street?"

"Because it's the only one open for travelers entering the plaza. It's guarded, but all you have to do is call out my brother's name. His name is Otón. He will hear you, I promise. When he asks, say that his little brother Emiliano has sent you. That's me. Now leave this place! Run, if you can."

"Run? Why?"

"Because word has reached us that a battle will soon begin, right here on this high plain. The foreigners will soon attack us."

Tila spoke up. "¡Un momento, muchacho! How do you know a battle is going to happen?"

The young soldier made a sucking noise with his teeth, "Ay, you're wasting time! Listen to me! I know the Frenchies are coming because General Porfirio Díaz passed the word a while ago. We're going to take a stand right here in defense of Fort Loreto and fight the intruders. The battle's going to happen when the sun rises." He then pointed north toward the road coming from the city of Mexico. "We know that the attack will come from that direction."

Without another word except for muttering muchas gracias to the young man, the sisters, arm-in-arm, turned and headed toward Puebla. They didn't run, but walked briskly, all the time keeping their eyes on the eastern horizon, where a pale light told them that the sun would soon rise.

The Chontal sisters made their way to Calle del Mercado only to find it clogged with a milling crowd of agitated women and tearful children. Soon the unexpected press of bodies overwhelmed the sisters, nearly separating them. One of them tried to shout for Otón, but it was useless because the wailing and prayers of those alarmed people drowned out any one voice. When the sisters realized that they might be trapped in the tangle of bodies, they struggled to make their way beyond the swarm, but soon they realized that it was impossible. They decided to give in to the press of the crowd that was headed for shelter in the cathedral. The only thing left for them to do was to use their strength just to cling to one another.

As the first rays of the rising sun tinted the heights of the cathedral's bell towers, suddenly and without warning the first artillery blast shattered the air. It was so powerful that it shook the ground under the hysterical crowd, making most people lose their balance. As if the explosion had been an earthquake, the impact rattled windows and cracked the adobe walls of houses lining the street. A terrified howl went up from the women, and soon prayers mixed in with weeping. ¡Dios Santo! ¡Virgen Tonantzín! ¡Socorro!

Just as horrified as the multitude that pushed and pressed, Tila, Lula and Chelo yielded to the hysterical frenzy that scooped them up so that their feet no longer touched the ground, and, without knowing how it happened, they were carried up to the tower. Once there, the sisters, still clinging to one another, were smashed against a corner wall facing an open veranda. They were crying and disheveled, their faces smeared with dust and sweat, and they too joined in the praying that went on in Spanish and other tongues:

Zapoteca, Tlaxcalteca, Mixteca, Chontal. Gods were invoked, the one that inhabited the cathedral as well as the ones that dwelled on the great teocalli of Cholula and other sacred pyramids.

The sisters stayed there the rest of the day, covering their ears against the relentless artillery bombardments. Whenever those barrages momentarily broke off, the sisters plucked up courage to take quick glances down toward the fort where they believed men were slaughtering one another. What they saw was beyond what they had ever seen: hordes of warriors clashing, one side in blue and red uniforms, the other in white cotton pants and straw sombreros.

From where they stared in disbelief, the Chontal sisters saw rearing, shrieking horses, the gleam of bayonets and machetes, disabled cannons on broken wheels, bodies of men and mules shattered and entangled, muskets and artillery relentlessly spitting fire. Above the mayhem, the terrifying din of screaming men and animals cut through the billows of yellow gunpowder smoke which, at times, was so thick that nothing was visible. When those clouds broke up, it was only to again show the unceasing rampage.

The deadly battle dragged on throughout the day. As the sun was setting, there was sudden silence; the cannons had stopped their deadly booming. The sisters gawked at each other and then looked over at the other women, many huddling their children. Some had kept their eyes clamped shut, afraid to look; others would not take their hands away from their children's ears, hoping to mute the sounds of slaughter. They were all suffering from hunger, thirst and the extreme need to relieve themselves.

When silence carpeted the battlefield, the women responded as if they had been a single person. Eyes snapped wide open and then rolled from one side to the other, eyebrows lifted in disbelief; all of the women held their breath. A frantic voice then shattered the calm; it came from somewhere down on the street.

"¡Corrieron! ¡Los franceses corrieron!"

Minutes passed before the terrified women were convinced that the French had really fled. When it happened, they got to their feet, some patting different parts of their bodies and that of their children just to make sure that they were not bleeding or wounded. Others looked around, disoriented and not knowing what to do.

The sisters were just as lost but pulled themselves together when they saw one of the women get to her feet and sprint down the winding staircase toward the cathedral's front portal. Behind her, all the others followed, pushing, shoving and desperate to get out of the tower. The sisters likewise scrambled to their feet and followed the distressed women down to the front portico. Once they reached the exit, everyone flooded out, shoving, tripping and frantic to free themselves and their children.

Once outside, everyone scattered in different directions. The Chontal sisters, however, were lost, not knowing which street to take. It was too late to ask anyone, as all who had been trapped alongside them had vanished into the shadows of dusk.

Foul cannon and musket smoke pervaded the darkness and gloom. The sisters gagged and their eyes watered, obstructing their vision even more. They walked unsteadily, like blind women, clinging with their hands flat against walls, groping their way down a street until they stumbled onto a tiny plaza with a fountain sustaining a thin trickle of water. The sisters heard the water before they saw it, but that was enough. They rushed to the anticipated sound, and there they drank and splashed water on their burning eyes.

Somewhat refreshed, but still not knowing what to do next, they crouched in silence on the cobblestones, trying to get their bearings. In a few moments they heard faint sounds, like huaraches scraping on cobblestones, but the darkness was too dense to make out who was moving. Chole, Lula and Tila got to their feet and groped their way to where their ears pulled them.

"¿Quién va?"

Just as Tila asked who was there, silhouettes appeared out of the gloom. Slowly the outlines became the figures of women, their shawls tightly wrapped around heads and shoulders, each one walking behind the other in a column that followed the woman at its head.

"We're looking for our men."

The voice was mournful but evidently determined to find a missing husband, a brother, a son. Hearing those words, the sisters hurried to join the procession and arm-in-arm they descended all the way to the battlefield. Although they hadn't lost anyone, they resolved to search for Emiliano, the young soldier they met earlier.

It took only a short time for the women to reach the site of the battle where campfires were now burning. The stench of blood mixed with mud and gunpowder, as well as the dreadful sound of groaning, led them to the fringe of where countless bodies lay. Darkness shrouded the mound where the conflict had taken place, but by now the scattered campfires cast off enough light to outline prone men being helped by those who had survived the horror.

The other women disappeared into the gloom while the sisters, tripping and falling, went from one cluster of men to another in search of Emiliano. They stepped over horse carcasses and still-smoldering wagons, as well as huge chunks of debris that had fallen on bodies. The sisters' long skirts were by then matted with mud and gore, their faces streaked with sweat and their feet painfully bruised because their huaraches gave them little protection. Regardless, they pushed forward, calling out the young soldier's name.

"Emiliano! Emiliano!"

Each sister went from campfire to campfire calling out the young soldier's name. Finally, a hoarse voice muttered, *"Allá, allá."*

The sisters came together to follow the way pointed out by the voice and found Emiliano sprawled out among other bodies. He was seriously wounded, a black stain spreading on his shirt, but he was still alive and able to speak. Without uttering a word, the sisters clustered around him. Two of them took him in their arms, while the third sister disappeared into the darkness. Soon she returned from somewhere with a gourd filled with water, and when it was pressed to his lips, the boy drank greedily. After a few minutes they saw that he tried to smile. Despite the darkness and his injury, Emiliano recognized the sisters.

"¡Ganamos! ¡Mandamos a esos demonios blancos a la chingada! ¡Viva mi general Zaragoza!"

His voice was soft, but he spoke each word so distinctly and with so much energy that it convinced the sisters that he would walk away from that killing field to live to be an old man, and even to go on to be known as one of Mexico's patriots. His brief words, spoken so clearly, engraved themselves deep in the breasts of the sisters.

"We won! We sent those white demons to fucking Hell!"

Emiliano lived long enough to tell the sisters of the relentless cannon fire the French had used against the Mexicans and, despite their pleas not to talk, he used his last minutes to paint the unspeakable picture.

He recounted how his fellow defenders, all of them tribal brothers, armed with old muskets, machetes and even farm tools, had assaulted the uniformed white faces, shocking them with their howling and then cutting off their heads. He went on to murmur that, more than anything, it was the wild shrieking of the Yaqui Indians that utterly terrified the French troops because they had heard the rumor that the Yaquis were cannibals. Emiliano told how it had taken their people all day, but in the end it was the bravery of General Porfirio Díaz, himself of the Zapoteca people, that had turned the tide in their favor.

Emiliano didn't die alone but in the arms of the Chontal sisters, who held on to him as if holding him would keep him alive. Chelo grasped his head in her lap while Lula wrapped her arms around his shoulders and Tila cradled his legs and feet in her hands. At that moment they loved him, although they knew nothing about him except that he had helped them find their way that early dawn and that he was like them, un indio.

The sisters went out to forage for whatever scraps they could use for Emiliano's burial: a few planks here, ripped leather reins from under the carcass of a dead horse, a tattered piece of canvas for a shroud. When they returned to Emiliano's body, they put together a stretcher from the pieces they had found, and after that they rubbed his face and arms to clean off the mud and smoke. When they were finished, the sisters wrapped his body in the canvas shroud, placed him on the makeshift bier and, between the three of them, lifted their load. Under that burden, the women picked their way across the scarred battleground, hoping to join the funeral cortege that would soon begin.

Praying for Emiliano as he began his journey back to his ancestors, the sisters trailed behind men and women who still searched for the bodies of loved ones. The searchers held torches high. Against that light, the living became shadows advancing in ghostly motion. Whenever the searchers found their fallen warriors, they silently gathered the remains and moved on to join the funeral march, inching its way over the mutilated earth toward the ground now designated as a cemetery. Tripping and stumbling, the long column wound its way toward the holy ground that was waiting to receive the dead.

Torches burned against the smoke-laden night, their glow outlining the long procession of stooped mourning figures who just the day before had caressed the faces and hands of their loved ones. Out of grief and respect, women pulled their shawl low over their brows, nearly covering their faces. Men removed their sombreros out of sadness and reverence for the bodies being committed to the earth. High above that cortege, above the floating stench of spilled blood and the silent echo of screaming men and animals, the mournful murmur of prayers for the dead spiraled to the heights. From there, those supplications made their way to the summits of the ancestral teocallis of their ancient land.

Lula, Tila and Chelo followed the mourners to the place where a pit had been dug. There they lowered Emiliano's remains so the boy soldier would rest with his comrades who had perished. Their skirts in tatters, their muddied huaraches barely hanging on to their bruised feet, the sisters pulled their shawls tightly around their heads for protection against the early morning chill and in grief for the passing of so many of their people. Vaguely aware of a priest's mumbled Latin prayers drifting toward them from somewhere, they hardly paid attention. After a while, they turned their backs on those foreign words.

As the sisters moved away from the battle scene, they realized that they had not thought of what to do next nor where to go. Just then a man stepped out of the gloom, where he had been staring at the three women. It appeared that he wanted to speak but didn't know what to say, so he just gawked at the sisters.

"Señor, ¿qué pasa?" It was Tila who plucked up the nerve to urge him to speak.

"You women should not be alone. These parts are too dangerous for us all."

"We know. But we don't know where to seek shelter."

"Head for the capital right now. Don't lose time! It is the safest place for all of us."

"In what direction?"

"Follow the crowds. We're all going there to escape the invaders who will return to seek vengeance for having lost this battle."

The man vanished into the gloom, leaving the sisters wide-eyed by trying to get a clear glimpse of him. They were still uncertain about what to do next. There was more they needed to ask him, more they wanted to know, but the man had disappeared just as mysteriously as he had appeared.

Tila moved away from the crowds that were by then on the move, and her sisters followed her, each now showing the distress of not knowing her next step. Tila didn't speak but her face reflected her sisters' anxiety. She kept quiet for a long while.

"We must do what the man said. The city will give us the shelter we need, and what's more important is that we can disappear into its busy streets."

Chelo's voice was husky when she responded to her sister's plan. "How can we disappear with these clothes on? Most anyone can tell that we're Chontal and that will lead the Acuña dogs straight to us."

"Yes, Tila's right. We should try to disappear into the streets." Lula, usually quiet, spoke up. "You're right about our clothes, Chelo. Maybe we can find something else to wear."

"What do we have to trade off?" Chelo was becoming more convinced that Tila's plan would not work.

"We have our belongings. I think some women would give us a skirt or a huipil in exchange for one of our own. We've also got the knives."

Tila listened as her sisters blurted out their ideas. "Hermanas, you're both right. We must change how we look and make it difficult for the Acuñas to find us. So let's mix in with all the people moving toward the city, and start right away to try to exchange our clothes. It must work."

When Tila, Lula and Chelo reached the outskirts of the capital, there was nothing about them to tell others that they were of the Chontal people, although it was clear that they were indias, but so were the majority of those surrounding them. By the end of the trek, the sisters had mingled in with the multitude that drifted onto the streets of the city and into labyrinthine barrios and arcades that provided a natural refuge for anyone seeking asylum.

Chapter Six

El Zócalo

When Tila, Chelo and Lula walked away from the killing fields of Puebla that terrible dawn two years earlier, they kept on the move until they reached the capital. Once they found themselves on the crowded city streets, they asked over and over where they might find work.

"What kind of work?"

"We do all things: cleaning houses, or preferably cooking. What else did you think? We're decent women."

"Well, don't get angry. I was just asking. Why don't you go to the convent over there? Maybe they can help."

So they knocked on the tall doors of the Convent of San Jerónimo, where an old nun directed them to one of the finer households in the area of Guadalupe. There the sisters were given work in the upkeep of the many bedrooms of a grand home. They were happy to find work so quickly and got down to their tasks with diligence, all the time making sure to keep indoors away from the danger of detection. They stayed there until word spread that hands were needed to clean the living areas of the National Palace. Rumor had it that a new emperor and his wife were soon to arrive and, although the sisters had no idea about what an emperor might be, much less what the wife of such a person would be like, they headed for the Zócalo to look for work in the huge palace.

The sisters were brought on as part of the mass of footmen, drivers, cooks, kitchen boys and scullery maids. Chelo, Lula and Tila considered themselves lucky: they were hired right away as chambermaids, and they, like the rest of the servants, were accepted weeks before the grand arrival of the new masters.

From the beginning, the Chontal sisters did their best, but what they did hardly made a difference because the place was shabby and in dismal condition. It was a discouraging task because the palace, constructed hundreds of years earlier during the Spanish viceroyalty, had been through terrible times. During the early part of the century, when the Spaniards had been ejected from Mexico, the residence became a barracks, and soldiers along with their horses had trampled floors and stairways, damaging every surface with urine and other waste. After that, the palace was abandoned for years, nearly forgotten, until waves of governments and administrations, along with their politicians, generals, ministers and even vagabonds occupied the once regal premises from time to time.

When Emperor Maximilian and Empress Carlota made their entry, the palace was still in shambles, and no matter how many hours were put into scrubbing, wiping and even applying fresh coats of paint, the mildew, dust, rust and cracks on walls and ceilings still presented an impossible task. An odor exuded from corners and niches, sickening people. In the end, all the servants were convinced that it was impossible to eradicate the stench, no matter how much soap and scrubbing went into the task.

Directing that uphill enterprise, from the insignificant to the most important details was a mayordomo, a fastidious little man whose name no one knew. He stewarded the army of servants with an iron fist. He walked about in quick, short steps, his back straight and stiff, and he always wore the same threadbare frock. Under his eagle eye, Indian servants and workers were always on the alert as he constantly prowled the corridors and rooms, overseeing the work being done even in the most out-of-sight recesses of the palace. He hardly spoke to his workers, but rather clapped his hands in fast, slapping sounds to show disapproval. The servants

knew he was approaching when echoes of his clapping hands rico-
cheted off the walls. He was always critical of the work being done.

The mayordomo, without bothering to learn names, simply
addressed the workers as tú indio or tú india. When he did speak
to a worker, he would let him or her know that he was a mestizo,
not a common Indian, and that he was a direct descendant of the
last viceroy's favorite manservant. Although his underlings kow-
towed to him, behind his back they jeered and mocked him, always
referring to him as the pinche mestizo.

The best times came when the servants gathered in the kitchen
to make fun of that "damn mestizo." They competed with one another in imitating him, but the favorite mime was usually Chelo, who
copied his creepy steps and his stiff back better than anyone else.

On the morning of the entrance procession of the imperial
couple, the servants worked diligently up until the mayordomo
was spotted leaving the palace heading toward the crowd out front
in the Zócalo. The minute word spread that he was out of sight, the
swarm of servants bolted upstairs to claim a space at the windows
overlooking the large central square, and it was from there that the
Chontal sisters got their first glimpse of Carlota, the woman who
would share a connection with them so deep that it would last until
the end of their lives.

The sisters watched as Emperor Maximilian and Empress
Carlota entered the Zócalo. As they looked on, vivid memories of
suffering and death on the fields of Puebla were still with them.
Those feelings clashed with the fascination they were feeling as
below them the spectacle unfolded of the French celebrating their
rule over Mexico. The hated franceses, who had killed so many
natives at Puebla, were parading their power over the land of the
Chontal sisters and millions of other indios, mestizos and criollos,
whose victory at Puebla two years earlier was now erased. Yet the
sisters and thousands of others like them were incapable of pulling
their eyes away from the lavish display.

Lula had managed to get a tiny spot at a window; she signaled
her sisters to squeeze in next to her. They did it only after pushing
and shoving their way through the throng of other eager servants

who were also struggling to catch a glimpse of the new rulers. Once squeezed in, the sisters knew they were the lucky ones because they were safe above the hordes amassed down in the Zócalo, where people were pressed together with barely a tiny space between one another.

Garlands and floral arches festooned archways and entrances, as did countless brilliantly colored banners that fluttered against the sky. Dazzled by the beautiful decorations that had transformed the Zócalo, the servants craned their necks, stretching them in every direction, hoping to make out the dignitaries who preceded and followed the royal couple. The emperor and empress rode in an elegant open carriage pulled by four matched, prancing Lipizzaner stallions, each with a quetzal feather in its crest. All the other notables were on foot, the more important ones ahead of the carriage and the lesser ones bringing up the rear.

"¡Miren, el arzobispo!" Lula cried out, pointing to the prelate. As soon as she gasped out the words, all faces snapped in that direction. The archbishop and the other church dignitaries surrounding him were robed in cloth-of-gold and silver vestments; their peaked miters were encrusted with precious stones that glittered in the sunlight. Altar boys and monks vested in long white chasubles flanked the clergy, each holding an incense burner suspended on filigreed chains. They aimed the burners toward the priests, showering them with the aromatic fragrance, and then the smoky billows wafted toward the awe struck mob that, not understanding the gesture, flinched and turned away.

Emperor Maximilian was wearing the ornate uniform and gilded sword of a Mexican general. Around the fringes of a feathered military cap, his hair flowed in the breeze. His golden hair amazed the multitude of indios more than anything else. Empress Carlota also astonished everyone with her beauty. Her sky-blue silk dress fit her slender figure perfectly, and most of the crowd found it difficult to turn their eyes from her.

Behind the imperial carriage followed the other important figures, almost as dazzling in their finery as the ecclesiastics. These were the mestizos who had taken for themselves grand titles of nobility. Theirs was a special place in the cortege; it had been their faction that paved the way for the creation of a Napoleonic empire in Mexico. Finally, to emphasize and to protect the authority of these illustrious men and women, splendidly uniformed French and Belgian soldiers stood guard around the vast plaza. Their swords and bayonets, meant to intimidate as well as to impress the potentially unruly crowd, shone in the sunlight.

From their high perch, Tila, Chelo and Lula gaped at the slow-moving figures ceremoniously making their way toward the grand cathedral to their right on the Zócalo. The planned ceremony was about to begin and tones of a choir were already drifting from the interior of the church. A Te Deum, in gratitude for the safe arrival of the imperial couple, was soon to be chanted, followed by the papal benediction recognizing Maximilian and Carlota as the new rulers of the land. Giving that special blessing was the privilege of the archbishop, along with the approval of the elite mestizos and *criollos* of the city who were called upon as witnesses.

Outnumbering the dignitaries by thousands was the horde of Indians that were crammed shoulder to shoulder in the Zócalo. Not only was the ground swarming with people, but every balcony and window overlooking the crowd was also jammed with onlookers. Boys, as if hanging from tree branches, clung to the highest perches of the bell tower and balconies of the cathedral, as well as from the massive façades of the National Palace and the Monte de Piedad, the pawnshop that served as the main bank.

There was hardly a free space anywhere because the front walls of all of the buildings ringing the giant square were alive with people gaping at the procession. As far as anyone could see, there stretched a sea of brown faces, men clad in the white shirts and pantaloons of their tribe and donning worn-out straw sombreros, and women dressed in tribal garments, the huipil and rebozo shawls indicating which pueblo or hacienda they were bound.

As the procession sliced through that multitude, the mestizos were the first to notice a hush extending through the massive crowd. Those powerful men worried because it was not like the humble ones to hold back from shouting out their sentiments in celebration. The truth, however, was that the multitude was not there in celebration, but out of curiosity. They had come to see what their new masters looked like, so they simply gaped in deep resentment.

What the mestizos, as well as the prelates chose to ignore, and what Maximilian and Carlota were incapable of realizing, was that the throngs surrounding them were men and women who had not forgotten the battle of Puebla nor that their country had been invaded. Among them were survivors of the Puebla battle and other conflicts, people who grieved that their heroic actions had come to nothing because los franceses had returned. They, los indios, were once more the ones on the bottom. They had been displaced once again by a new order, one that was not truly new but a repetition of the suppression brought to their land when the first bearded white men arrived in Mexico.

Among the multitude were women who harbored profound bitterness because of the loss of a husband or children, not only on the battlefield but also because of other unjust misfortunes. They had lost the security of their dwellings and were now forced to come to the capital in search of work. Side-by-side with those women were men, uprooted, homeless, many of them maimed and reduced to begging, indios who harbored unspeakable hatred for the French —a loathing now nourished even more by this show of grandeur and superiority. Because it was happening there, on the same sacred ground where their ancestors had erected temples and worshiped their own gods in their chosen way, the hostility of those indios deepened and manifested itself in silent anger.

"¡Viva México, cabrones!"

The scream rose above the mass of people when their hostility could no longer be contained. It exploded and more howling erupted from the hearts of that swarm of people. The manifestation of pride alongside the curse echoed over and again until it became a giant wave of wailing hurled against the intruders. The rage became so threatening that the ministers and officials, alarmed and fearful for their welfare, quickly herded the dignitaries into the safety of the cathedral. When that was done, the cathedral's portals were slammed shut against the very people for whom the church had been built. Scrambling to regain a semblance of order, the Te Deum of thanksgiving was chanted, followed by the benediction, while soldiers roughly disbanded the mob of swearing, cursing people.

When it was over, Lula, Chelo and Tila, along with all the other servants, returned to their tasks. There was little time left before the emperor and empress arrived to spend their first night in the palace. The sisters were charged with putting the last touches on the sleeping quarters and the private chamber of the empress. They went to work making the bed and bringing in fresh water for her toilette, placing flowers in vases and, most important of all, making certain that the area was aired and dusted by the time the beautiful young empress arrived.

Chapter Seven

L ife as the empress of Mexico began for Carlota. Events had swept her into the national palace that morning after her carriage had inched its way through morose throngs of brown faces and faded shawls. Carlota yearned to get closer to the multitude that had surrounded her because she knew that they were the people of her empire, but servers and officials had kept her apart and unreachable. She had been showered with flowers and garlands. Banners waved triumphantly above her in a show that contradicted the expressions on the faces of those people who stared at her in silence. Bewildered, Carlota occasionally glanced at Maximilian, looking for an explanation, but she saw only satisfaction pasted on his face. He appeared more interested in the ornate architecture of the buildings they passed, remnants from his ancestors' days as monarchs and viceroys of Mexico.

By the end of the procession, she had become aware of a disturbance that had broken out deep in the heart of the huge crowd, but suddenly she and Maximilian had been hastily rushed into the cathedral. Once inside, she waited for an explanation, but no one came forward, as if the shoving and cursing had not happened, as if she didn't have eyes to see the clenched fists or ears to hear the hostile screaming. So the empress waited, expecting to be informed, but all she received were stony expressions, leaving her so puzzled and irritated that she hardly paid attention to the Te Deum and the service that followed.

After that, Carlota's day had been crammed with ceremonies, receptions and introductions during which her hand was kissed countless times, and she was bowed to as well as flattered endlessly by ministers, mayors and generals. There was even time set aside to meet her ladies-in-waiting, who wasted no time surrounding and showering her with adulation.

Throughout the day, Carlota took time to observe Maximilian. Each time she looked at him he appeared elated, even energized by the goings on; but hers was the opposite frame of mind. With every passing moment, despite the fawning representatives and the exaggerated show of welcome, she felt a growing apprehension.

In the beginning, Carlota had desperately desired to be empress of Mexico, but then she experienced a glimmer of doubt when the representatives of the conservative faction first approached Maximilian, hoping to coax him into accepting the imperial crown. Why would Mexicans desire an Austrian ruler, she asked herself. She grew even more anxious when she and Maximilian landed at Vera Cruz to find only deserted streets. Her doubts redoubled that day when she focused on the real people she and her husband would rule, not the flatterers around her. These thoughts drained Carlota and forced her to want to escape the festivities.

Unknown to the empress, outside the night sky was bright with exploding fireworks, but on the ground instead of celebration, the Zócalo was packed with the same curious, dejected mob of indios aimlessly shuffling from one side of the square to the other, still wondering what the day's events meant. Inside the palace, the spirit was different. Although the banquet was finished, the dancing and socializing were still in full swing. Carlota knew that she was expected to remain at the center of the festivities, but she was exhausted and depressed. She found it beyond her strength to continue, so she bade a good night to the distinguished company. Responding to deep courtesies and bows, the twenty-four-year-old empress made her way out of the illuminated ballroom and headed for her bedchamber.

She longed to be alone, but her ladies-in-waiting trotted behind her with heels clicking rhythmically. Yearning for privacy, Carlota was exasperated by the sound of their steps. She tried to overcome her dark mood, understanding that those women were a required part of her position. At that moment, however, she only saw them as invaders of her privacy, inordinate gossipers and chatterers. Carlota wanted more than anything to be rid of them, especially as they circled around, trying to engage her in meaningless small talk.

As they neared her bedchamber, Carlota tried to discourage the women from following her, but they would not listen, choosing to believe that it was out of kindness that the empress was dismissing them. They were not ready to give up what they considered their hard-earned privilege. When Carlota became convinced that the twittering women intended to stay with her, she gave up any attempt to conceal her irritation and angrily swept into her room, only to find that it was not empty.

The Chontal sisters were waiting, having just completed their tasks. As the giddy ladies entered, the sisters froze, pasted against the far wall. When Carlota caught sight of them, she stopped to stare. All day she had wanted to get closer to the natives of her empire, but that had not been possible because of the wall of mestizos shielding her from them. Now, standing within arms-reach of those three women, the empress felt a thrill.

Carlota suddenly remembered her entourage and decided that this time nothing would keep her from dismissing them. She wanted to savor this encounter without interruptions or excuses for getting rid of the three Indian women. She turned to glare at the attendants and then dismissed them with a determined flick of the wrist. The ladies-in-waiting had no choice but to obey their mistress' command, and they left the chamber unsure of why they had been dismissed.

Backed shyly against the bedchamber wall, Lula, Tila and Chelo stared at the young empress and then lowered their eyes. They had never stood so close to such an elevated personage. Just knowing that they were in the presence of the grandest woman of their land nearly robbed them of breath. All they wanted to do was bolt from the room, run and disappear into the cavernous recesses of the palace.

The four young women stood pinned to the floor. Carlota examined her charges as the indias risked glances out of the corners of their lowered eyes. Their beauty dumbfounded Carlota. It was so different from anything she had seen before. They were diminutive in height, just like her. Their heads were gracefully crowned with thick black braids interlaced with colored ribbons. Carlota's poor eyesight forced her to step closer to look at their faces, their fine broad foreheads highlighted by sweeping eyebrows that nearly met at the bridges of their noses, as if a single eyebrow crossed from one temple to the other. Their eyes were elongated ovals set on their sides with pupils so large that there was hardly any surrounding white. Those eyes were brilliantly black, as if carved from flint, and they were set above high cheekbones under which were wide mouths outlined by chiseled lips.

Carlota was captivated by the color of the women's skin—it was like nothing she had ever seen. Their complexions, a rich brown, seemed as smooth as silk to her eyes. Doubting what she was seeing, the empress stepped even closer to the sisters and reached out her hands to touch Lula's face. Startled by that gesture, Lula jerked back, but then immediately stepped forward to allow the empress' fingers to touch her face.

When the empress lowered her hands, it was the sisters' turn to look at her, and they did so with a childlike naturalness that disarmed Carlota so much that she allowed what in others would have been unforgivable audacity. She remained still as the three women looked at her, taking in every detail from the top of her head down to where they imagined her feet were; the long dress made it impossible to see what was beneath it.

They took in Carlota's height, which was almost like theirs, although her hair combed high on her head made her seem taller. They saw that the empress' hair was the color of chocolate and that it coiled in soft curls along the hairline in tiny strands twisting around the base of her neck. They studied her eyes that were round, large and luminous; except that she blinked so often that she had the look of a frightened bird. Her nose, so different from theirs, was thin and her mouth was small and round. What astonished the sisters most of all was the color of Carlota's skin. It was so white and nearly transparent, like the white flowers that flourished along the banks of Lake Xochimilco.

The trance was broken when the empress moved away to slide onto a small chair in front of her dressing table, and from there she gazed into the mirror. She was not looking at her image but at Chelo, Tila and Lula's reflection. Finally, Carlota looked at her own face in the mirror and at the same time she motioned for the sisters to come closer. As if pulled by the same string, they reacted at the same time. As they approached her, Carlota let them know with her hand that they should remove the pins from her hair. They obeyed, and a cascade of light-brown hair tumbled down Carlota's shoulders, to the astonishment of the sisters.

Carlota finally broke the silence while still looking into the mirror. "How are you called?"

The sisters noticed the strange way that the empress used her words, but they understood. Too shy and frightened to speak, they lowered their eyes. Carlota sensed that they were afraid and patiently waited. Finally the answer came.

"I'm Tila, and these are my sisters, Chelo and Lula."

When Tila spoke, Carlota could not tell who it was that had spoken. Still seated on the stool, she swiveled around to face them.

"That's all? You have no family name?"

"No, Majestad."

The empress tilted her head to the side and shrugged. "Very well. If that's the way you like to be known, then let it be."

By now she had gotten to her feet, and the sisters saw her sway slightly. They understood that she was exhausted, and they headed for the door with the intention of leaving.

"Don't leave. Won't you attend me?"

Chelo looked at Lula, who then turned to Tila who then returned her sisters' startled looks. In a moment they curtsied respectfully.

"Sí, Alteza."

Silently, the sisters set about helping the empress out of her bulky dress. Next, they undid the laces of her corset and removed it along with layers of shifts and smaller garments. Reaching into the wardrobe, a nightgown was retrieved along with the robe that was placed at the foot of the bed. Chelo poured water into the porcelain basin to bathe Carlota's neck, face, hands and arms; the gown was then slipped over her. When she was seated on the bed, Lula washed and dried her feet. As a last step, they positioned the young empress onto the bed and placed a coverlet on her so that she could sleep.

It was a quiet first encounter, as if those women had known one another for years and were in a relationship that needed few words. As they attended the empress, the Chontal sisters moved from one detail to the other, silently making their way about the bedchamber. They seemed to know the place where Carlota's things were kept, that it was all a repetition of what had been done countless times. The empress, hushed and serene, responded as if those hands had cared for her before.

Those brief moments were the beginning of an unlikely friend-ship that at first was marked by curiosity and apprehension. It, nevertheless, would bind the three sisters and the empress of Mexico for more than six decades, a tie destined to last until the end of their lives. The same naturalness and simplicity that marked that first encounter would deepen with the years and, although their friendship was improbable because race and class separated them, those differences neither interfered nor diminished the bond that would in time unite them.

On that first night when these sentiments began to take root, the sisters finished what had to be done and prepared to leave the empress. As they headed for the door, however, Carlota's voice once again stopped them.

"Hermanas, wait! Bring your bedding so that you may sleep here in the room with me."

Puzzled by Carlota's command, the sisters first looked at one another and then turned to stare at her, an unspoken question stamped on their faces. Unperturbed, the empress waved her arm to let them know that they should do as she asked. When the sisters still looked confused, she told them simply, "I sleep alone."

Chapter Eight

Most visitors to the National Palace were unaware that its underground foundations held a warren of tiny rooms and cubicles interconnected by a maze of narrow hallways. In times of conflict, when one army or another occupied the palace, the upper floors were reserved for officers and staff members, and the subterranean spaces were assigned to the roughnecks and misfits that composed the regular ranks, whether revolutionary or federalist. When Maximilian's empire took shape, those underground cubicles were set aside for the use of servants, maids, kitchen boys, cooks and whomever else it took to run the giant edifice.

When Tila, Chelo and Lula were hired as maids, they were given one of those cramped enclosures to share. Although confining, they liked it because it reminded them of the room they had shared during their childhood at La Perla. It was small but it was where they slept and kept their clothes and other belongings. It was their own space and, more importantly, it gave them a place where they could speak openly in their own tongue and be themselves. Whenever they had time off between chores and duties during the workday, the sisters made sure to come together there to rest and talk about what they had seen and heard.

On the morning after spending the night in the empress' chambers, the sisters scrambled out of sight to meet in their underground hideaway. When they closed the door they kept quiet for a long time. It was obvious that each one was having a hard time putting thoughts into words and that silence made the cramped room grow stuffier. Lula reached up to the small opening to let in some air.

"I don't like her!" Her blunt words broke the wall of silence that was keeping the others from saying what was on their minds. "I don't like her eyes. I don't like the way she smells."

"Smells? What are you talking about? You're being silly."

Tila had flopped on the bed and let her huaraches slip off her feet while she looked at her sister with half-closed eyelids. She was attentive to Lula's words although she sensed their direction.

"I mean that she smells like the rest of them, those women that hide their faces and bodies behind fans and under ugly dresses."

Out of the corner of her eye Chelo gave Tila a nod of understanding. They knew that although years had passed, Lula's hatred of anyone with white skin was a result of the ordeal inflicted on her by Arcides Acuña. It was a fire that burned hotter as she grew in age.

Tila sat up and fixed her eyes on her sister. She knew that words caused Lula pain so when she spoke, it was only because it was important to her. More than ever aware of this, Tila studied her sister's face with more care on that day than at other times. She saw that Lula's expression was still young yet in many ways aged, that it was soft yet hardened.

"Hermana, what are you really saying?"

"I'm saying that the empress intends to turn us into her maids, to tie us to her as close as she can. I'm saying that I don't want that to happen."

"Why not?"

"I cannot give you reasons! I just don't want that to happen."

"She hasn't even asked us. What makes you think she will?"

"I know it because I feel it!"

"Lula, be reasonable!"

"I am being reasonable!"

By now Chelo was growing impatient and wanted to change the direction of the conversation. It was not the first time her sisters spoke this way about different matters, and she knew that it used up precious time, sometimes wasting all of their free periods. She intervened to break up the give-and-take.

"Hermanas, what will we do if the empress does command us to be her maids?"

"If she really commands it, then we have nothing else but to obey." Tila's usual practicality broke into what her sister was saying.

"That's not true. We can return to one of the homes in the city where we're sure to find good work." Lula showed that she was determined not to stay with the empress. "We did it before and we can do it again."

"Lula's right." Chelo backed up her younger sister. "Tila, what would keep us from leaving this place now? All we have to do is gather our things and leave."

"I wish it were that easy, but it isn't. Both of you are forgetting that we are hunted women, that we have murdered one of the patrones and that the Acuña family will not stop looking for us until they find us."

Looking intently at Tila, Lula blurted out, "You're thinking that it's my fault, aren't you? You're saying that it's because of me that you and Chelo must remain in hiding."

"No, Lula, I'm not thinking that way. How could I blame you for what the three of us did? Remember that Chelo and I stabbed the vile man as many times as you did. We are all responsible, and I don't regret it even a little."

"Then what are you telling us?" Chelo's eyes had become tight slits.

"I'm saying that giving up our place here is not a good idea. I want you both to remember that becoming the empress' maids would provide us with protection against the long arm of the Acuñas. It would bury us deep in the powerful heart of the new masters. The way I see it, the empress has a much more powerful influence than that of the Acuñas. I say that we would be well hidden and protected. Don't you see? It would be the last place to look for us. I tell you both that we can be safe as long as we stay with the empress."

Chelo and Lula fell silent. They were weighing Tila's words, even searching for something that might be a better idea, but they found nothing to propose. After a while, the sisters looked at their older sister, and Tila caught the meaning in their eyes.

"Does this mean you agree with me? Lula, what do you say?"

"I had not thought of it that way. Hermana, I don't want to stay here but I see that you're right. We're safer here. I'll change my mind and say yes."

"Chelo?"

"Yes. I, too, agree."

"Then it's agreed that if the empress orders us to stay on as her maids, we will remain at her side."

"For how long?"

"For as long as the Acuñas exist. Maybe for the rest of our lives."

As the sisters rose to make their way back to the empress, Lula said, "Why doesn't her husband sleep with her?"

Tila paused at the door and murmured, "I don't think anyone knows."

Chapter Nine

I carry the memory of that night inside me like a faded picture. Its lines are blurred and vague, yet the image remains unchanged. Although no one knows this part of my story, I often return to it. It happens on my first night with Maximilian, when the wedding ceremony and celebrations are over and night has closed in on Laeken Castle.

Its corridors and chambers are silent except for creaking walls and sighing passageways. Outside, the frozen wind whispers as it sways the dark trees surrounding the castle, and the forest animals have found their niche for nighttime slumber.

In that gray unclear picture, I see myself still a girl, one that has already read master historians and philosophers but who is as yet ignorant of what it is that a man and a woman do when together for the first time. I watch Maximilian standing in front of me, smiling and breathing heavily. After a while the images in the picture stir, and I see him as he removes his clothes for me to observe his naked body. That sight shocks me, makes my body shudder. I have never before seen a naked man.

In that memory I gaze at his body, its marble-white skin, its parts covered with hair. I'm stunned. My mind scurries in different directions until I feel faint. He then raises his hands and removes my gown until I too am naked. I feel ashamed of my nakedness and try to cover it. Without thinking, my hands hover over my breasts and then travel down in an attempt to cover myself. When Maximilian realizes that I'm mortified, he laughs a laugh so loud and coarse that it echoes off the walls of the chamber.

Suddenly, Maximilian takes hold of my hands and pulls them toward him, forcing my fingers to touch his intimate parts. That sensation disgusts me so much that it forces me to pull away, with every intention of running from the chamber, but he takes hold of me. When he lifts me, I'm powerless to escape. All I can do is kick and push, but it's useless. My resistance only arouses him more.

I turn away from that memory, but the images always return, and I again watch as he throws me onto the bed and rolls on top of me, nearly suffocating me as he thrusts his mouth over mine. I feel a sense of panic and am compelled to shove him away. It's only when he attempts to get between my legs that I match him kicking and scratching.

As if playing a game, Maximilian laughs, makes faces and jeers at my struggle. When I cry out for him to stop, he continues to laugh but now with contempt. Finally, one of my feet lands on that vulnerable part and he springs away in pain and shock, whimpering like a little boy.

He then curses me in his crude language; but, more than anything, the expression on his face is one of outrage, one that says that he is an archduke, a prince never before denied, much less rebuked. Maximilian stands by the bed, naked, breathing heavily, with blood trickling from the scratches on his chest. I see hatred in his eyes, a loathing that he is able to hide later on when we are in the presence of others, but never when facing me alone. In his eyes I see the determination that never again will he be so humiliated. The images fade away and the memory evaporates.

Chapter Ten

December 1864

The National Palace

A lthough married to archduke Maximilian for seven years,
Carlota was still a virgin when she faced Colonel Alfred van
der Smissen for the first time. It was December 1864, the empire's
first Christmas in Mexico, and the court was celebrating. The
mood was festive and optimistic. Reports streamed in affirming
that the pretentious little Indian, Benito Juárez, had been routed
along with his ragtag followers, and Mexico was firmly in the
hands of Emperor Maximilian. At least, that was what the French
generals along with their Mexican counterparts guaranteed.

The audience chamber at the palace was colorfully decorated
with pinecones and thick branches brought down for the occasion
from the surrounding volcanoes. Multicolored garlands hung from
the vaulted ceiling. Thousands of lit candles transformed the huge
hall into a close reproduction of what most of those men and
women had left behind in Europe.

Along with plentiful food and sweets, the Mexican Christmas
treat, *ponche navideño,* was generously served from elegant fonts.
The punch was a blend of fruit juices and the native liquor called
mezcal, a drink that quickly relaxed stuffy manners. Music flowed
from a loft above the gathering where a chamber ensemble played
cheerful seasonal melodies.

Laughter and smiling faces surrounded Empress Carlota, who dazzled the court in a lovely gray silk gown highlighted with lavender tones. She hardly needed to bring out her finest jewelry, her beauty being more than ever captivating and provoking envious glances and quick words exchanged behind women's fans. The gentlemen consumed her with devouring eyes.

It was on this occasion that Colonel Alfred van der Smissen's first encounter with the empress took place. As he nervously stood in line waiting his turn to approach the imperial couple, he took comfort telling himself that the other officials ahead of him were just as tense.

To calm his agitation, Smissen reminded himself that his was a special mission: He had been sent to the Mexican imperial court to serve as the commander of Empress Carlota's personal guard. Thinking of this momentarily settled his nerves, but then he realized that curious eyes were on him. When he saw that people were inspecting him and whispering about him, he felt his nerves slipping again and, although he tried even harder to appear unaffected, the clenching and unclenching of his gloved hands gave him away.

When it was his turn to step forward, the colonel approached the imperial couple and bowed low, respectfully. Upon raising his eyes, they interlocked with those of the empress. The attraction of the colonel and the empress was immediate and unexpected, and utterly confusing to both of them.

Captivated by her, he found it nearly impossible to take his eyes off her face, all the time fighting a powerful urge to fall to his knees and kiss her hands. He was finally shaken from his daze by a voice behind him saying something. He suddenly realized he was expected to address the emperor and empress.

"Majesties, I'm honored to be standing here. I am your servant, Alfred van der Smissen of the Belgian Foreign Legion." His voice was dry and raspy.

Maximilian eyed him carefully and stiffly smiled at him, but all Smissen knew was that Carlota's eyes were burning into him. He turned to face her and, almost speechless, he mumbled a few flat, meaningless words.

Empress Carlota allowed herself to gaze at Smissen openly, without any inhibition, and immediately wanted him with all her strength. She struggled to regain her composure despite a compelling desire to take his face in her hands and kiss his eyes and mouth.

The colonel was not a handsome man. His head was too large for his stature, and his forehead, tapered at the temples, was emphasized by a receding hairline that made him look older than he was. His eyes narrowed when he was concentrating, giving him an arrogant expression. His shoulders sloped considerably, causing his uniform and decorations to hang in an untidy, rumpled manner, robbing him of the dashing appearance most military men desired.

Neither handsome nor elegant, Smissen nonetheless radiated a manliness that was not lost on women. By the time he bowed respectfully before the young empress, the colonel had already distinguished himself in the field of battle, gaining for himself the respect of his men and superiors. He was known to be an officer willing to take risks but never at the cost of those under his command. Aside from his courage, his ambition also was reputed to be impressive.

Because it was his first introduction to the court, Smissen felt himself obliged to pull away from the empress to mingle. As he wove his way through the crowd, Carlota's eyes remained riveted on him, following him from one side of the chamber to the other. She studied his walk, how he held himself, how he responded to others, how he smiled.

When Emperor Maximilian signaled that the celebration was over, Carlota noticed Smissen bowing low in her direction. She returned his gesture with a deep curtsy and then forced herself away from the chamber. Followed by her ladies-in-waiting, she headed for her bedroom with her heart beating so hard that it affected her breathing.

Carlota gruffly dismissed her ladies at her dressing room door, allowing only the Chontal sisters to undress and prepare her for the night. After the sisters loosened her hair, she stood arms out-stretched, allowing her clothes to be removed but refusing to speak while she withdrew into a dark mood.

Respecting her silence, the sisters finished their tasks without saying anything. In that stiff silence, sounds seemed louder than usual: splashing of water in the hand basin, opening and shutting of drawers, creaking of shutters shifting in the night breeze.

After a while, this time looking into Carlota's eyes, Chelo asked, "¿Está triste, Emperatriz?"

These words momentarily drew Carlota out of her sullen mood. "No, Chelo, I'm not sad. I'm thinking."

"Are your thoughts sad, Majestad?"

"No. My thoughts are in conflict."

The sisters exchanged glances but said nothing more. When they finished helping the empress into her bed, they readied their sleeping mats, snuffed out the candles and settled in for the night. It was not long, however, before Carlota's voice made them think that she was calling them. At first her words were faint, then became stronger and at times agitated. The sisters sat up thinking she was calling out for assistance, but no, she was talking in her sleep. They realized that she was having another of her recurring dreams that often made her mumble incoherently, sometimes tearfully.

The sisters didn't know that their mistress was dreaming of Alfred van der Smissen, that in the dream she was abandoning herself to him without inhibition and taking pleasure from his body. It was a dream so real that, when she awoke, its memory made her feel ashamed for sinning in thought if not in deed. Nonetheless, Carlota clung to that dream.

That morning, Carlota was pulled from her reverie when Lula opened the curtains and pushed out the shutters to allow sunlight to flood the bedchamber. Carlota kept her eyes shut hoping to extend her reverie, but she knew it was over. Again refusing to speak, she remained silent from the moment she left her bed and even as the sisters helped her bathe, dress and comb her hair. When that was done, she walked out to a small terrace where she stood daydreaming.

After a while Carlota went to her desk to sip chocolate, absent-mindedly turning pages, scribbling occasional comments on documents, but she found it nearly impossible to concentrate, her thoughts returning time and again to Alfred van der Smissen. She knew that somehow she had to resist the forbidden longing she was experiencing but found that it was beyond her strength. She felt overpowered by the need to talk about the sensations that had taken hold of her. She longed to have someone close to her who would listen without judging her as sinful and guilty, but she had no such confidante or intimate friend.

At that moment, Tila approached to pour a fresh cup of chocolate. On an impulse, Carlota decided that it would be la india who would help her cool the fever raging inside her.

"Tila, do you dream?"

Bewildered, Tila looked at the empress and tried to decipher the meaning of her question. She took a few moments to respond.

"Yes, Alteza, I do."

"Are your dreams so real that you believe they are true?"

"Yes. Sometimes."

Tila was poised with her hand holding the jug of steaming chocolate in midair. Her face expressed thoughts that went from bewilderment to curiosity.

"Have you ever had a sinful dream?"

"Majestad, I do not understand what that word means."

"Which word?"

"Sinful."

Astonished, Carlota put down the quill she held and stared at Tila. She waited a few moments to reflect especially on the tone of la indias' voice when she uttered the word *sinful*. Was it possible for anyone not to understand the meaning of that word?

"Tila, when you have a dream of something forbidden, that is what is meant by sinful."

"Majestad, I still don't understand."

"Sinful can be a dream of desiring someone, a man for instance. When you want with all your strength to lie with that man, when you want pleasure with him, when you picture yourself doing prohibited deeds with him, when you surrender to that hunger that is what is meant by the word sinful."

"I see. Yes, I have had such dreams."

"Then you have had sinful dreams."

"But, Alteza, how can such dreams be sinful if they are only dreams?"

Tila's face was open and sincere, like that of a child expecting a clear and simple answer.

Carlota had been certain that her lustful dream had been sinful, but now she felt that conviction beginning to slip and shift in the wake of Tila's guileless question. After all, it had been but a dream and if this was to be the extent of her pleasure, then why consider it sinful? She really had not done anything wrong, had she? Still there was a force that compelled Carlota to believe what she was taught from childhood.

"Because thoughts often lead to deeds."

"Majestad, I think that dreams are dreams and deeds are deeds. They are separate. Also, we are not asked what dream we want, it just comes to us. If it is filled with pleasure, then it is a gift."

Intrigued by Tila's uncomplicated logic, Carlota wanted to hear more. She wanted to believe that her impure dream might not be sinful after all.

"Tila, do you not believe that people commit wicked acts?"

"I do."

"Like what? Give me an example."

"Like when a man taints and ravages the body of a woman, despite her struggle and effort to stop him."

Carlota's face drained of color. "Tila, do you know of such a woman?"

Tila opened her mouth, but at that moment Lula slipped into the chamber.

"Majestad, your secretary is here to read your agenda."

Lula inadvertently cut off her sister's answer, leaving both the empress' and Tila's thoughts dangling. Carlota was left to question her understanding of *sinful* and Tila wondered what intense desires were assaulting her mistress.

"Very well, Chelo. Show him in."

Frustrated, because Carlota wanted to pursue her conversation with Tila, she was nonetheless forced to put aside those thoughts for the time being. When the young secretary walked in, he stood stiffly by the side of the desk while the empress glared at him with the flat unfriendly stare that often intimidated her servants. She tightened her lips as she took in his badly tied cravat and his ill-fitting morning coat, unabashedly showing her distaste while focusing her eyes on his thin moustache and goatee. She mentally noted that one of his sideburns was longer than the other.

"Señor Secretario, please take a seat and read the agenda, if you would."

Carlota struggled to dispel her rudeness, but she was so troubled that her voice sounded hoarse and unpleasant. The young man, obviously nervous, sat on the edge of the chair and carefully opened his portfolio. He began reading the list in a monotonous voice.

"The emperor left for Cuernavaca early this morning . . . "

The secretary's voice faded in and out while Carlota's mind drifted.

"He requests Your Majesty meet with the minister of finance . . . "

Incomplete sentences made their way into her consciousness, but when she tried to fit the loose words together they didn't make sense.

" . . . planning a discussion for funding new uniforms . . . palace guards . . . the mayordomo in charge of repairs . . . Borda Residence . . . Chapultepec Castle . . . And the final point concerns Colonel Van der Smissen."

Throughout the jumble of words, Empress Carlota stared at nothing in particular with obvious boredom until the colonel's name reached her consciousness. When she heard that he was scheduled to meet her in just a few hours, she sat up with her heart pounding so hard that she thought the secretary surely heard it. She glared at the startled man. The expression on her face confused him, and he returned her look not knowing whether to smile or frown.

"Your Majesty, have I said something wrong?"

"No, no, you haven't. I'm just a little surprised. What is the nature of the colonel's audience? He was introduced to us just yesterday."

"Well, I supposed he needs instructions from Your Majesty since he is designated as your personal guard."

"I see . . . yes . . . that must be it. Thank you. Is there anything else for today?"

"No, Majesty, unless you have letters or other matters for me to attend."

"No. That will be all. We'll meet tomorrow at this time."

When the secretary left the room, Carlota got to her feet in such a hurry that she nearly knocked over the chair. She needed air. It was hard for her to breathe in the room, and she again made her way to the terrace to ponder the situation. Should she cancel the interview with Smissen? If she did, what would be her reason? Would it not be postponing the inevitable? He was, after all, her appointed personal guard.

The easiest thing would be to send Smissen away, she told herself. On the other hand, why should she do that? Did she not desire to be with him? Why should she not do what she wanted? She was an empress, was she not? However, she was a married woman forbidden impure thoughts and sensations, such as the ones that came to her in the dream and even at that moment. Tila's responses returned to Carlota, prompting her to put an end to her useless uncertainty. It struck her that she was being childish. It was her duty to meet with Smissen, just as it was her obligation to meet that old bumbler, General Bazaine, and the stuffy finance minister. It was all part of her duties, and she would conform to what was expected of her.

After those thoughts, Carlota did do what was expected of her that day because she was deeply involved in the empire's governance. As usual, she convened a council meeting and kept scheduled appointments, all the time prepared with pertinent questions and comments. Even when it came to her face-to-face meeting with Alfred van der Smissen, she kept her composure, although inside of her a tempest raged. Thereafter, whenever he was out of her sight, he was in her every thought.

Chapter Eleven

During 1864 Maximilian's imperial forces won one decisive battle after another, convincing even the most skeptical that the empire was destined to remain in Mexico. With the successful siege of Oaxaca in February 1865, the empire had reached its peak. By this time, life for the imperial couple had become routine. The Borda residence in nearby Cuernavaca was renovated and made ready, as was the Castle on Chapultepec Hill in Mexico City. Carlota, Maximilian and their household vacated the National Palace to relocate to the new residences. Prying eyes soon noticed that when he chose to be in Cuernavaca, she remained in Chapultepec, and when he returned to the castle, she discreetly drifted off to the Borda residence. They were rarely together under the same roof. No announcement was made to explain this pattern, but people had eyes to see and mouths to talk, and soon the rift between the monarchs became fuel for raging gossip.

In the meantime, Carlota chose to rely on Smissen in his role of personal guard, but not before she mastered a manner that was friendly but remote. She made up her mind that the only fulfillment of the desire she felt for him was being close to him, to feel his gaze on her face and on her breasts and to bask in the warmth of his smile. She was finally able to find peace, once she determined that nothing beyond these harmless pleasures would ever take place between them.

As for Smissen, wherever Empress Carlota went, he was sure to walk a few paces behind her, and never did he betray any sign that might have drawn criticism. When she was in residence at Chapultepec, he was her escort on visitations to hospitals and orphanages. He always rode by her side when she made her way in an open carriage along El Paseo de la Emperatriz, excursions that often took them as far away as the cathedral. He was watchful as she distributed clothes and food to the poor, all the while witnessing how the gap between the rich and poor among her people saddened her.

On the days when it was Carlota's time to reside at the Borda Residence in Cuernavaca, it was Smissen who organized the tiny staff to accompany her. The Chontal sisters were the only ones the empress chose as her attendants, and he saw to it that a small guard was on duty to cover the daylong journey.

Once settled in that house, Carlota used her time to answer letters and inquiries during the morning hours, and, after a noon meal, she, Tila, Chelo and Lula boarded an open carriage and, escorted by Smissen, they explored the countryside, the small town and its markets. The four women enjoyed this so much that they usually did it for hours until sunset.

The exotic flowers that seemed to spring from stonewalls, terraces and sides of winding roads captivated Carlota. She hardly ever passed any of the lush bougainvillea plants that grew everywhere without pointing or stopping the carriage to cut off clumps of blossoms. Her fascination was just as great with the thick lavender-colored blooms dangling from giant jacaranda trees that flourished everywhere.

Carlota had two favorite outings: the first was to the palace erected during the Mexica Empire and afterward converted into a residence by the conquistador Hernán Cortés. Her other favorite was visiting the cathedral where she wandered through its atrium, vestibule and minor altars.

Mass and prayers were usually over by the time she visited, and the church was empty. It was a time when nothing moved except for the flickering of countless lighted candles. She loved those moments of quiet solitude, during which she would sit for long periods, admiring the ornate ceilings and walls from which faces of saints, monks, prelates and rosy cherubs looked down on her with gentle eyes.

More than anything, Carlota cherished those moments because they belonged only to her. It was a private time when she surrendered without inhibition to thoughts of Smissen and the longing for him that was constantly with her. There in the shadowy silence of the church, Carlota disentangled herself from the constraints of guilt and sin that had bound her from childhood and, in her imagination, she freely abandoned herself to her lover and his caresses. She had convinced herself that she was in control of those powerful feelings, that she could conjure and dismiss them whenever she chose. The empress told herself that her reveries took place only in her imagination and that at no time was she in danger of actually committing the sin of adultery.

It happened sometimes, however, that during those moments of quiet reflection she became doubtful, when it struck her that perhaps she was wrong and that she was not really in control, that perhaps the passion she felt for Smissen would one day overcome her willfulness. Wondering if on that day, she would surrender to him filled Carlota with a restlessness and nervousness she had not imagined possible. Whenever these thoughts nearly overcame her, she felt compelled to cut short her daydream and return to where her companions waited for her, chatting and enjoying the beauty of the surrounding gardens. After that, the little group returned to the residence to end their day, but Carlota's lustful desires, instead of melting away, remained locked in her body, constantly struggling against her formidable will.

One day what she feared, yet desired, happened. When she was about to go into the cathedral, she felt Smissen get close enough to murmur, "You fill my thoughts night and day." Thinking that she had imagined it, she turned to glare at him, only to find that he, indeed, had uttered those words. Shaken, she moved away intending to separate herself from him, but then she abruptly stopped to look back. It was a glance that invited him to come. He followed her.

What happened next came unexpectedly to the empress. In her reveries, Carlota had not allowed herself to imagine her response if ever Smissen made an advance, so when he did, she was overcome by an unexpected giddiness. She was helpless to take hold of her emotions, but she moved along the aisle toward the main altar, to the part shrouded in shadows. There she disappeared into the darkness.

In seconds, Smissen was so close to her that she felt his breath on her face and neck. Carlota didn't resist. Instead, she reached out to take hold of his hands and guide them to her breasts, and he instantly caressed them passionately. Wordlessly, and locked in an intense embrace, she and Smissen slid to the stone floor.

Carlota's daydreams had not prepared her for the passion that overcame her. Gone were all thoughts of sin and what was forbidden, of betrayal of vows and indecency. It mattered not that she was in a church, liable to be seen, to cause a scandal. Forgetting everything, she abandoned herself unconditionally to the powerful surge of desire overwhelming her. She had waited too long. She had resisted her impulses too often. She had been respectful of what others had to say for a lifetime.

Carlota surrendered to Smissen as he kissed and caressed her. His hands found their way under the folds of her gown until he undid her garments one by one. All the while, she didn't resist. When she felt his fingers probing the most intimate part between her legs, Carlota was overcome by pleasure and kissed him over and again while his free hand fumbled with his uniform's rough material, pulling at its belt and buttons until he freed himself. He mounted her.

When he penetrated her, she could not help groaning, causing him to murmur, "I've hurt you." Without speaking, Carlota let him know that she was not hurt, that he must go on. As if answering what he had said before, she whispered, "I can't stop thinking of you either."

After the first flash of pain, Carlota reached a pitch of pleasure that she could not have imagined even in her dreams. At that moment she desired only that her rapture would not end, that it would go on forever. The plunging rhythm of his body pierced her, going through her, spreading until she shuddered uncontrollably in response, and Carlota was transported to where she had never been. She was lifted upward to the heights of the vaulted nave of the church. She soared to where the gentle eyes of saints and archangels gazed at her, telling her that they accepted her ecstasy.

When their rapture ebbed, Carlota and Smissen stayed at the foot of the altar with legs and arms intertwined. Far from prying eyes or wagging tongues, they lingered in the silence of the empty cathedral. The late afternoon melted into sunset and the shadows of the centuries-old cathedral grew deeper, more elongated. It was Carlota who first got to her feet, rearranged her clothes and, without saying anything, drifted toward the entrance. Afterward, she and Smissen met over and again until the year ended.

Chapter Twelve

M^{*y*} *idyll ended abruptly and too soon. It happened when Napoleon reneged on his promise to support the empire with his army. When this change became obvious, his puppet, General Bazaine, became evasive whenever I broached the subject of the recall of troops. Maximilian chose to turn his back on the crisis by escaping to Cuernavaca to chase butterflies and sleep with his mistress.*

I wrote letters to Napoleon. I pressed him, reminding him of his solemn oath to aid the empire in every way. At first, he responded with polite advice and explanations: He recommended patience. He promised that very soon matters would improve. He reminded me that his own empire was in crisis and that the Prussians were on the march. But I would not be put off. Instead I intensified my letters.

Majesty, I will not hesitate to express my displeasure at this moment. I promise you that when I come face-to-face with you, I will remind you of how you have failed to honor your word! Even now I'm prepared to let the entire world know of your poor behavior.

Napoleon's responses abruptly ceased, causing me great frustration. Adding to that stumbling block, the archbishop turned on me when I proposed that the empire secularize at least part of the Church's holdings. Maximilian's ministers sided with the prelate, rejecting my proposal on the grounds that the empire did not have the right or the power to clash with the country's ecclesiastical hierarchy. I tried every way to achieve at least a partial secularization of Church lands, but in the end I was defeated as well as hated. Those superstitious hypocrites summed up their position in a few empty sentences.

We simply do not possess that privilege. What is God's is God's. No one has the right to cast envious eyes on those possessions.

As it turned out, the rejection of my proposal was not enough for my now growing number of enemies. Bishops and monsignors demanded that I remove myself from the business of the empire once and for all. I later found out that those same prelates ran to Pope Pius IX. He was scandalized. It was not until later that I discovered the depth of his rancor toward me.

And so it went for months. What followed was the collapse of my dream, its end signaled by the unplanned, needless battle in which an imperial force was humiliated. The small town called Tacámbaro was the site of the encounter that turned out to be an irreversible blunder.

Chapter Thirteen

The fate of the empire reversed in early April 1865 with Tacámbaro, the encounter that need not have happened. The unexpected turnaround began when a certain Señora Regules crouched next to a wounded follower of Benito Juárez, cradling his head as she gave him a drink of water. He was so young that his upper lip was only beginning to show signs of shadowy fuzz.

"Anda, hijo. ¡Bebe! Te sentirás mejor."

Her voice was soft and coaxing as she tried to get him to take at least a sip from the jug she held to his lips, although she did it despite the feeling that she was too late. He was losing too much blood. She held him close to her breast as she nervously looked up toward the rooftops surrounding the deserted plaza. It was from somewhere up there that a Belgian sharpshooter had shot the boy.

When that single gunshot sounded out, it panicked people so badly that they stampeded in different directions, desperately looking for cover. In their terror they abandoned the young soldier, who was sprawled out on the cobblestones. It was only Señora Regules who ventured from the safety of her home to come to help him.

When she looked away from the heights, she tried again to get the young soldier to take a drink, but she saw that it was useless—he was gone. His skin had turned grayish, and his eyes were rolled back, leaving only their whites visible. Shaken, the woman put down the water jug. As she was about to close the lids of the dead boy's eyes, she felt a vise-like hand grip her shoulder. The clasp was so brutal that it made her cry out in pain. Frightened, she looked up to stare at a handful of soldiers that she recognized as Belgian legionnaires, the ones that had been patrolling the back hills and woods surrounding the village of Tacámbaro.

"Treacherous old woman! You're under arrest! Come with us!"

Although the man spoke to her in French, Señora Regules understood him, but instead of giving in to his rough instructions, she abruptly squatted back on her butt and at the same time latched on to the body of the fallen soldier. With a speed that caught the soldiers by surprise, she rolled over, pulling the corpse on top of her so that the Belgians were forced to struggle with the weight of the two inert bodies. Her resistance incensed them so much that they shouted at her, then cursed and even kicked her in an attempt to separate her from the body. But Señora Regules clamped her eyes shut and suffered their abuse without letting go of the body.

In the meantime, the townspeople who had run away regained their senses, and they rushed back to the plaza. They appeared from behind doors and around corners getting back in time to witness Señora Regules' punishment at the hands of armed foreigners. People stared in stunned silence for a few seconds as their neighbor was pummeled, kicked and roughly pulled in an effort to separate her from the corpse that she would not let go.

Seeing how she clung to the body with such force, the soldiers dragged her and the dead man over the cobblestones, thinking that she would be forced to let go. They only left behind a path of smeared blood that alarmed the village people even more. The abuse didn't go on for long before the villagers exploded in rage, catching the soldiers by surprise, especially when they found themselves targets of flying chamber pots, vases, chairs and shoes that came down at them from rooftops. Heavier objects were soon hurled: rocks, stone handles of molcajetes, metates as well as jugs filled with boiling chocolate. The abusers were hit in the head, face and hands, cutting and searing those rosy complexions.

The din intensified with infuriated shouts until it became so powerful that the noise unnerved the soldiers. Still, they persisted in trying to separate the woman from the corpse, yanking at her until they pried her loose. Using her like a shield, the soldiers backed away, ducking and swerving, until they made a dash for their headquarters.

But the Belgian legionnaires were not yet free. Their brutality had unleashed the pent-up rage of those mexicanos, and an out-of-control rampage broke out. Men and women armed with whatever tool was at hand stampeded after the soldiers with the intention of freeing their neighbor. All the while the howling went on, spitting out insults in a language the Belgians didn't understand but knew that it was hate-filled.

¡Cabrones!

¡Hijos de la chingada!

¡Pinches franceses de mierda, suéltenla!

The wailing frightened the Belgians to the point that when they finally made it to the barracks, they were close to passing out from shock and fear. Once safe behind the heavily barricaded portals, the small garrison shut Señora Regules in a room hastily converted into a makeshift cell and prepared for whatever might come next.

Unknown to that garrison of Belgian soldiers was the fact that their comrades had committed an unmitigated blunder when they mistreated and dragged the female prisoner into that cell. The woman they had taken into custody was the wife of General Regules, a key juarista officer, as well as the commander of a force camped in the sierra above the village. The Belgian soldiers had no way of knowing that in a matter of hours that general would come at them with every juarista under his command, that they had inadvertently unleashed the battle that would reverse the empire's fortune and signal its ultimate collapse.

¡Ayyyyy, jijos!

¡Mándenlos a chingar a su madre!

The attack began when a piercing scream sounded just before dusk. It was a shriek so shrill and prolonged that it made the Belgians tremble in utter fear because they recognized it as a portent to their slaughter. It was the Yaqui whoop that Europeans feared even more than heavy artillery or armed cavalry. They braced themselves and scrambled to arms, knowing that they were few and that it would be over within minutes.

The Belgian makeshift headquarters was set up in the town's Municipal Palace. It had two floors and was large enough to house the one hundred fifty or so Belgian soldiers and officers, but it was vulnerable because of its oversized windows opened to the street, as well as a vast roofless patio at its center. Seconds after the war cry rang out, the front portals of the building crashed inward, and, at the same time, what seemed like waves of brown men clothed in white cotton pants and shirts spilled through the front as well as from above into the open patio.

The Belgian officers were caught off guard, and they froze. No one thought of taking Señora Regules and again using her as a shield or to hold her as a bargaining chip. Instead, the terrified soldiers fired their weapons without taking aim, hitting some guerrillas, but mostly striking walls and faded portraits of Mexican magistrates. The screaming, cursing, crashing of glass and stucco, intermingled with the blasting of weapons and slashing of machetes continued until a command sounded out above the uproar.

¡Basta, muchachos! Ya les partimos la madre.

The juarista victory was quick, clean and undeniable. General Regules rescued his wife while his men wiped out some one hundred Belgian legionnaires and took another fifty as prisoners of war to use as bargaining chips later on. Soon afterward, the townspeople got together and the celebration began. The streets of Tacámbaro filled with jubilant people welcoming their defenders. They threw flowers in the path of the guerrillas and handed them gifts of food and drink, chickens, eggs, anything to demonstrate their gratitude.

In terms of numbers, imperial losses at Tacámbaro were small, but for most mexicanos, the unintended and unplanned clash was a gift—it mirrored the battle of Puebla. Its message was clear: The invaders could be defeated. To the people of Mexico, the outcome of the victory at Tacámbaro also became a sign of a shift in the empire's fortunes. Soon the French invaders would be sent packing once and for all.

To the emperor and his French generals, the defeat was an unmitigated humiliation. They immediately strategized and decided that retribution had to be exacted from the juaristas, as well as from the people of Tacámbaro. It was resolved that Colonel Alfred van der Smissen, a legionnaire himself, was to lead a force to that town to chastise it.

Smissen gladly took command, but when he led his troops into the town, he discovered it was too late to gain anything. Its streets were deserted, its houses and fields uninhabited, and, instead of finding a force to encounter in combat, he found only emptiness. There were no guerrillas to do battle with, no one to punish. Dejected, but left with no other recourse, Smissen declared that he and his troops had achieved a victory. After that, he wheeled his forces around and headed for the capital.

Having signaled ahead that he was returning, Smissen and the legionnaires marched into the city expecting to be greeted as heroes. Their experience, however, was worse than the empty streets of Tacámbaro. Although the streets and plazas of the capital were overflowing, it was a sullen, long-faced crowd that glared at the foreign troops, and it was clear to Colonel Smissen that those people were more than ever resentful of the foreign presence on their land. Secretly proud and overjoyed with the intruders' humiliation, outwardly there was no whooping, no celebrating, only cold stares from that sea of brown faces.

Three women stood out from the rest of the crowd on that day when Colonel van der Smissen led his disgraced legionnaires back into the city. The Chontal sisters looked on with the rest of their people, but they were in turmoil because they understood that their lives were now seriously interlocked with that of the empress, and she appeared to be on the verge of defeat. It could be the end.

Tila murmured, "Es el fin." The man and woman standing in front of them turned and nodded. "Sí, amiga. Es el fin."

Chapter Fourteen

Tila, Chelo and Lula stepped into the atrium of the cathedral on Mexico City's Zócalo to wait for the crowds to thin out. They were surprised to find that others had done the same thing. The vast grounds leading to the church's entrance teemed with motion and noise. Children ran about playing and shouting while mothers called out for the little ones to be still. Vendors, seeing that here was an unexpected opportunity to peddle their wares, milled about, showing off sombreros, rebozos, huaraches and gadgets that everyday people used.

There were women merchants sitting at their regular places on worn-out blankets spread out with displays of tidy piles of lemons, bunches of green onions, chili peppers and unshelled nuts stuffed into paper cones. There was also plenty of food along with fruit beverages for sale at stands that had been hastily put together. In contrast to the moroseness that had met the colonel and his troops, the crowd was now festive.

"¡Arrímese, marchantito! Compre aquí lo que usté guste."

Loud invitations to come and buy clogged the air, clashing, roiling and creating ear-splitting racket. Mocking laughter and cursing aimed at the intruders intensified the commotion. People now felt free to openly celebrate the trouncing of los pelones at Tacámbaro.

The Chontal sisters leaned against one of the walls of the atrium, seemingly the only quiet ones in that milling crowd. Their eyes watched the coming and going of so many people, but their minds were on another matter. Chelo and Lula looked over to Tila, hoping for her lead on what to do next. Tila moved away from the wall and headed toward one of the cathedral's side entrances. There was a minor chapel tucked into a secluded corner of the church. It was wrapped in darkness except for a stand of burning candles, some newly lit and still tall, others nearly burnt out. The sputtering light from those tapers cast flickering shadows on a statue of the Virgin Mary, perched at the highest point of the altar. Next to it were other images of saints and angels that seemed to move in the fluttering candlelight.

When the sisters' eyes finally got used to the gloom, they made out that the place was isolated and that its one pew was empty. There was a silence so deep that it hurt their ears, after having been overwhelmed by the uproar going on outside. They sat on the bench and carefully pulled their shawls low over their faces to muffle whatever they said from any nosy eavesdropper. Lula and Chelo waited for their older sister to speak first, but when she kept quiet, Chelo came to the point.

"If this is the end, what about us?"

"Lower your voice. There might be somebody listening," Tila scolded in a husky whisper. "The end? We cannot be sure that it's the end. Who can? Maybe it is, or maybe it isn't."

The sisters sat shoulder-to-shoulder, whispering. Anyone would think that those women were huddled against one another murmuring prayers and petitions. Lula leaned toward Tila and said, "Well, I say that it's the end or nearly the end. It's in the air, in people's faces and, even if they don't say it out loud, it's what they're thinking. I can see it even in the empress' face and in her eyes. Anyone can tell she's afraid."

Chelo raised the hem of her shawl to get a good look at Tila's face to see if she agreed with Lula. She expected her to say that it was time for them to venture out to look for another place to live.

"I still say we should not make any foolish decisions without being sure that the outsiders will be leaving. We cannot yet be sure. I say, stay where we are."

"Why?" The other two voices chimed in.

"Because it's safe!"

Chelo squirmed in her place, agitated by Tila's words. She pulled back her shawl to expose her face, and her body showed her determination to challenge her older sister.

"Tila, are we never to be like other women? Are we never to have our own families, our own corner to live in, with people to care for and who care for us?"

"Hermana, we're marked women! We're assassins! We're not like other women!"

"Maybe the Acuñas have forgotten us." Lula's voice was strained, almost tearful. "We're nobody. We're three insignificant indias among the many that surround us. How do we even know that Don Baltazar is still alive?"

"¡Ay, hermana! We are not insignificant! We're the murderers of one of them, and it doesn't matter if el patrón is dead or alive; so long as just one of that detestable family lives, we will be pursued until we're found. And if the French intruders do leave our land that will only give the Acuñas more freedom to do what they want."

As Tila rattled off those words her voice rose. When she realized that she was nearly shouting, she abruptly stopped and nervously looked over her shoulder to assure herself that no one had been there to hear. Then, confident that no one was around, she went on, now more quietly.

"I say that we stay on with the empress. Let us wait and see what happens, and if the end for los pelones really comes, then we can make plans, but not before."

Tila waited to hear from her sisters, but when they said nothing, she shifted around in her place so that she was nearly facing them. She didn't have to ask what they thought because that question was pasted on her face.

"Very well, Tila. You're right, but only for now. I say that in the meantime, we prepare a plan to leave the empress when the end comes for the white intruders. When that time comes, we'll have to take the risk of living on our own."

Lula, quietly leaning against the pew, listened to Chelo. Just then a woman and a boy entered the chapel. When they saw that there were no spaces on the bench, they went to the foot of the altar, knelt, made the sign of the cross and began to recite the rosary.

The presence of the woman and boy forced Lula to lower her voice even more. "I agree. Let's wait and see and plan, but only for now. Some day we'll have to stop being cautious."

The Chontal sisters left the chapel, but not before taking time to look at the statue of the Virgin still shrouded in darkness and surrounded by her angels. When the sisters walked out into the atrium, it was bustling with an inviting crowd but they headed for the castle, a long way to go before night set in.

Chapter Fifteen

E mpress Carlota stood on the terrace overlooking the Valley of Anahuac. It was a sight that eased her tension and agitation. Noontime was her favorite time to gaze out on the city, that brief moment when sunlight streamed down and bathed it in a transparent, shimmering light. Carlota cherished this time of day, especially because the sight transported her imagination back to the times of the city's origins and what must have been its past grandeur.

She was vaguely aware of her ladies' chattering behind her as she thought about her precarious empire. The shameful episode at Tacámbaro had now receded in the aftermath of more recent humiliations, too many to remember them all: la Carbonera, Chihuahua, El Guayabo and other battles that had left the empire weakened and humiliated.

Carlota could not keep her thoughts on such harmful events for long, and she turned her mind to Alfred van der Smissen who had become the center of her world. She lived for the times she and he journeyed to Cuernavaca where they were free of gossip and prying eyes. That village had become their retreat, the place where at night they fell asleep in each other's arms, listening to the soft sounds of owls and crickets.

As if hypnotized, Carlota often lost herself in thoughts of their days together, when they strolled along the shimmering pools of the Borda residence, walks filled with the fragrance of orchids and other exotic flowers that often incited them to intimacy.

As often happened when she stood at the terrace reliving her memories, bitter thoughts intruded and pushed that happiness away. She shuddered, remembering the pain she had experienced when Smissen was called to wage battle at Tacámbaro. He had returned safe and untouched, but the agony caused by his absence was irrevocably seared onto her mind. She was afraid of another separation, afraid that she was incapable of bearing the grief of losing him.

Returning her gaze to the city below, Carlota thought of her two years as empress. She lifted her head to look up at the castle's turrets, improved by Maximilian's and her own touches, but she was forced to turn away. The sun was too bright. The empire had brought about some improvements, but not the essential ones, such as education reforms, improvement of roads and even reformation of the Church. Carlota had tried to promote those issues with the emperor's council, but her agenda had been rejected repeatedly.

The empress narrowed her eyes and returned to gaze down at the immense valley. From that vantage point, she made out the massive volcanoes. The city sprawled at their base, a city larger than any she had seen in Europe. Her eyes focused on the causeways and wide avenues laid out by the kingdom's native designers. To this network Maximilian had added an impressive boulevard, cut through forests and hills to connect the castle to the Zócalo. As if spellbound she stared and, as always when looking at that magnificent city, she felt elated.

Her satisfaction was cut short, however, when she gazed over to where her ladies were seated, cheerfully exchanging words about the embroidery they were doing. Carlota turned away when she felt a sharp flash of irritation brought on by their giddiness, a silliness she resented at a time when she was hounded by worries that caused her persistent headaches. Biggest among those worries was

Benito Juárez, the illusive indio who caused the empire constant alarm. In the beginning he was waved off as a harmless nuisance, but now it was undeniable that the masses of her people still considered him to be the president, although she found it difficult to explain how that could be, since he had abandoned his office. Benito Juárez had fled, along with his entire cabinet, without leaving at least a minister to represent him.

Now rumor had it that he was somewhere up north. It was said that he was possibly positioned at Torreón, or perhaps Piedras Negras, or was he in the Texas wilderness? Wherever the little man was, he refused to meet with Maximilian, despite repeated invitations, and he continued to press his followers to harass the French.

The bitter memory of the defeat at Tacámbaro again broke into Carlota's mind, forcing her to rub her forehead. Perhaps even more unsettling was that because of Juárez's stubbornness, the United States was now voicing serious disapproval of the empire. This frightened her more than anything else.

Sickened by these thoughts, Carlota again rubbed her forehead, trying to ease the headache that was tormenting her. She remained very still, as if planted where she was, struggling against the sinking feeling that usually followed these distressing thoughts. Her stomach began to churn and brought on a strong wave of nausea, but she fought it off as she did on those mornings when she was forced to leave her bed to vomit into the hand basin.

Carlota had enough of those thoughts, so she turned to leave the terrace but gestured to her ladies to stay. Leaving the women behind, the empress disappeared into the shadows of the inner corridor and headed for a small patio that connected with her sitting room. From there she rang for a servant. When a footman appeared, she asked for the Chontal sisters to join her.

Carlota sat down to wait for them, leaning her head against the headrest and gazing with half closed eyes at the beauty of that tiny corner of the castle. The shaded patio was quiet, except for the splashing of the fountain, and she closed her eyes to listen. After a few minutes she opened her eyes to look at the beauty of the lush plants surrounding her, fascinated by their exotic colors. For an instant she was transported somewhere far removed from her worries, and she wondered if there were plants in other lands that came close to the beauty of these flowers. In a while her eyelids drooped again, and she forced herself to forget the stress that had threatened to overwhelm her minutes earlier.

The soft patter of huaraches brought Carlota back. When the sisters appeared, she motioned for them to sit on the fountain's ledge. Before speaking, the empress looked intently at them, thinking that it was now two years since they had agreed to be her only attendants. It was they who looked after her needs, private and public, who cared for her when she was in poor health; they even knew of her encounters with Smissen. The sisters were brave enough to stand by her during her frequent outbursts of rage and fits of nervousness when no one else dared come close to her. This intimacy led to her ease in revealing her fears to the sisters.

"Hermanas, what are people saying?"

"Majestad, what people?" asked Tila, who was always the leader.

"Those on the streets, in the marketplace, in churches, in the kitchen."

The sisters, sensing the mood of the empress, looked at one another

"They dislike you." Tila was honest.

"Why? In my heart I'm their mother."

"Alteza, there are so many women who have lost their husbands or sons. The men rage because they feel they have been robbed. They have to beg for their tortillas."

Carlota's eyes widened. What she was hearing didn't surprise her, but it did frighten her. She paused for a few moments to reflect.

"Do they hate me?"

"Some of them do because they know that it is you who governs."

"Me? What about the emperor? What do those gossiping tongues say about him?"

"They say that he spends his time capturing butterflies in his little net," Chelo blurted out.

Carlota pondered the truth of those words. "Do the people laugh at him?"

"Sí, Majestad, but not only for that. Tongues wag about how he also pursues and captures pretty indian girls."

Carlota stared at Tila with inflamed eyes that were made worse by the headache that had returned more painful than before. Maximilian's womanizing was not a surprise; she had known about it soon after they were married. It was something he would not give up, despite being infected with the abominable sickness that made him ill at recurring times. What, in truth, humiliated and mortified her the most was that his ways were a source of gossip in public places.

Carlota leaned back in the chair and closed her eyes to wonder what was being said about her own relationship with Smissen. She would not risk asking because she was afraid of the answer.

Silence enveloped the women. Only the fountain's murmur filled the air, and all the while Carlota felt her heart racing. This latest detail, along with the other catastrophic news, explained why she and Maximilian had grown so unpopular among their subjects. She asked herself who was more to blame: he or she?

As if in answer to her question, Chelo broke into her thoughts. "Alteza, con respeto, we will say that you, more than the emperor, have angered the people."

Taken aback, Carlota sat up to face her. "Why? In what way?" Her voice was low and sharp.

"Because they are poor and hungry, and you are so rich."

This time Carlota's breath faltered, and she felt a dull, suffocating feeling in the pit of her stomach. She had overheard whispers that claimed that her spending was excessive and too costly. But hearing it from Chelo's lips stunned her. She was aware that the court gossiped about the manner in which she had refurbished the castle. She knew that it was said that everything she touched became an extravagant misuse of money, that her clothing, carriages and stables were a wasteful expense, even beyond the ways of the wealthiest. But it was only now that she understood that criticism of her spending had seeped out, reaching all the way down to the streets.

Hearing this unnerved Carlota. She had wanted the opposite. She desired to show love for her people, not disregard. It was for that reason that she traveled to remote parts of the empire, not holding back from mosquito infested jungles, making her way over nearly impassable roads that jarred her bones and sickened her stomach. But now she was hearing that her style, so natural to her, had become the heart of anger and gossip, even more heated than the emperor's laziness and appetite for native women.

"If I have made the castle and other things beautiful it's because it's appropriate for an emperor and empress to live in such a manner. Would those gossiping tongues have us live in huts?"

"No, Majestad, but people think that you have gone too far."

Lula's words rankled Carlota until her impulsive temper flared. She angrily got to her feet and swiveled in different directions, looking for an object, anything to fling at the sisters, but there was nothing. Instead she lunged toward the farthest corner of the terrace, putting space between her and them. Her face had reddened and her lips pinched into a thin straight line. She had reached her limit. Too much was going wrong, and she could no longer listen.

"It is you, Lula, who have gone too far! You and your ungrateful sisters!"

"Perdón, Alteza, but you asked us to speak."

"Leave me! Get out, the three of you!"

Without a word, the sisters moved toward the inner part of the chamber. When they were almost out of Carlota's sight, she called after them. Her voice was now toned down and under control.

"Wait! Come back!"

The sisters looked at her and sensed that she was desperately trying to regain control of herself, so they returned. Carlota went back to the chair and sat down, closed her eyes and tried to hold back the tears that nonetheless streamed out and rolled down her cheeks.

The women sat facing each other in silence. When Carlota regained her composure, she spoke in a whisper, forcing the sisters to lean forward.

"I asked what is being said and you responded, but I became angry. Now I want to know more of what my enemies are saying about me, so don't be afraid to tell me more. Believe me, I need to hear what you have to say."

There was an uneasy pause while the sisters looked at one another and then nodded. Finally, Lula spoke up.

"Much gossip is about you not sleeping with the emperor and that you will never conceive a child."

"Lula, where did you hear this talk?" Carlota's voice deepened and her body stiffened against the chair.

"Alteza, servants have long tongues, and we have good ears. No secrets are hidden from maids and footmen, and they spread what they hear in kitchens and dark corridors."

Carlota could hardly believe her ears. Suddenly, the seditious juaristas and their successes, even the foolish French generals, as well as the cunning French emperor, receded. It all became inconsequential, even petty, compared to what she was hearing. Unable to speak, she gaped at Lula, who went on speaking.

"The maid who knocks on the bedroom door each morning, the other one who serves the coffee, her helper whose duty it is to open the curtains, and especially the ones who make the bed, they know more than anyone else because it is the bed that tells the truest story. Bed sheets reveal what cannot be denied. They know that the emperor sleeps alone when he's in the castle "

Carlota sat up stiff and unmoving. Her eyes bulged and she clenched her hands into fists. Suddenly her head snapped in the direction of the sisters to glare at them. They, more than anyone, knew that she didn't sleep with the emperor. They were witnesses to what she and Smissen did in the cathedral, as well as in the chambers of the Borda residence.

"You say that it's the servants that are spreading this poisonous gossip? Who else apart from them is taking part in this malicious talk?"

"Even more than your servants, Majestad, it is your ladies and others of your court who whisper behind your back. They gossip that it is not that you are barren but that you don't sleep with your husband."

Mortified, Carlota licked her lips and clamped her eyes shut, refusing to look out on such a world. She was profoundly ashamed that her intimate life was a source of gossip, not only in the kitchen, but also in the privacy of her chambers. How could she not have known it? Outrage thrashed her heart and the more she reflected, the more she blamed herself. It was her fault because she had behaved in unguarded ways. She had allowed indecent eyes to spy and long tongues to wag.

With her eyes still clamped shut, Carlota imagined that she overheard the vulgarities exchanged in laundry rooms and over boiling pots. She well knew that servants had no pity when it came to gossiping about the private lives of their masters. As if she were present, standing hidden somewhere in a darkened corner of a kitchen, she caught sight of sleazy winks and wicked glances sliding from eye to eye.

And what about her treacherous ladies? Carlota's vivid imagination recreated lewd words about her and Maximilian, passing from mouth to mouth, snickering behind fans about unsoiled bed sheets and about a bedchamber that didn't echo with the moans and sighs of lovemaking. She now saw that her servers as well as the court mocked her behind her back.

Feeling intense humiliation, but at the same time blaming herself for allowing her privacy to be at the center of the scandal, Carlota felt lost. She desperately needed to shift the blame, to find someone else to accuse or hurt, so she unfairly snapped at Lula.

"It's not your business nor anyone else's if Maximilian and I do, or do not, share the same bed. Furthermore, I forbid you to ever speak of this again."

"Majestad, you asked."

Carlota had stopped listening. As if she had been in a deep sleep from which her companions had awakened her, she now felt sick and hurting. She got to her feet to walk to the edge of the veranda, but her legs were trembling so violently that she feared her knees might buckle. She reached out and clung to the banister.

Carlota looked upward at the sky where the sun was now slipping into its western cradle. She then turned her gaze down at the city she had grown to love, imagining the comings and goings of her subjects at that moment. She closed her eyes. Behind swollen eyelids, she saw candles and lamps being lit in homes, in churches, along archways linking plazas and street corners.

Empress Carlota returned to the chair to sit, lost in thought. She was again thinking about the imminent collapse of the empire, but even more about the pernicious gossiping. Just as tormenting was the deeper secret that she hid, the reason for the nausea as well as the changes in her body. Soon her condition would be evident, but people would know that it was not Maximilian's child. There would be no celebrations in honor of the long-awaited heir. There would only be shame for her and scandal for the empire.

"Hermanas, what else are those evil tongues saying?"

"They whisper about you and el coronel belga."

The Belgian colonel! The Belgian colonel! Those words drummed in Carlota's mind over and again because they confirmed what she had feared. Her relationship with Smissen was out, and there was nothing that could be done to put that secret back into hiding.

Carlota knew that it was not her companions who had betrayed her, but rather she herself with the looks she shared with Smissen, unveiled, unguarded glances filled with love and longing. She had carelessly shown her love for him with her gestures, her smiles. Those hungry gossiping vultures had detected every detail.

Carlota said no more. Instead, she surrendered to the approaching night chill. The sky had turned from crimson to pale blue. The cicadas and other night creatures were intoning their nocturnal song in the gardens and forests surrounding Chapultepec Castle. Night had begun its descent on the Valley of Anahuac.

Chapter Sixteen

When word leaked out that the empress was gravely ill, the rumor spread that she was bewitched. In a matter of days, the castle was alive with talk of how she perceived shadows where there were none and that she heard voices even when she was alone. It was whispered that the empress screamed and ranted, that she pulled her hair until the skin on her head bled, that she threw herself on the floor, twisting in pain, and that not even her Indian maids could help her.

It was not long after news of Carlota's symptoms circulated that the imperial household was gripped in fear. It was suspected that a dose of toloache had been slipped into her morning chocolate at a moment when the sisters were not vigilant or had been deliberately distracted by someone. When the news spread through the corridors, chambers and kitchens, what at first was a dim suspicion soon turned to utter certainty. Everyone was terrorized because, if the empress was infected, the mysterious illness or poison could strike again.

"The empress is bewitched!"

¡La emperatriz está embrujada!

There was no doubt that the spell cast on the empress was induced by toloache, a powerful concoction put together by skillful sorceresses. It was common knowledge that only witches held the secret of the dark root that thrives in dry stony ground. The plant is unusually stunted, with twisted thorny branches that give off a prickly fruit stuffed with tiny black seeds. At night those seeds become infested with nocturnal insects that carry the infernal slime to the unsuspecting.

Toloache is scarce, growing in hidden crevices at the foot of volcanoes. It is so difficult to find that only the most cunning of witches knows how to detect it. Those same witches know that the ancients used toloache to provoke passionate love in the object of desire. They know also that if used in excessive doses, the drug distilled from those black pods is known to induce madness or even death.

In the streets of the city and in its marketplaces, the rumor of Empress Carlota's spell ran wild from stall to stall where the peddlers of herbs and roots gathered. When they heard the symptoms, those healers affirmed that it could be nothing but toloache that had bewitched the empress. From garbage-strewn alleyways, the gossip slithered its way back up into the castle's kitchens, where cooks, scullery maids and even errand boys, wide-eyed and terror-stricken, made the sign of the cross as they wondered who had done such an evil thing to the young empress.

The elders claimed to know the answer. The guilty one was Concha Sedano, known as India Bonita, the emperor's favorite mistress who was insanely jealous of the beautiful Carlota and who feared that the emperor might leave her to return to his wife. The Sedano woman, the toothless ones said, was the daughter of a clan of witches and sorcerers, cruel people who stopped at nothing to harm anyone who thwarted their wicked ways. For such people, the ancient use of toloache was their usual revenge.

Empress Carlota's subjects did not doubt what the elders said about the powers of toloache. They knew that a witch's skill easily crossed family and class lines, that it respected nothing, not even the privilege of an empress, and they knew that unless a more powerful potion was brought in to counter the powers of the drug, Empress Carlota would descend into irreversible lunacy and soon die.

The Chontal sisters were among those who didn't doubt that their empress had been bewitched, but they were also aware that it was not the only thing that had sickened her. Serious matters were accosting Carlota. She was devastated because Emperor Napoleon finally did what she most feared: he reneged. Adding to her grief, General Francoise Bazaine and his young bride abandoned Mexico for France. This was followed by another desertion: The French emperor recalled Colonel Alfred van der Smissen, who followed the order without losing time. He put together his gear and left only a note filled with words of love and reminiscences, along with a postscript promising he would wait for Carlota in Brussels. The magnitude of so many betrayals that had helped cause the empress' curious illness was evident to the sisters.

On one of Carlota's worst days, Chelo, Tila and Lula disregarded her inexplicable orders to keep away and came to help with her needs. They knew they could make themselves useful, especially since she was carrying a child that was also exposed to the poison.

When the sisters entered the room, they tiptoed cautiously over the tiled floor, trying not to be heard. They reached the empress, who was pacing, lost in thought, and they stood for a time to observe her. If Carlota was to be helped, they were the ones to do it. As she walked throughout the chamber, she mumbled and ranted strange words. She was disheveled and her clothing was rumpled, even soiled. Her feet were bare and dirty.

The sisters were alarmed to see the empress in that condition. The poison was having its effect, they reasoned, and they had to act quickly to undo its evil. Finally, Chelo found the courage to get Carlota's attention.

"Alteza, we're here."

Startled, the empress turned in different directions trying to detect where the voice had come from. As Carlota stood in the middle of the room, the sisters noticed how rapidly the pregnancy had advanced. They were even more alarmed, remembering that with each hour the toloache was penetrating further into every part of her body. But what made the tiny hairs on their necks stand erect was Carlota's face. Her eyes were reddened, her pupils dilated and her lids swollen. Her complexion was pasty, her cheeks sunken and her lips dry and cracked, although her tongue tried to moisten them over and again.

Her usually lustrous hair was dull. It draped limply on her shoulders, and this, more than anything, gave her a haggard, aged appearance. Carlota blinked at the sisters, trying to see through blurred eyes until she finally realized who they were. When she recognized them, she showed relief, not the anger they had feared.

"You've come." She spoke as if the sisters had intentionally kept away, as if she had forgotten that it was she who had commanded them to keep away.

Although bewildered, the sisters put aside their confusion and moved closer to Carlota, committed to never leaving her side again. Not even the terror of becoming targets themselves could intimidate those sisters, now resolved to find the potion that would counter the evil effect of the drug.

Chelo and Lula led Carlota by the hands toward a chair. Tila settled her down, gathered her hair away from her damp neck and bound it high on her head. They didn't speak as they went about removing Carlota's soiled gown to sponge her arms, shoulders, breasts and the rest of her fevered body as well as her feet.

She, too, was quiet; her eyes were closed and her head reclined against the back of the chair, while she surrendered to those ministering hands. At one point, Chelo put the palm of her hand on Carlota's belly. When she felt movement, she looked at her sisters to confirm that the child was alive.

As they performed that silent ritual, the women again experienced the same emotion they had felt the first time they had assisted the empress, with the difference that the bond that drew them together had grown, as if a bridge had spanned the edges of their different worlds, connecting them unconditionally. In the midst of the empress' collapsing world, she and her companions clung to one another simply and quietly, because there was no one else. They were alone. They needed one another.

As they led her to the bed, Carlota still didn't speak, except for words that she repeated from time to time. "It's the end. The empire's doomed. The child will be lost." At other times she murmured, "He left me. I'll never see him again. I'm alone." After that, she said nothing else.

The sisters looked at one another in understanding—the news of the Belgian colonel's departure had run wild as soon as it was known that the foreign soldiers were departing. However, a greater fear than a fleeing lover now weighed heavily on the sisters.

"Hermanas, what's happening to me?" Taken by surprise by Carlota's question, the sisters interrupted what they were doing.

"You have been bewitched, Majestad," Tila whispered.

"Bewitched! How? Who could have done this to me?"

"It is said that Concha Sedano is the one. The emperor's favorite."

Carlota sagged limply into the bed, closed her eyes and drifted off, making the sisters think that she had lapsed into the death-like stupor induced by toloache. Suddenly Carlota contorted, arched her back and violently pushed her belly up, only to fall back onto the bed. She let out a piercing scream with her mouth grotesquely opened, tongue stretched out and trembling in pain. Carlota's shrieks grew louder, rippling and bouncing off the chamber walls. Blood saturated her gown so fast and so profusely that she looked on the verge of death.

Carlota's ordeal lasted hours, until the fetus dripped from between her distended thighs. Only then did she stop wailing, and she fell into unconsciousness. Chelo took the tiny body in her hands and raised it to show it to the others. It was a girl child, nearer to her final term than to the beginning. Although fully formed, she was dead.

The sisters knew what had to be done. Putting aside their sadness, they went about the business of washing and changing Carlota. After that, Lula went to the door to call a maid, another india.

"Amiga, keep vigil over the empress. We will return soon."

With the wrapped bundle hidden, the sisters walked the nearly deserted corridors of the castle. The usual flurry of maids and servants was missing, as if something was about to happen. The Chontal sisters hurriedly descended the rear stairway until they reached the kitchen's back door leading to the herb and flower gardens. It was there that they searched until they found a quiet place where lush white flowers grew under an ancient tree. Tila, Chelo and Lula got on their knees to dig with their hands until they reached the depth they wanted. Finally, panting, sweating and with soiled hands, they rested. When Lula was about to lower the bundle into the earth, something compelled them to pause.

"The child should have a name before she meets the gods." Tila's voice was muffled. "It should be a name that will bring joy to her mother every time she thinks of her daughter."

The sisters looked around for inspiration until Chelo bent over to pluck a white flower with an especially lovely bloom.

"Let us call her Tlazoxochitl. Even the gods will welcome their newest precious flower," she suggested.

Having chosen a name, the sisters lowered Carlota's daughter into the grave, packed it and, while still on their knees, recited a final prayer for Precious Flower in their native tongue.

Go, Beloved Daughter, to the region where light begins and there scatter your flowers. Go to the land sown with seed and there also scatter your flowers. Scatter your flowers, Beloved Daughter, until you reach the gods.

When Lula, Tila and Chelo returned to Carlota's room, they found the empress still unconscious, making them even more anxious to go out immediately in search of the only sorcerer who had the power to cure their mistress. Tila turned to the maid who had been watching over the empress.

"Stay with her. Let nothing take you from her side. You will allow no one to come into this room. You will not give her anything to drink or eat. Nothing! Not even water! If you do, we will know, and then only the gods will be able to help you. Do you understand?"

"But how will I be able to deny entrance if one of the ladies comes to the door? Me, a poor india?"

"Bolt the door! Pretend you cannot hear! Do whatever comes to your mind! Anything! The lady will soon lose patience and leave anyway."

The sisters disappeared into the gloom of the corridor. The sun was by now setting, and already long shadows were creeping up the side of the hill toward the castle. Despite the rapidly descending night, Tila, Chelo and Lula began their long trek toward Tepito, the infamous dwelling place of witches and sorcerers

The sisters had by now armed themselves with the name of the only sorcerer powerful enough to challenge the Sedano tribe. It was in Tepito, that squalid barrio, that he performed his rituals. Everyone was aware of the dangers lurking in that labyrinth of grimy alleyways and hovels. Knowing that it was the only place where they could find el yerbolero, compelled the sisters to search him out. Tila led her sisters down the steep hill away from the castle to search the entire night, if necessary, for the man who could tell them what herb or root could save Carlota's life and mind.

At the bottom of the hill, the sisters ran into a peddler packing his cart with what was left of his wares: pots, pans and other kitchen utensils. His burro was hitched, waiting patiently for the signal to head home for the night.

"Indias, where are you going?"

"To Tepito."

"¡Ah, jijo! That's far away and dangerous."

"Sí, Señor."

"Well, as long as you understand, jump on and I will help you on your journey."

"Gracias, Señor."

The sisters climbed into the cart, grateful that the peddler was willing to take them all the way to the edges of Tlatelolco. With a click of his tongue, the man got the burro to give a hefty pull, and the cart lumbered toward the Zócalo. Once there, the cart moved past the cathedral, where it cut over a little to the left into the warren of dark crooked streets now beginning to empty for the night. Lanterns on posts were lighted, and some people held torches to light their way to wherever they were going.

The cart creaked at every turn of its wheels, more so when it slipped into a rut, making the pots and pans crash against one another. Hardly noticing the rough jolts and swaying, the sisters didn't complain. Instead, they rolled with the cart as it pitched from side to side. When the long ride came to an end, the peddler turned to the women huddled against the rear of the cart. He saw that they were dozing, despite the rough ride.

"¡Epa, indias! This is it." The man's voice startled the sisters. They reacted, alert right away, jumped out of the cart and thanked him again for his kindness.

"Gracias, Señor."

"You're welcome. Can I be of more help?"

"Possibly. Do you know of a healer by the name of el yerbolero?" asked Tila.

"Healer? Sorcerer is more like it! I know of him, but you must be very careful with that man. Everyone knows that he's dangerous."

"Thank you again, but we need him. Where can we find him?"

"There. Through that little street."

For a moment the peddler hesitated, apparently concerned for the women, but then he shrugged his shoulders, raised his sombrero and flicked the burro's rear end. The cart lurched into the darkness while the sisters stood looking toward the shadowy street pointed out by the peddler.

"Tila, I'm afraid. Aren't you?" asked Chelo.

"Yes, sister, but what is to be done? The empress will die if we don't do something. Lula, why are you so quiet? Are you so afraid that your tongue is stiff?"

"I'm afraid." That was all Lula was able to squeeze out of her dry mouth.

After exchanging those whispered words, the sisters pulled their shawls low over their brows and disappeared into the inky gloom. They trekked over slimy uneven cobblestones, holding on to one another, knowing that they were in the heart of a forbidden slum, where thieves, beggars, sorcerers and other outcasts took refuge. With each step, Tila, Chelo and Lula remembered that Tepito was a place where even those in charge of enforcing the law thought twice before penetrating. Nevertheless, the sisters plunged into that squalid place because they had no choice. Nothing was going to stop them from finding the cure for Empress Carlota's bewitchment.

Night had fallen but streets, sidewalks and doorways were filled with people, faceless shadows that appeared and disappeared from nowhere in particular. Even more frightening was the silence that wrapped itself around those mute phantoms. The usual chatter, loud talk and laughter of ordinary streets were missing. An eerie quiet shielded the fronts of houses, as well as their windows that looked out onto the street like empty eye sockets.

The sisters didn't allow themselves to be intimidated by the bleakness of those streets. Instead, they went from person to person asking the whereabouts of el yerbolero. One or two people shook their shoulders and mumbled that they didn't know of such a man. Others rolled their eyes in disbelief. Most of them simply turned their back and walked away.

After a while of so much disregard, the sisters were close to losing hope, when their attention was drawn to a soft whistle coming from an alley at the end of the street. They followed the signal and found an old woman who was so shrouded by her shawl that only her long nose was visible in the gloom. When she spoke, she lisped through toothless gums.

"Indias, why are you searching for el yerbolero?"

Chelo, Lula and Tila sensed that at last here was someone that might give them information. They formed a circle and surrounded the woman to press her farther into the dark alley. They kept quiet for a while, taking in her short hunched body as well as the rags that covered her. When they spoke, the sisters did so in whispers.

"Old woman, do you know where we can find him?" asked Tila.

"Before I answer, tell me your reason for searching for him."

"No! You tell us now where he is or you will regret it," threatened Tila.

"What will you do to me if I don't tell?"

Three clenched fists appeared under the hag's long nose. And then with unexpected speed, those fists opened, reached deep under the old woman's dirty shawl and grabbed her braids.

"If you don't tell, these braids will be torn off your old scull. What do you say?" grumbled Chelo.

"¡Ay! You're hurting this old woman. Have a little respect and I'll lead you to the place."

Her voice was shrill, more frightened than in pain, but with her braids still in Chelo's grip, the old woman led the way to the sorcerer's den. All along the way, the old hag squealed, ¡Ay! ¡Ay! ¡Ay!

The women trudged along dark, crooked streets until the old woman stopped in front of a heavy wooden portal. She scratched at the door with overgrown fingernails until it opened slowly on creaking hinges. All four stepped gingerly into a large room with smoked-smeared walls and a high-vaulted ceiling. The floor of the place was earthen and littered with tattered baskets, broken boxes, even remnants of what had been a chair. The only light in the chamber came from the glow radiated from a fireplace that was cluttered with blackened iron pots and kettles. One of them was boiling so hard that it was overflowing, letting off a hissing whistle.

When they got inside the room, the old woman squirmed and pulled until she shook herself free from Chelo's grip, only to fall from the force of her resistance. Before the sisters could react, the hag crawled on her hands and knees toward the darkest corner of the room, where she squeezed in behind a man who was squatted next to the fire. The sisters' eyes adjusted to the gloom in time to see her disappear behind his back and snuggle there, as if she had been a mouse taking cover in its nest.

With the old woman out of sight, the sisters' eyes shifted to the man. It had to be the yerbolero. As if in unison, their spines tingled and their eyes became saucers. They stood holding on to one another, trying to fight off their fear. The man glared at them, silently waiting for them to say something. Somehow the women drew courage and returned his stare.

El yerbolero was dressed like other men: white cotton shirt and pants, with his feet strapped into worn-out huaraches. The sisters looked at him and saw un indio who was neither old nor young, neither thin nor fat, and because he was squatting, they could not tell if he was tall or short. In the fire's flickering shadows, his face appeared to be made of carved wood, and his eyes were like those of the idols of their ancestors.

As the man examined the sisters, they thought that the pupils of his eyes were so black that they must have been obsidian stone, not flesh. His moustache was scraggly, hanging limply from the edges of his wide, thin-lipped mouth. His skin was even darker than their mahogany-toned complexions. Most frightening of all were his fingernails that were overgrown and curved like the talons of a vulture.

"What are you called?" the man asked.

"I'm Tila. These are my sisters Chelo and Lula."

The man asked no more about names, but only went on glowering at them, evidently trying to decipher their identities while he examined them from top to bottom.

"Why have you come here?"

"To talk to you."

Only Tila spoke and el yerbolero narrowed his slanted eyes. He took a long pause before saying anything, all the while keeping his eyes riveted on the three women. He finally gestured for them to squat down on the floor.

"How did you find me?"

"We asked."

"What do you want of me?"

"Our señora has been put under a spell, and we know that you can save her."

"Who is your señora?"

"La Emperatriz Carlota de México."

"She's our enemy. Why should I save her?"

"Because she has been sickened with toloache by Concha Sedano, the daughter of the tribe of sorcerers who claim to be stronger than you."

El yerbolero didn't react to the mention of the notorious tribe of witches and warlocks. He merely kept his eyes on the sisters, apparently still trying to read their thoughts and intentions. At last, he slanted his eyes yet more and nodded, letting them know that he was ready to take up the challenge of proving his own powers.

"If I save her, what will you give me in return?"

"We have no money."

"What do you have?"

"Our loyalty."

When the sorcerer heard those words, he broke his steely image and gawked at the sisters in disbelief, but then in an instant his face returned to its wooden expression. After a few moments of thinking, he leaned his head to one side to look at the sisters with an expression that had become different.

"There's something else besides loyalty that I will accept in payment."

"Señor, speak." Again, it was Tila doing the talking.

"If I heal your señora, you'll have to bring back something that belongs to the Sedano woman. It matters not what object it is, as long as it has touched her skin."

Expecting a more daunting condition, the sisters looked at one another, puzzled. After some hesitation, they asked to be allowed to speak privately. El yerbolero assented, and they shuffled into a tight circle to face one another. They huddled and whispered until they came up with a plan.

"We agree, but because our señora is near death, the cure must begin soon. We give you our oath, on our knees and in the name of Tonantzín that we will get something that has clung to the skin of that evil woman to bring to you. But first, the cure."

El yerbolero turned to the old woman, who was dozing against his back. She became alert as soon as he whispered something into her ear. Her shawl had slid off her head, revealing stringy gray braids that she tried to cover as she got to her feet and shuffled to a table in the far corner of the room.

The sisters, still on their knees, stretched their necks in an effort to see what the hag was doing, but because she was shrouded in a shadowy niche, they saw very little. They heard only the opening of clay jars and the clinking of what they thought were spoons. Not long afterward, she brought el yerbolero two pouches, which he took and signaled the sisters to come closer to him. They obeyed his order and he handed Tila one of the little bags.

"You must first make a tea with these yerbas. Make certain to brew it in a clay pot, enough for two cups. Make your señora drink every drop. When she does, she will vomit so much that you will think that death has come for her. But be not deceived. She will not die. She will instead be cleansed of the poisonous toloache."

Handing Chelo the second pouch with such care that the women knew its content was precious, he gave them his last instructions. The sorcerer barely whispered, and they had to gather so close to him that they could feel the heat radiating from his body.

"This is yerba santa. Brew it in a separate clay pot and again make enough for two cups. Before giving it to your señora, wrap her in a heavy shroud, just as if she had died and you were preparing her for burial. Her entire body must be covered except for her nose and mouth. After she drinks the yerba santa, she will sweat profusely. After that she will fall into a deep sleep. Again you will think that she is dead, but you will be wrong. It will be a sign of her descent to Tezcatlipoca's underworld, down there where the dead reside.

Once in Mictlan, your señora will travel on a pathway that will take her to face her fallen ancestors where she will ask them of their suffering and punishments, and they will ask about her own deeds. She will then weep and agonize because of what she hears, but you, indias, must not be frightened, and above all do not abandon her. She will be that way for many hours until she awakens. When that happens, she will remember nothing of her journey to the underbelly of the world. After that, she will be well and her mind will be safe."

With no more to say, Tila, Lula and Chelo got to their feet, holding their precious bags and bowed low in acknowledgment of el yerbolero's wisdom. When they reached the doorway, they turned to him and silently let him know that they were grateful.

"Señor, we will be back with the object we have promised."

"I have no doubt. In the meantime, remember that the Sedano witch will know everything. She will rage and claw at your door while you minister the cure. She will attempt to break into your enclosed chamber. She will do everything to destroy you and your señora, but she will be helpless, because my power surpasses hers."

Chapter Seventeen

Their return from Tepito was long and hazardous, but the Chontal sisters arrived at Chapultepec before sunrise. The pouch containing the precious yerba santa was tucked deep between Tila's breasts. Chelo protected the other bag, and Lula trekked ahead, leading the safest way back to the castle.

As they began their ascent up Chapultepec Hill, the sisters were nearly run over by a rush of carriages going in the opposite direction. They were vehicles loaded with officials and their wives, all of them with desperate expressions on their faces. Most were disheveled and showed signs of having dressed hastily. Carts piled high with valises, boxes and pieces of furniture followed the coaches. Adding to the pandemonium were soldiers, some on foot and others mounted on horses.

Scrambling maids and servants, charged with protecting their masters' belongings, struggled as they pulled the reins on horses and mules, slowing down movement to nearly a standstill. The din caused by that turmoil was so intense that the sisters had to shout just to hear one another above neighing horses, crunching carriage wheels and yelling people, all of them obviously frantic to flee.

Afraid that they were falling into the same panic without knowing the reason, but trying to find out what had happened to cause the frenzy, the sisters asked one person, then another. No one paid attention, either pushing away or simply refusing to pause long enough to answer. It was not until they shoved their way against the current that the sisters finally reached the back entrance of the castle, where they found a kitchen boy.

"¡Epa, muchacho! ¿Qué pasa?"

"Everyone's leaving."

"We can see that for ourselves. Tell us why they're running."

"The emperor and his generals have left to do battle against the juaristas and he's taken all of his soldiers. The court and even the city are unguarded."

"Where did he go?"

"To Querétaro, I think. Now everyone is scared because President Juárez's people are on their way here to kill all the Frenchies."

"Is everybody running?"

"Yes, everybody except for a few maids and the women and men who are to go with the empress."

"Go? Where?"

"Back to where she came from . . . I think."

"Gracias, muchacho."

Bewildered by this unexpected turn, the Chontal sisters moved over to an out-of-the-way corner and there they formed a tight huddle. Although there was no one nearby, even the boy had disappeared, they whispered, wagged their heads and agitatedly gestured with their hands. How could it be that the empress was to return to her land when she was near death? Everybody knew it. The trip to Vera Cruz was itself long and dangerous, and the towns on the road to the port were infested with the black fever. How could her ladies care for her when they were more concerned about their own welfare?

¡Ay, Santo Dios! Doubts filled the sisters with a powerful urge to join the fleeing mob, but the thought of Carlota, that she was alone and that they had promised to see to her cure, cut short their apprehension. Without anything else to say, they stopped whispering and headed for Carlota's chamber.

The corridors were empty. As they approached the empress' rooms, the sisters heard unusual chatter and scraping coming from a room. Lula paused to stick her nose into the room's open door and saw the ladies preparing for a long journey. In that brief instant, her sharp eyes took in trunks, piles of dresses, shoes littering the floor, undergarments hanging out of drawers. Unexpectedly, one of the ladies jerked her head in Lula's direction. Lula tried to slide out of view, but she was not quick enough. A heavy hand grabbed her shoulder.

"¡Mira, india! Why are you sticking your nose in what's none of your affair?"

"Señora, con respeto, the Empress Carlota is our affair."

Rattled by Lula's audacity, her two sisters quickly grabbed her and all three disappeared into the darkened hallway toward Carlota's chambers. They had to pound on the door before a voice responded.

"¿Quién es?"

"Amiga, we've returned. Open quickly!"

The maid opened the door, her face filled with fear, but it faded when she realized that the Chontal sisters had finally returned.

"Amiga, you waited for us."

"Sí. I said I would. The empress is not herself. She's been in another world all the time that you've been gone. She screams and calls out names that I don't recognize, then she falls back into the shadows of her spirit, only to twist on the bed in great pain."

"We'll help her. We found el yerbolero, and we have la cura, but we can't waste time. Will you help us?"

"Sí."

"We need a brazier, wood, water and two clay pots. Go to the kitchen and bring those things quickly. You'll need help. Look for a boy that was there a while ago. He's probably still hiding down there, so look everywhere for him, even under the stove. He'll help you. ¡Pronto! We don't have time to lose."

The maid did find the boy, and together they carted the things to begin Carlota's cure. As soon as they delivered their load, the frightened boy sprinted out of the room and vanished, but the maid stayed with the sisters to help. Outside, the din of the fleeing mob was diminishing, although there was still some leftover racket that rose to where the empress lay unconscious. Clopping hooves, clanging swords, creaking carts mixed with high-pitched female voices and husky male shouts.

Ignoring the commotion, the women set about their task. One started a fire in the brazier, another put water to boil and the others undressed Carlota to wash her perspiration-soaked body. When that was done, one of the sisters cradled her while another spooned the first herbal brew into her mouth, causing her to retch. They waited until Carlota stopped vomiting. When that passed, she was heavily shrouded, and with that the second tea was given to her.

So it was that the women worked silently in the darkened room with the light of the burning embers in the brazier and the only sounds of splashing water, the muted rustle of covers and heavy breathing.

Suddenly, a scratching at the door shattered the quiet of the chamber. At first the sound was faint, but then it became a powerful clawing until the women thought that the door might splinter into pieces. They stopped what they were doing to gawk at the door, and when Chelo made a move to open it, Lula grabbed her arm.

"Stop! It's the Sedano woman. She's come to attack us just as el yerbolero said."

The scratching grew even louder until it became a terrifying pawing and pummeling, but when it was ignored, a fearful moaning began. It seemed to creep into the room from under the door and to seep in around its hinges.

¡Ayyyyyyyy! ¡Ayyyyyyy!

"Hurry, hermanas! Close the windows and the terrace door. Lock everything. Nothing must come in. Not light, not even air."

No sooner had Tila uttered those words than the banging shifted from the door to the outside windows and the terrace. Just as if Sedano had wings to fly, the pounding now went on from the outside of the bedchamber. Like a bat, the sorceress seemed to be clinging to the exterior walls of the castle, assisted by what must have been a dozen demons at her command to hammer at every window. The beating and shrieking intensified until it became so violent that Carlota's bedroom shuddered and vibrated as if struck by an earthquake.

The women were terrified, but they would not interrupt the treatment. Carlota's life depended on it. They chanted prayers in their native tongue, reciting incantations to Tonantzín and Coatlicue as they labored, even though the howling and banging went on for hours until the evil spirit spent itself. Finally, there was silence.

The cure took hours to complete, but at last it was done. The exhausted and traumatized women had toiled without rest from sunrise to sunset, but they had followed el yerbolero's instructions step by step. Now there was nothing else for them to do but stand guard over the empress, who was shrouded and laid out on the bed as if ready to be buried.

Carlota's companions, although exhausted, watched closely, knowing that she had descended to the deepest regions of Mictlan, where she was mingling with those who inhabited the kingdom of the dead. Among them were her ancestors who would guide her back to this world of sunlight. There, too, Carlota would find her beloved daughter, embrace and kiss her. Together, mother and daughter would live in an instant the lifetime that had been denied them.

The women by now were free of the terror that had filled them during the night and now they could think of Carlota's recuperation. Suddenly, a loud knock at the door jarred them out of their thoughts. Terrified that it was again the Sedano witch, the sisters recoiled and braced themselves. It was only when they heard a familiar voice calling out from the other side of the door that they relaxed. They remembered that the empress was expected to be preparing for her journey to the coast. Lula went to the door, opened it and cautiously made certain that it was one of the empress' ladies.

"Is the empress ready for the passage? "

"No, señora, she is not."

"When will she be ready?"

"She needs more time."

"How much more time?"

"Maybe tomorrow."

After that, knocking at the door by Carlota's ladies went on periodically, and each time the lady went away more and more exasperated. Each time she returned, she was more impatient and eventually on the verge of anger, but nothing could be done. The empress was indisposed, and the traveling party had to wait.

As Carlota recovered, the agitation and commotion in the hallways and chambers outside her room quieted until it finally stopped. The castle emptied, leaving only the party assigned to accompany the empress to Vera Cruz, where a steamer awaited to transport the empress and her retinue to France.

On the second day after her cure, Carlota opened her eyes and finally returned to where Tila, Chelo and Lula were waiting for her. Just as the yerbolero had foretold, she spoke of nothing nor did she appear to remember anything. When that happened, the sisters knew that she was almost herself again, despite some disorientation as she looked around with vacant eyes. They saw also that Carlota's face had changed. It was older, a shadow of pain was cast over it. When she tried to get out of the bed, she was so unsteady that she was forced to lean back on the bedpost.

More time was needed for her recuperation, so the Chontal sisters silently went about packing her belongings. In the meantime, without knowing why, Lula looked over to Carlota's bed and found her standing quietly on her feet without any help. The sisters immediately dropped what they were doing and gathered around the empress.

"Alteza, not so soon." Chelo was at Carlota's side before the others. "You're too weak."

"I can stand. Look!"

Carlota raised her arms to show that she was firmly on her feet. "What has happened?"

"You were very sick, Majestad," answered Chelo.

The empress looked around the room, taking in the folded bundles of undergarments, shoes, dresses and all the other things that were to be packed.

"What is all of this?"

"Majestad, prepare yourself."

"For what, Tila?"

"For the journey back to your land."

The empress looked at Tila, trying to focus on her words, but time was needed before her memory returned. Maximilian had banished her from Mexico in retribution for refusing to accept the adoption of Agustín and Salvador de Iturbide, grandsons of the deposed emperor of Mexico, Agustín de Iturbide. The older boy was to be designated successor to the Mexican throne because Carlota and Maximilian had failed to have a son of their own. She now remembered how they had quarreled bitterly over the issue. Maximilian's failure to persuade her to accept the adoption finally led to his command that she leave Mexico.

Carlota recalled it all, but now after nearly dying, the importance of the empire had diminished for her. She realized that at the moment she cared very little about leaving Maximilian. At any rate, her exile was set and unavoidable. After a few moments, she shrugged her shoulders and withdrew into silence.

"Alteza, let us help you dress."

Chelo's voice brought Carlota back. She gazed around the room as if for the first time, but said nothing. She lowered her eyes to examine her body, ran her hands over her belly groping for what had been there before. All the while, her expression was of growing awareness until she understood what had happened. When she swayed from side to side, hands reached out to help her, but she gently pushed them aside. After a few moments, Carlota steadied herself.

"Is it lost?"

"Sí, Majestad," Chelo answered.

"A girl or a boy?"

"Una niña, Alteza. We prayed over her before we buried her."

"Did you give her a name?"

"We named her Tlazoxochitl. It means Precious Flower in your tongue."

Carlota said no more. Thereafter, she kept the loss of her daughter buried deep in her heart. She never spoke of it until she was an old woman, when she finally opened her heart to let out its hidden sadness. It was on the day of her death, sixty years later at Bouchout Castle, a medieval fortress hidden in a remote Belgian forest. For the present, however, the young empress would prepare to leave Mexico, but not as soon as her entourage expected. She needed more time.

"Who's in charge of my transportation to Vera Cruz?"

The sisters looked at one another but it was Chelo who had that information. "The lieutenant now at the head of your guard. I don't know his name, but I know who he is."

"Please go and inform him that the empress will not be ready to travel until two days from today. He's to pass that information on to the ladies preparing to join the retinue."

As Chelo made for the door, Carlota stopped her. "Before you leave, Chelo, I want to ask you and your sisters if you would accompany me on this voyage. I don't know where it will end. I know only that if you do choose to come with me you will always have the means to return to your land. That I promise you."

Hiding the confusion Carlota's words caused them, the sisters curtsied and left her chamber.

Chapter Eighteen

Tila, Lula and Chelo slipped out of Carlota's chambers and headed for an isolated sitting room, where they could speak privately about the empress' request.

Chelo sat down on a low chair and pulled her shawl closer around her shoulders, as if she had just felt a current of cold air whip into the room. Her face, like that of her sisters, showed signs of serious fatigue and lack of sleep. She spoke with a drowsy voice.

"Where is she going?"

"Back to the land of her birth, I think."

Tila was sitting on the edge of an overstuffed armchair, more uncomfortable than at ease. She spoke almost in a whisper.

"Hermanas, this makes me afraid. What would we do in a strange land?"

Lula had perched herself on a stool facing a darkened fireplace. As she spoke, her eyes roamed around the room taking it all in. It was small but ornate, a place meant for people to chat or read, back in the days when the court was still thriving.

"I haven't forgotten that we agreed a short time ago that when the foreigners ran away, we would take it as a sign to leave in search of a new life. That day has come, but now I'm not so sure. My heart has changed."

Surprised, Tila was quick to ask her sister, "Changed? In what way?"

"I'm sad to see the empress so afflicted."

"Why have you changed?"

"I don't know. Maybe it's because someone hates her so much that she was poisoned and nearly died. Maybe it's that, like us, she is marked and hunted."

Chelo and Tila, taken aback, stared at their sister. They had not expected Lula to ever feel sympathy for the empress.

"You have never spoken this way about the empress."

"No, I haven't. Maybe I've changed now that I've seen her suffer so much fear and pain. I think I know what she's feeling. For me, she's now different."

Chelo let her shawl slip away from her shoulders as she pushed closer to the edge of the chair. She was intrigued by the change in Lula.

"I see her that way, too. She lost the child and nothing will ever erase that pain. Think of it, we were the ones designated by Tonantzín to place the girl in her resting place. In years to come, people will come and go over that grave buried beneath flowers without knowing that the daughter of a distinguished lady is buried there. We will be the only ones to hold the secret. Does that not tie us to the empress more than anything else? I think it does."

Lula agreed with her sister. "We also witnessed the anguish and pain she endured giving birth to the little girl. We saw that the empress loved the child, but suffered her loss with patience."

Tila's thick eyebrows furrowed; they nearly became a straight line. It was clear to her that her sisters were on the verge of agreeing to join the empress in banishment, but she felt that it was her obligation to point out at least one strong reason why they should not take that fearful leap into an unknown world.

"Hermanas, you're saying that we should consider going with the empress. Is this so?"

"Why shouldn't we?" answered Lula. "Like us, she is alone. Like us, she has no one to trust. Why should we abandon her now that we have saved her life? We should have thought of that last night before we decided to face the dangers of el yerbolero and the evils of Sedano."

Lula's words were enough to convince Tila, and she turned to look hard into her sister's eyes. She knew that Lula was right. The three of them had gone a long way, doing for the empress what women did only for someone like a sister. Yet something about Lula's transformation still baffled Tila.

"Lula, what has changed you so much?"

"All I know is that I want to help her. I don't want to abandon her."

"I see it that way too." Chelo was now wide awake. "After all, we have been her companions for three years. She has preferred us to the conceited ladies of her court, and she has even taken us into her confidence. Think of it, hermanas, we know her most intimate secrets."

After that, the sisters sat in silence, pondering what their next step should be. An eerie quiet had invaded the castle, except for sounds drifting toward them from outside. Shouting, whistling and gruff orders reminded the sisters that the last wagons were being loaded. Those would be the carts for the transportation of cooks, kitchen boys and maids, and all the other hands needed to assist the empress, her ladies and staff. That last minute flurry told the sisters that there was no more time for talk if they intended to accompany the empress. It also reminded them that there was now a change for the day of departure.

"Chelo, you'd better go now to inform the lieutenant of the empress' change of mind." Tila spoke softly but with renewed energy. "Before you do that, let's not forget that we have to fulfill our part of the bargain with el yerbolero. When you return, we'll take care of that step. We have time."

The sisters got to their feet and slipped out of the sitting room and into the isolated corridor. They linked arms and headed to their room to put their knapsacks together. Their minds were made up, there was much to be done, and there was no time to lose.

Chapter Nineteen

Empress Carlota fell into a depression while on the road to the port of Vera Cruz. She mourned the death of her daughter. She grieved over the loss of the only love she had ever possessed. Her dream of the empire had collapsed, leaving nothing in its wake except emptiness and turmoil. And now she felt abandoned—the Chontal sisters had not joined her entourage, as she had hoped.

Now, more than ever, Carlota was hounded by a serious distrust of people, a nagging fear of being harmed by unseen enemies. She knew that anyone could get close enough to poison her, and the specter of the sinister drug that had pushed her to the verge of death and madness stalked her at all times. Complicating her mental distress was a chronic stomach disorder that she endured almost constantly since her face-to-face encounter with that poison. The aftereffects of the cure concocted by el yerbolero stubbornly lingered, afflicting her with a sour, bitter ache in her gut. Carlota patiently endured that pain, but she recognized that if the sorcerer's cure had saved her life, it had also forced her to journey deep into her soul. This alone was a murky experience that haunted her nearly every night, making her fear the coming of darkness.

Known only to Tila, Chelo and Lula, the empress had undergone a profound transformation that had left her fearful of eating food prepared by hands of strangers. Consequently, Carlota survived mostly on unpeeled fruit, nuts and small amounts of wine. It became a pattern with her to sit in front of a plate of food and allow it to go untouched, no matter how delectable. She often walked away from sumptuous dinners without explanation to her hosts, baffling those around her and fueling rumors of her eccentric, irrational ways.

Fear forced Carlota into a solitude that left her with a grievous sense of loneliness, a condition that could have been alleviated by the company of those of her entourage but whom she deliberately rebuffed. The group charged with securing her safe conduct to Vera Cruz was small, but instead of welcoming her companions' presence, she rejected everyone. They had no way of knowing that she was so conflicted, that she found anyone's nearness intolerable and that she had grown to prefer the safety of her solitude. Of course, they whispered behind her back, trying to explain her eccentricities.

Carlota's entourage included several ladies-in-waiting, all of them French or Belgian or Swiss. In addition to her ladies, a grand chamberlain figured prominently, as did her treasurer, her secretary, numerous servants, a physician, a personal cook and a squadron of Belgian legionnaires. Among all those people there was no one that Carlota trusted.

The trek from Chapultepec to the port city turned out to be brutal. Interminable rain, flooded roads that often compelled the entourage to leave their coaches and walk long distances in driving rain and mud. Once, the luggage wagon overturned and became mired in mud for hours until teams of mules could be rounded up to haul it back on track. On top of that hardship, there were other terrors that gripped the group, the most glaring of which were the nightly rest stops that posed the risk of yellow fever infection, the dreaded vómito negro. Of course, there was the constant threat of an attack by juarista guerrillas.

The entire time, the empress remained withdrawn, seemingly impervious to the hardships experienced by the others. Whenever she spoke, it was usually to complain that her real companions were not with her, and she stubbornly insisted on asking for the whereabouts of the Chontal sisters, despite always getting the same answer.

"Majesty, they're not included in your train of companions."

"Why not?"

"They chose to return to their native town. It seems they were afraid."

It was a lie meant to isolate the empress from the three Indian women, and she knew it. Unknown to her and to the rest of the entourage, the sisters were following Carlota. They were hiding in the cargo wagons and blending in with the local inhabitants whenever they walked. By whatever means they contrived, the sisters always managed to catch up with the party by the time it stopped for the night. At the end of the day, the sisters found a stable with straw to sleep on and a kitchen in which to help in exchange for tortillas, beans and a little fruit juice. This was enough to keep them going the next day, hoping to find the right moment to link up with their mistress.

As the journey progressed, Carlota's depression turned into an irritability that she expressed by treating her people brusquely. Whenever she spoke, she lashed out sarcastically in a haughty manner, and she often demanded that strict protocol be observed. If ever any member of her party happened to be late for a meal, that person would have to go without eating at her command. At other times she became icy, morose, refusing to speak even when confined with others in the coach or at meals when it made everyone uncomfortable and nervous.

Ultimately, her rudeness made those around her also bad-tempered. To make things even more confusing, at other times Carlota inexplicably abandoned her grumpy, brooding behavior and became giddy, chatty and almost flirtatious. When in this mood, she demanded that everyone share in her frivolity. If anyone resisted, that person then became the brunt of her anger, and then the cycle of unpredictable behavior began all over again.

Before the journey ended, Carlota caused two major incidents of outrage among her entourage. The first happened when, without explanation, she ordered her ladies to leave the coach to walk on foot while she remained on board. The women obeyed her command, but after hours of struggling on foot through sweltering heat, caked mud and roots, the ladies wept out of frustration and anger. Some nearly fainted from fatigue. The women became so resentful after that incident that they maliciously grumbled behind her back, giving life to more gossip about her irrational behavior.

The other episode took place when the company arrived at Orizaba, where they were put up courtesy of the mayor and his wife. A special dinner was organized with a guest list that included the town's dignitaries and their spouses who, brimming with pride to be invited to such an auspicious event, came elegantly dressed. Most of them arrived in stylish coaches driven by liveried servants. It was, everyone agreed, a fiesta fit for an empress.

When it was time to sit down at the table, without excusing herself and in defiance of the strict code of behavior that she was expected to follow, she walked out of the mansion and headed to the plaza, where she sat down under a jacaranda tree to gaze up at the stars. There were witnesses to what she did, and because no one could explain away the rudeness of her behavior, it only fueled the rumors that she was indeed losing touch with reality.

Carlota's actions that night not only shocked and offended her hosts but it mortified her staff, and if there were still one or two members of her entourage who had before harbored, even secretly, a little good feeling for her, this last embarrassment canceled those sentiments. Her ladies were especially filled with vengeful thoughts that spilled out in constant criticism, especially because they considered her a traitor to her royal class and lineage. Each one vowed to leave her as soon as they set foot on French soil. In the meantime, however, they prattled maliciously.

Tongues wagged without pity almost constantly, and the harping grew louder as days passed. The ladies-in-waiting were incensed. Nothing could extinguish the insult that burned deep inside of them because they knew that the empress considered them frivolous fools.

They might have been frivolous, but they were not fools, and those women would not be satisfied until they witnessed Carlota's ruin. Their nasty, unforgiving comments went on until the unkindest one of all was murmured, the one that would stick to Carlota until the day of her death.

"She's gone mad!"

Empress Carlota was aware of the spiteful yapping that went on behind her back, but because she was trapped in a cage of grief, she retreated inward, not caring what was being said of her. Instead, she yielded to the plan of boarding the ship that was waiting to transport her to France. Word had spread that she was on her way to press the French emperor and the pope for support for Maximilian, but that rumor was far from the truth. She had no intention of asking for any more assistance. What she wanted was to understand why those men had invested so much effort and capital in the empire only to withdraw it without explanation. Carlota was convinced that once she heard the answer to that question, she could go on with her life.

When the empress and her train arrived at Vera Cruz, they found the city nearly deserted and in the grip of unbearably humid heat. Vultures ominously circled over the island prison of San Juan Ulúa. There were no officials to bid her a happy voyage nor were there women dabbing tears from their eyes because of the departure of the empress. Missing also were children to present her with flowers and to sing lyrics that told of how much she would be missed. Instead, there was only the officer who wordlessly showed Carlota onto the rowboat that took her to board the Empress Eugénie.

The oppressive climate and the snubs saddened Carlota, but she preferred to be alone anyway. When she was greeted by the ship's captain and shown to her cabin, she took refuge in it and banned anyone from her presence, ordering that only cabin boys bring fruit or drink.

When she felt the jolt of the ship weighing anchor, Carlota gazed out to get a last look at the black-green tropical shore that silently moved away from her. Only then, in the isolation of her cabin, did she allow herself to weep for the Mexican empire of her dream. She cried for its brown, mysterious people whom she had hardly gotten to know, and her heart ached for the vanished passion she had experienced in the inner shadows of the cathedral. She wept for the lost daughter that love had planted in her womb, the child that she was leaving behind buried in the same soil on which she was conceived. She grieved for herself because she knew that she was locked into loneliness and that there was no way out.

Empress Carlota had no way of knowing that at that moment of sadness, news of her departure was flashing from Vera Cruz to every remote town and village throughout Mexico. It would have broken her heart to know that there was unrestrained rejoicing among the people of that land, and that her Mexican children were dancing for joy because she was gone. At that moment Carlota had no way of knowing that men in tattered straw sombreros and women clad in huipiles and rebozos were sitting around campfires, strumming guitars and singing a corrido that grew longer, bawdier and more vulgar with each rendition.

Adiós, Mamá Carlota,
Narices de pelota.
Que se larguen los franceses,
¡Adiós! ¡Adiós! ¡Adiós!

FRANCE and ITALY

1866-1867

Chapter Twenty

*A*nxiety overwhelmed me. obsessed, I paced the cabin. My dream had lasted less than three years, a mere thousand days, a grain of sand in the existence of that ancient land of volcanoes and ferocious gods. I grieved.

Had I known while on that fateful voyage that Maximilian had written to his mother claiming my madness, perhaps my thinking might have been different. Perhaps I would have prepared myself, instead of surrendering to regrets and recriminations.

That infamous letter reached Europe ahead of me. Only too late did I discover that other letters were written as well, and those repeated Maximilian's damning words. By the time I set foot on French soil, a snare of unimaginable magnitude waited for me, and I was unprepared.

Chapter Twenty-One

July 1866

Dearest Mother,

At this moment, I need to share a terrible secret regarding our Charlotte. The truth is that I'm afraid her passionate nature has driven her to a place from which there is no return. Charlotte has lost her mind.

Her behavior has been so erratic as to attract the attention of the Court. She's rude, loud, intrusive, and when I made the mistake of asking her to conduct council meetings while I was away on business, she browbeat the councilors in an attempt to have them pass laws and rulings without even consulting me. Naturally, her behavior alienated the officials.

The same is true of her ladies, who complain that she shuts them out in preference for Indian hags that are so unkempt and dirty, that no one can bear the stench they bring into any room.

One episode finally confirmed to me Charlotte's madness. When I told her of my intention to adopt the two Iturbide boys, Agustín and Salvador, in order to groom the older as my successor, she ranted and howled with rage. She became irrational! What else am I to do in the face of her barrenness?

As I write this letter, Charlotte has embarked on a voyage to confront Emperor Napoleon, as well as the pope, on what she perceives as their betrayal. She might appear at your doorstep with the same claim. If that happens, I beg you to remember her mental condition. I also implore you to keep her madness a secret.

Your loving son,

Max

July 1866

Dearest Sister Eugénie,

I have received word from Maximilian, telling that our Charlotte has gone mad. He is experiencing the shame and hardship of having to conceal what is clear to the entire world. He has alerted me that she, accompanied by filthy Indian females, is on her way to confront you and Louie regarding what she considers your betrayal. It seems that in her derangement, she is also planning to confront His Holiness Pope Pius. She is prepared to announce to every court in Europe that you have defaulted on your promises and, therefore, have exposed her and Maximilian to the vengeance of the natives of that land.

Eugénie, I beseech you to keep secret Charlotte's lunacy. Perhaps there is still time to pass it off as a dreadful disease contracted in that dark land from where she's returning.

Your loving sister,

Sophie

July 1866

Dear Husband Louie,

I have distressing news. As incredible as it may sound, it must be believed because it comes from Empress Sophie of Austria. I have today received a letter in which she reveals that Charlotte has lost her mind.

My maids are at this moment packing my things. It is imperative that I join you as soon as possible because, along with the pitiful news about Charlotte's lunacy, came the message that she is coming to France with the intention of confronting us. According to Sophie, Charlotte, in the company of a pack of Indian females, is making her way to France. She has apparently got it into her demented mind that the turmoil going on in Mexico is our fault.

She also blames the pope. She insists that it is we who are responsible for the debacle in Mexico. Oh, blessed Mother of God! How I wish I had never heard the mention of that wretched land! Where do you think she got that outrageous idea? Or maybe she's blaming me! Louie, do you think she's blaming me? I know that others have flung that accusation, but you know that it's untrue, don't you?

I must join you immediately so that we can plan. We must come to a decision as to what we will do when Charlotte appears. Or has she already come to you? Has she? Ah, Louie, you wouldn't keep that from me, would you? We must be of one mind as to what we will do regarding that unfortunate woman. Will we bar her from entering the palace? Or if we allow her into our presence, what will be our approach? Kindness? Understanding? Or will we be stern and remind her that it has been her own inordinate ambition that has thrust her and her abject husband into the situation they're in? Whatever our stance will be, it must be a united one.

Louie, keep the news regarding Charlotte's madness a secret because if it becomes known, you and I will be the first to be blamed.

Your loving Eugénie

July 1866

Your Holiness,

It is with alarm that I write these lines to you. Eugénie has notified me that Empress Charlotte has gone mad! And if that were not bad enough news, we have been informed that she is on her way to Europe to confront us regarding our so-called culpability for the collapse of her ill-fated empire. Your Holiness, have you heard anything in this regard? Has Maximilian communicated with you? I understand that Charlotte has said that she is intending to face you on this matter also. This alone tells me that she has gone utterly insane.

Eugénie and I view this terrible affair as a calamity, brought on solely by Maximilian, and especially Charlotte. They might have been successful monarchs if they had only practiced a drop of wisdom. Instead, he dedicated his time to the design of dress uniforms and to chasing butterflies alongside his mistresses, and she squandered the Mexican people's patrimony on decorating that atrocious castle on the hill. Begging Your Holiness' forgiveness for what might seem as an indiscretion unbecoming a gentleman, but she, too, is quite well known for her dalliances with her Belgian bodyguards.

France has done its utmost regarding the Mexican Empire. We now face the Prussian menace, and there is no choice but to inform Charlotte, if and when she approaches us, that she must pack off her pride and lamentations to face the consequences of her frivolous ways.

I await word from Your Holiness. In the meantime, I beg that you keep this unfortunate affair private, especially regarding Empress Charlotte's madness. It should be kept a secret out of respect for her family, as well as Maximilian's. I fear that widespread knowledge of her lunacy would become the cause célèbre of the century.

One more thing, Your Holiness: It is said that Charlotte consorts with any number of Indian women of ill repute, namely sorceresses, and that she even practices their vile superstitious ways. I beg you to be aware of this if you have the misfortune of being confronted by her.

Your most humble servant,

Louie Napoleon III

Imperial Highness Franz Joseph,

You have, by now, received the most disastrous notice regarding your sister-in-law, the Empress Charlotte of Mexico. I have it from the most reliable of sources that she has gone mad. My heart grieves for her and your brother, Maximilian, as well as your entire illustrious family. For my part, I can say that my conscience is clear, for I have at all times tried to guide and counsel her in the ways of the Almighty God. I understand that she and a handful of Indian women are on their way to Europe, and that your Highness is one of her targets. It seems that in her lunacy, Empress Charlotte has delusions regarding Maximilian's place as inheritor to your throne. The tragedy is that she is spreading the rumor that you have usurped your brother's place.

I share this sad news with you so that you may deal with your mother, Empress Sophie. We all know the great love she has for all her sons, but especially for Archduke Maximilian. There is no doubt that this alarming news will ultimately reach her, and no one knows how she will respond. For our part, Almighty God will be our guide in all matters. I am but His humble servant, as well as the shepherd of His holy flock. I'm assured of His infinite wisdom in all matters. I say this because I understand that Empress Charlotte is also intent on confronting this humble servant with her delusions. I bid you to keep Charlotte's madness a secret. Widespread knowledge of it would no doubt cause great scandal.

Pius IX

Chapter Twenty-Two

AUGUST 1866

France

The last train from Saint Nazaire to Paris had departed by the time Empress Carlota stepped onto French soil that August afternoon. Except for the town's mayor and his wife, missing again were the welcoming committee, the guard of honor, even Napoleon's personal envoy, demanded by protocol to welcome the Empress of Mexico, failed to appear. Carlota's ladies-in-waiting, male staff and chambermaids swarmed the pier, all of them disoriented and without an inkling of what to do next.

The empress was exhausted, as were the others of her entourage. All they wanted was to find a place to rest before continuing the long stretch to Saint-Cloud. More than fatigued, Carlota was humiliated by the snub, but she hid her frustration and did not acknowledge the obvious slight. When informed that she and her party had to wait until the next day to depart, she felt her nerves, already frayed, begin to give way, but she resisted that setback as well.

Carlota, by now suffering from an intense headache, noticed that members of her party were melting into the crowd, leaving her to deal with the mayor and his wife. She pursed her lips in irritation. On the other hand, she admitted that she would have liked all of them to disappear for good. In the meantime, the luggage barge was moored, and gangs of stevedores began the work of unloading, filling the area with vulgar shouts and cursing as they worked.

The mayor, hoping that the empress was unaware of the swearing, nervously wiped sweat from his face with an oversized handkerchief, all the time trying to build up enough courage to speak to the empress.

"Majesty, we've taken the liberty of hiring coaches for you and your ladies. They should arrive momentarily."

"And where are we to go?" Carlota's voice was icy.

"Ah! We have a very fine hotel in our esteemed city. Since we're now an official port city, we've made sure to have appropriate accommodations for other visitors of similar importance."

It became instantly apparent to the mayor that his words had implied that there were others equal in importance to the empress. His face went pasty when he saw her expression of displeasure.

"What I mean, Majesty, is that there have been one or two other dignitaries in whom Saint Nazaire has taken pride, although no one of your stature."

When the mayor realized that his words were only making matters worse, he shut his mouth and turned to his wife with a face that implored her to say something. She, however, turned away, pretending not to understand. They were both suddenly yanked from their ordeal by a sight that neither the mayor nor his wife could explain; their eyes bulged trying to focus on what they thought were apparitions from another world. It was a disheveled trio of women who had emerged from behind the stacks of just unloaded luggage.

"Savages!"

The mayor blurted out the only word that came to him. He then realized that these apparitions were making their way toward them, arms linked and walking in small steps. In the late afternoon sunlight, their colorful dresses glimmered with brightness and their skin shone as if it had been fine-polished mahogany wood.

Carlota was glaring at the mayor when she saw the expression of shock overcome him. She whipped around to see what he was gawking at and instantly recognized Chelo, Tila and Lula. They had followed after all. The sight of those sisters instantly dispelled Carlota's headache as well as her frustration and irritability. She even forgot about her antipathy toward the people surrounding her, suffocating her with their artificial ways.

The empress felt an impulse to run to her companions, take them by their hands, embrace and hold them to show her relief, but a lifetime of strict training in protocol held her back. Carlota remained planted, ramrod straight, awaiting the approach of the three women. Only her eyes betrayed what she was feeling when the sisters curtsied in front of her.

They, in contrast, smiled broadly at their friend while the mayor and the other onlookers gawked in disbelief. After a few moments, Carlota asked for her coach. When it pulled up to the landing, she gestured for her companions to climb in with her, provoking even more dismay in the mayor.

"Majesty, are you certain that you want these people to ride with you?"

"I'm certain. But before that, please call my secretary and treasurer. I need to speak to them."

By this time the mayor was so bewildered at what was happening under his nose that he decided to turn his attention elsewhere. He made his way over to the pack of disoriented travelers and called for the empress' treasurer and secretary. The two men followed him to see what instructions awaited them.

"Mister Secretary, I want you to dismiss my ladies-in-waiting at once. That is, the ones who are still to be found, since I see that most of them have already disappeared. Retain only two chambermaids to serve me from here on. The same pertains to my physician. Is this clear?"

"Of course, Majesty. What about me?"

"You'll remain in my service, of course. I'll need you. Mister Treasurer, you'll also stay on in my service. Your duties will include adjusting the number of rooms needed for our suite in this city, in Paris and in Rome, and all stops needed in between. Please make sure that each of our servers receives adequate compensation, which includes my Mexican assistants."

"The Indians, Majesty?"

The Treasurer seemed dumbfounded to hear that the native women would be part of the empress' entourage.

"Yes, the Indian women as well. Now, if neither of you gentlemen has any further question or concern, let us board our coaches and head for the hotel. I'm extremely fatigued."

"Majesty."

Bowing deeply, the two men mumbled the word in unison. They had been given instructions to be completed as soon as possible, so they scrambled to get to any vehicle that would take them to the hotel ahead of the empress.

Once in the coach, Carlota and the Chontal sisters rode in silence until they arrived at the hotel and were shown to their suite. At the hotel, bystanders eyed the unlikely companions the empress had with her. The three sisters ignored those curious and even hostile looks, and followed the head attendant to their rooms. He then informed them that Her Majesty's luggage had arrived.

"Majesty, do you wish tea to be brought in?"

"Yes, thank you."

When all was settled and the women were left alone, only then did Carlota, Tila, Chelo and Lula become themselves.

"Were you far behind?"

"Never, Alteza. We made sure to know wherever you were and that you were safe."

Carlota gazed at the sisters, showing a mix of gratitude and amazement at what they had done. She also felt the stress that had built up inside her over the last weeks begin to dissipate and, more important, she sensed that now her courage would somehow return.

"Gracias, hermanas. Now, you may help me undress."

As if the sisters and the empress had not faced a hazardous route from Chapultepec to Vera Cruz, as if weeks of stifling confinement on the steamer had not happened, as if they had not come from one world to another at the expense of a brutal crossing over a vast ocean, the sisters began their usual tasks. They removed the pins from Carlota's hair, brushed it so it lay on her shoulders and then, in their natural way, they took off the empress' rumpled clothes to bathe her neck, arms and feet.

The sisters worked quietly while Carlota, eyes closed, surrendered to her companions' care, feeling grateful for the gift of trust they brought with them. When she felt the coolness of a nightgown slipping over her, she broke the silence.

"Hermanas, you're now in my world."

"Yes, Alteza."

"Will you regret it?"

All three looked at Carlota, but it was Tila who responded. "No, Majestad."

Carlota spoke no more. Neither did the sisters add anything to what they had said. Instead, the women took a little tea and nibbled at what had been brought in to eat. After that, the Chontal sisters prepared themselves to retire for the night. When they were ready, Carlota asked for the lamps to be turned down, and the women slept.

Chapter Twenty-Three

AUGUST 1866

Saint-Cloud, France

Empress Carlota sat facing Empress Eugénie as they waited for Louie Napoleon. The trip from Saint Nazaire to Saint-Cloud had fatigued Carlota. Nonetheless, she was in an expectant mood. She looked calm, but beneath the surface she was fighting off the irritation that she and her attendants had been put up at a hotel instead of the palace, as would be expected. This snub, on top of the same treatment at Saint Nazaire, rankled her.

Louie Napoleon was late, and while waiting for him, Carlota noticed Empress Eugénie's nervousness. She seemed to have something on her mind, almost on the tip of her tongue. Carlota watched her as she fidgeted with her handkerchief, now and then eying Carlota anxiously. Finally, Carlota spoke up.

"Highness, is there something bothering you?"

"No, Majesty. It's only a matter of my remembering a letter I've recently received from Empress Sophie, telling me of your arrival."

The mention of a letter from her mother-in-law aroused Carlota's curiosity, and she wanted to know at least something of its content.

"Oh? My arrival? How kind of her. What else does she say?"

"Nothing of great importance, except that you're traveling with unusual attendants."

"Unusual? How so?"

"Well, she writes that your maids are native women."

"That is so. I wonder what's unusual about my being attended by people native to Mexico. Does she say?"

"Oh, no, no! She doesn't say any more than that they're very different."

Now Eugénie's nervousness and her hints caught Carlota's full attention, so she pursued the matter. She leaned forward in the chair to get closer to Eugénie, but she did it so fast and so unexpectedly that the movement apparently startled the jumpy empress, who shrunk back, eyes wide open, as if expecting Carlota to do something violent.

Eugénie blurted out, "Majesty, please don't do anything you might later regret."

Not knowing that her mother-in-law had warned Eugénie of her madness, Carlota was startled by the empress' reactions. Naturally, she wanted to know more, but when she asked for an explanation, Eugénie sat back, crossed her arms and refused to say anything else. There was nothing else Carlota could do but keep quiet, all the time resenting the awkward silence while they waited for Louie Napoleon.

During that stiff interlude, Carlota tried to dispel the uneasiness that Eugénie's strange remarks had planted in her by looking at the elegant chamber in which they waited. It was high-vaulted with graceful floor-to-ceiling windows that looked out onto classically trimmed lawns, trees and plants. The room was decorated with elaborate gilded trim, spectacular mirrors, polished parquet flooring and an impressive pink marble fireplace that was crowned by a baroque era clock.

The settees and other divans, although upholstered in up-to-date fabrics, dated back to the time of Louie XV, as did the small marble-topped tables placed strategically for the use of visitors. It was obvious that the chamber was meant to impress with its ornate stylishness

Empress Carlota, however, was not overwhelmed by such elegance. She had, after all, been born into similar luxury, and the castle at Chapultepec did not suffer in comparison. Once she had examined the decorations, she returned to thinking of her mother-in-law's letter, as well as the impending meeting with Louie Napoleon. Time dragged, and the clock's ticking became louder, reminding Carlota of the valuable time she was wasting.

Carlota shifted in the chair, feeling her impatience grow. To dispel the mood, she again turned her attention to Eugénie. She discreetly looked over to where the empress sat pouting. Everyone knew how sensitive Empress Eugénie was about her appearance. For a few moments, Carlota put discretion aside to take a good look, and it struck her how much Eugénie had diminished since she had last seen her.

Empress Eugénie's face had sagged noticeably, and her hair, once known for its luxuriousness, had thinned noticeably. Although her dress was of the finest fabric and cut, it did not fit in the perfect way for which she was famous throughout Europe. The jewels she wore were brilliant, but they sat awkwardly on her throat and ears. What cast a truly worn-out appearance over the empress was her body. Her shoulders drooped. Gone was the straight-backed haughtiness that she used to look down on whomsoever she addressed. Carlota also noticed that Eugénie had lost the graceful glide for which the ladies of the French Court were famous; instead she dragged her feet as she walked.

Eugénie's eyes unexpectedly snapped over to Carlota and revealed her irritation at being the focus of a critical inspection. Carlota instantly felt a sharp sting of embarrassment because she had been caught staring. In an effort to dissimulate, she turned again to scan the elegant chamber from top to bottom.

To Carlota's relief, Louie Napoleon finally appeared. His secretary and valet preceded him, but when he came into Carlota's full view, she saw at once that he, too, had diminished since she had last seen him. He carried himself like a stooped old man; gone was the famous swagger. His uniform hung on him as if he had lost considerable weight, and his goatee was streaked with gray.

Despite those signs of aging, Napoleon made a show of energy and vitality, but this appearance betrayed extreme weariness, so much that Carlota felt an unexpected pang of pity. She wondered if the crisis in Mexico was responsible for the decline in him, as well as in Eugénie. He approached Carlota, smiled seductively as in years past and bowed deeply to kiss her hand.

"Your Majesty. I'm delighted to see you. I hope your crossing was pleasant."

As Napoleon uttered those words, he looked into Carlota's eyes. His eyes were flinty and cagey, and the flash of pity Carlota had just experienced evaporated. Those eyes put her on the defensive, and she braced to play the cat-and-mouse game for which Napoleon was famous.

"The crossing was as might be expected, Sire, tedious and at times hard on the stomach."

"Ah, yes, the stomach. At any rate, Majesty, we welcome you to France. I hope you have found your accommodations satisfactory."

"Majesty, I'm grateful to be in France and, of course, for the exquisite accommodations at a hotel. It is a welcomed change from this palace."

Carlota deliberately allowed her sarcasm to come across. When she saw that her words had landed a blow, she relished the brief moment, especially when he glanced over at Eugénie who was in obvious discomfort. Napoleon recovered quickly and, smoothing down his goatee, he turned toward a window and addressed the two women in an artificially jovial, lighthearted manner.

"Such a lovely day! My Lord, I'm so thirsty. Ladies, do you care for a glass of orangeade?"

Eugénie accepted, but Carlota turned down the offer. Napoleon let the valet know what he wanted and at the same time he dismissed the secretary with a flick of his wrist.

"Majesty, please come with me to my office. Dear wife, join us."

Carlota and Eugénie followed the emperor into an adjoining chamber. It was smaller than what Carlota expected, and it was austere compared to the previous room. There were maps of different continents and countries tacked on the walls, and the desk was overflowing with documents and books. Except for the rush of daylight that streamed through the windows, the place would have been bleak and unwelcoming.

"Please, ladies, take a seat." The emperor pointed to a small sofa that was wide enough for two people. "Here we can speak in confidence without being bothered or interrupted. Tell me, Majesty, what are your plans for the near future?"

Carlota riveted her eyes on his to let him know that she would not be intimidated by diversionary chitchat. When she answered, her voice, too, had taken an artificial tone, just like his.

"My schedule will take me to the Vatican, Sire. I have been granted an audience with Pius."

"Oh? May I ask what the nature of that audience might be?"

Carlota put on a startled look, as if she could not imagine how such an indiscreet question could be asked. When she was confident that Louie had adequately interpreted the meaning of her expression, she responded, "I'm afraid that the matter is quite confidential, Sire."

The emperor frowned as he sat down behind his desk and stared out the window without saying anything. Minutes passed while Carlota felt anxiety building up, but still no one said anything until Napoleon turned to her, his eyes again slanted and suspicious.

"Well, Madame, it was you who requested this interview. I'm listening to whatever you need to say."

Carlota, caught off-guard by his sudden shift of mood, reproached herself for not being on guard, but she rapidly regained her balance. This was the first move of the game and it was her turn.

"Majesty, the Mexican Empire, yours and our empire, has collapsed because you have withdrawn your troops. I would like to understand the reasons for your unexpected change of heart."

"Come now, Majesty. You're allowing your female side to get the better of you."

Napoleon's grin and his condescending tone rankled Carlota, but because she recognized it as a tactic meant to derail the focus of what she was saying, she let the demeaning comment pass. She went on to pursue the topic.

"Majesty, what was the reason for reneging on your promises? I need to understand."

Napoleon's smirk melted away, and he jerked to the edge of the chair, making it squeak shrilly. His cagey eyes shifted and then blurred, obviously trying to focus on Empress Carlota, but then he turned to Eugénie who sat inertly, as if pasted to the sofa. He wet his lips and drummed his fingers on the desktop, trying to hide that his hands were trembling. Finally, he took a deep breath.

"Madame, our Creator has fashioned us separately as men and women. We men perform certain tasks on this earth, and your gentle sex does others. Women, sadly, were not given the capability to deal with reasons, much less understand them. Who am I to question the will of our Creator?"

"I'm not understanding you, Sire."

"Of course not, Madame. I don't expect you to follow what I'm saying, which is exactly why I never speak about reasons with women. You're incapable of understanding reasons."

Now it was Carlota's turn to push forward onto the edge of the sofa. Napoleon's words were hitting her with such force that she could no longer endure Eugénie's body pressing in on her side. Although she felt her heart pounding, she knew that she had to keep control of her voice and respond carefully.

"Sire, try me. Give me one reason that explains why you broke your promise and see if I can or cannot understand. Give me one reason why you have gone back on the words you wrote, letters that I have in my possession. Once you give me that reason, let us see if I can understand it or not."

The emperor blanched and opened his mouth, but nothing came out. In that instant the doors swung open and the valet entered, silver tray in hand, bringing three glasses of orangeade. Napoleon had inadvertently gained time for him to compose himself.

When the valet offered the tray, Napoleon grabbed the glass and greedily gulped down its contents at once. Eugénie took hers, but seemed so disturbed that she sipped just a little. Carlota shook her head when the valet offered her the glass. He placed it on a small table by her side, bowed to the three monarchs and backed out of the room.

Napoleon, by now in command of himself, spoke. "Majesty, why do you mention those letters? What are your intentions?"

"My intentions are to remind you, Sire, that you promised many things but recanted, and now the Mexican Empire has collapsed. The main responsibility for that fiasco has come to roost here at your front door."

The emperor, eyes bulging, glared at Carlota until he came up with a sharp retort, and so what began as a discussion between two sovereigns deteriorated steadily to an over-heated argument. They hurled recriminations of past offenses at each other. They referred to forgotten promises, and they even intimated that there would be dire repercussions.

The debate then became a shouting match that soon bordered on incoherence, all of it lasting more than an hour until fatigue finally silenced both emperor and empress. Through it all, Eugénie stared without uttering a word, mouth open, now and then getting to her feet to pace the small space of the office.

When Napoleon realized that Carlota would not allow him the last word, the emperor finally reached his limit. He pounded a clenched fist on the desk with such force that documents and books shifted from one side to the other. With that, he sprang to his feet and shouted in a voice so worn-out that it was little more than a croak.

"Charlotte, how dare you speak to me this way? It's not your place, Madame, to question me or accuse me of anything. Do you hear?"

By this time Carlota was also on her feet, but she was still in control of her voice and her mind. "Sire, I am Carlota, the Empress of Mexico, your peer, and it's from that truth that I dare to make statements and ask questions to which I have not been given a response, not even as a courtesy."

"You *were* the Empress of Mexico." With that comment Napoleon circled the desk and headed for the door. Once there, he turned to Carlota and in a loud voice declared, "This interview is ended!"

Suddenly the scene was over. Napoleon stormed out of the study without another word, leaving the startled women stranded. Eugénie turned to the door and silently escorted Carlota out of the room and down the imperial stairway to the front entrance. She gave the order for a coach to come immediately, with instructions that Carlota was to be taken wherever she wanted. When the horses and carriage pulled up under the portico, Eugénie curtsied low for Carlota who, instead of doing likewise, looked hard into Eugénie's eyes. This time her words came with difficulty. She almost stammered.

"Eugénie, what else did my mother-in-law say in her letter?"

"Charlotte, please forget that I mentioned the letter. It's not important."

"I don't believe you! Every word that comes from that woman regarding me is usually hurtful. Tell me!"

Feeling overwhelmed by Carlota's insisting, Eugénie slipped. "She's not hurtful. She's only concerned for your health."

"What about my health?"

"Charlotte, there are doctors that specialize in certain parts of the human body. They're known as alienists. If you would only agree to see one of them."

When she took in Eugénie's words, Carlota's voice became so loud that it rose above the racket of crunching wheels and clattering hooves. The startled stable boys and coachmen turned around to stare at her.

"Alienists? You mean doctors that probe the human mind? Did Sophie say that I'm mad?"

"I'm sorry, Charlotte, I cannot reveal that to you." With those words, Eugénie turned and disappeared into the palace. It was the last thing she ever said to Empress Carlota.

Carlota arrived at the Grand Hotel profoundly shaken. She was a woman not yet twenty-seven, but she had aged during those hours. Her face had broken down, sagged around the cheeks, her forehead had creased and her lips pursed like those of a much older woman. Her stomach was churning, and fear gripped her. Carlota was in complete turmoil, angry and afraid, but more than anything she was torn by extreme confusion.

When she entered her suite, she found the sisters waiting for her with food and wine they had purchased at a local marketplace. At first Carlota didn't want anything, feeling her stomach would turn, but then she accepted a glass of wine to calm down the terrible storm assaulting her nerves. Afterward, the sisters helped her out of her clothes that were damp with perspiration. All the while, she was locked in moody silence.

Afterward, Carlota sat down at a window overlooking the Luxemburg Gardens and tried to pull herself together. She remained withdrawn while she sifted through the details of her clash with Napoleon and with the devious, cold-blooded Eugénie. What was the meaning of their words but, more importantly, the unspoken, countless subtleties and innuendos? She had grasped at once Napoleon's roundabout chatter as a transparent way of derailing her focus, but she asked herself what the cunning emperor had been getting at when he spoke such rubbish about women not being capable of understanding reason. Was he not the one who had written her countless letters praising her intelligence and diplomatic skills?

Why, she asked, had he been his old seductive self at the beginning of their encounter, all sweetness that turned into bitterness? Why had he then become a quivering, irritated mess? What was he hiding? What was Eugénie scheming when she talked about a letter from Empress Sophie, that embittered old woman who had never forgiven Carlota for taking away her golden boy? If one such letter existed, could there be others? Were there letters that claimed she was mad? Above all, the mention of alienist doctors truly set Carlota's teeth on edge.

In the end, Carlota could not come up with answers to so many questions, except that she was certain it was pointless to pursue the French monarchs any further. She admitted that she had failed in that regard. To be sure, she had not received the answers she desired, but she had to move on.

Exhausted, Carlota looked over to where her companions huddled, sharing her turmoil. The empress gazed at them and experienced a moment of awareness she had not felt before. She didn't know where the sisters had come from, nor who they were, but that they had emerged from nowhere. Carlota understood that, in a mysterious manner, they had crossed her path to strengthen her when she was on the verge of foundering. She gestured for them to come sit by her.

Chapter Twenty-Four

*A*lthough Louis Napoleon and Eugénie offended me in many ways, they did provide my entourage a special train from Paris through Burgundy, then across the province of Lyon and finally over the Alps into Italy. Once the frontier was crossed, the train sped through Milan, Turin, Florence and onward to Rome.

Fall was approaching. Along the route, trees blazed with tones of orange, red and gold, as did the fields nearly ripe for harvesting. I gazed out the window and surrendered to the sway of the train until I fell into its clanging rhythm. As if in a trance, I looked at the beauty of the passing landscape, but in the recesses of my mind I was haunted by images of cactus, volcanoes and brown-skinned enigmatic people.

I felt confused, but no matter how much I examined my feelings, the cause of that bewilderment eluded me. Had I possessed the power to discern the movements of my spirit at that moment, I might have realized that it was fear gnawing at me, not confusion. I didn't understand that I had valid reasons to be fearful. I should have seen that yet more snubs, more resentful faces, more gawking eyes and malicious whispering waited.

I didn't see that deeper, more significant matters were there for me to examine. I failed to recognize that I needed to scrutinize my motives: Why was I dealing with the very men whom I knew were my enemies? Why was I exposing myself to ridicule and even betrayal by putting myself in their hands?

Years would pass before I plumbed the inner recesses of my soul deeply enough to answer those questions. As of that moment, as the *train raced toward Rome, I could only struggle to gain at least some clarity.*

Those thoughts sickened me, and I put them aside. I retreated instead into a fanciful world in which I found myself on a journey, a time when I would never again have to face anyone. I even fantasized that the train would take flight until it reached the moon and stars. Perhaps up there I might be rid of the fatigue and melancholy that withered my spirit.

Chapter Twenty-Five

AUGUST 1866

Rome

Carlota's daydream was cut short. The train would soon pull into the station where the real world awaited her. She shook herself free from the trance and, when she felt the sharp jolt of the train stopping, she took a deep breath and got to her feet, prepared to descend from the coach to face whatever was coming.

What was waiting took Carlota by surprise. When she, her companions and entourage stepped onto the platform, a reception of unexpected grandeur greeted them. Her heart raced when she saw cardinals dressed in full regalia, their scarlet robes resplendent with gold chains and flowing capes brilliant in the Roman sunlight. At their side, standing at attention were decorated military officers with feathered caps fluttering in the breeze. Over to the side were officials dressed in fine frock coats with decorations pinned to their lapels. Tall hats gave them all a distinguished air. Along the length of the platform stood an honor guard uniformed in the pope's colors. Their breastplates and unsheathed swords also shone bright in the sun. Behind that illustrious welcoming party stood a ten-piece brass band belting out rousing Mexican anthems.

Carlota saw that a line of policemen was on hand to hold back a throng of curious onlookers who had read about the arrival of the Empress of Mexico and wanted to see what she was like. But it was the Chontal sisters who captured everyone's attention. Few onlookers having never seen a native of the world from across the ocean. They had read about brown-feathered people in books and even seen similar figures in the theater, but never had any of those onlookers seen a native of flesh and blood. People stared without inhibition, and the sisters became the talk of Rome for days.

In contrast to what had awaited Carlota at Saint Nazaire, here was a welcoming speech filled with affectionate and respectful words, along with the final touch of a little girl who shyly handed the empress a colorful bouquet of flowers. The young empress was overtaken by a wave of surprise, gratitude and happiness. Gone for the moment was the confusion and melancholy she had been experiencing just minutes earlier.

As for Lula, Chelo and Tila, they felt intimidated by the sight of so many uniformed and robed men. They had witnessed the pomp of the French parades in Mexico, but the size and opulence of this display dwarfed anything they had ever seen. The sisters saw that most of the dignitaries and the crowd had their eyes riveted not on the empress but on them, and they stared back unabashedly, grasping the shock they produced in these Europeans who still perceived people like them as savages.

After the reception was over, Carlota and her companions were helped onto an elegant open carriage and began their ride to the Albergo di Roma, the luxurious hotel where an entire floor was reserved for the empress and her retinue. When Carlota signaled the sisters to join her in the carriage, a wave of murmurs swept over the dignitaries, but neither the empress nor her companions seemed to notice.

The route to the hotel was filled with waving banners and cheering crowds. The uproar filled Tila, Lula and Chelo with unease, more so when they took in the vast palaces, buildings and fountains filled with marbled muscular men and other strange images with horns and wings. It crossed the mind of each of the sisters that no doubt the great Teocalli of Cholula must have looked as grand before the Bearded Ones covered it with dirt.

Although exhilarated upon arriving at the hotel, the women were tired and looked forward to silence and privacy. The empress' luggage had been delivered by the time they were shown to their suite, and the sisters proceeded with their usual routine, oblivious to the luxury surrounding them. They moved about with ease, just as if they were in their small room at La Perla when they were little girls. When they were satisfied that Carlota was ready for bed, they produced, from somewhere, a bundle of bread and cheese and from elsewhere a pitcher of water.

All this time the women had been quiet, even when they sat down to eat. The empress was apparently lost in her own thoughts, as were the sisters. After she had eaten, Carlota turned to them.

"Hermanas, you've never spoken of your childhood or of your birthplace. You know about me, but I don't know anything about you."

With food still in their mouths, the sisters looked at Carlota in amazement, as if she had uttered words in an unknown tongue. After a few moments, Lula and Chelo turned to Tila, expecting her to say something. She took a sip of water and swallowed. Carlota noticed that her voice was softer than usual.

"Alteza, we don't know where we were born, neither do we know who our mother and father were. What we do know is that we spent our years as girls in a place called La Perla, and it was from there that we traveled to Puebla, and then to the city where our path crossed yours."

Carlota kept quiet as if expecting to hear more, but when her silence went unanswered, she cleared her throat and spoke. "Well, we all have secrets, and keeping them to ourselves is a privilege we each have. Perhaps in years to come I'll tell you all my secrets and you will tell me yours. In the meantime, because I owe you my life, and because it was you who buried my beloved Precious Flower, I will trust you as I trust no one else. Likewise, I want you to trust me above all others."

Lula and Chelo again looked to Tila, urging her to speak, to say something that would reflect what Carlota had just said.

"Majestad, we trust you above all others already."

"Thank you, Tila. Also, I want you to know that from here on, I will not eat or drink anything except what comes from your hands. I'll depend on you to go out in search of food wherever we are. Bring it to me so that together we may eat and drink only what we know is safe. I caution you. Because we're in another world, don't think that poison doesn't exist here. It does. It can be found everywhere, especially in the hearts of evil people. Do you understand what I'm saying?"

"We understand."

"Good. Now let's sleep because tomorrow we'll meet with the most important man in this world we call Europe."

Chapter Twenty-Six

AUGUST 1866

Rome

Pope Pius IX sat near an oversized marble fireplace. His heavy-lidded eyes stared at the painting of Raphael the Archangel, but his thoughts were concentrated on another letter he had received that morning from Emperor Louie Napoleon in which the emperor listed new details about Empress Charlotte that disturbed the pontiff. He sighed deeply as he absentmindedly chewed his thumbnail. When he realized what he was doing, he pulled his hand from his mouth and straightened the heavy gold chain and crucifix hanging around his collar. He was robed in a white pelerine and cassock that emphasized his large stature and portliness.

Pius scanned his surroundings. It was a room he favored because it was not large, but neither was it small, and its paintings were more to his liking than others throughout the Vatican. Most of those other pieces overwhelmed him with their exaggerated size and usually tortured subjects. Here, in his private reading room, he made it a practice to take time to rest between tasks by gazing at paintings by Titian, Raphael and, his favorite, El Greco's San Andrea. Pius was fond of contemplating the saint's tapered fingers, his elongated neck and sublime expression. How did the artist achieve that look? Pius asked that question every time he turned to the painting.

The pope also admired the highly decorated vaulted ceiling that resonated with the echo of his footsteps on the ornate marble floor. He often stopped mid-step just to relish the gilded molding that framed the doorways and windows. It was not unusual for him to take time to study the intricacy of twisting plaster vines and leaves that decorated the walls. Each time he looked at that filigreed work, he marveled at the crafting of such beauty. Pius often found himself secretly wishing that he had been born an artisan, someone with the gift of creating such loveliness.

The furnishings of the room were also just right, he thought, with the proper number of settees and tables, and his desk was perfect. It was just large enough to hold the countless documents that streamed in daily. Yes, he loved that room. Pope Julius II designed it, he had heard.

"Such a long time ago."

Pius sighed deeply as he slowly rose from his armchair. Arthritis was already making headway into various joints of his body, but he fought it off by reminding himself to keep on his feet as much as possible. He walked to the double doors that opened out to a small terrace overlooking the piazza. From that vantage point, Pius took in a full view of Bernini's colonnades, at that moment bathed in early morning sunlight. As he looked down at the scene, he marveled at how the sun cast shadows that created an illusion of countless moving columns. Those reflections curved around the piazza like two arms arched and ready to embrace the throngs that often assembled there.

The pontiff turned away from the terrace and headed for the desk, where he had placed Napoleon's letter. He had evaded rereading it long enough. It was filled with a description of Napoleon's interview with the Empress of Mexico. The details were so disturbing that Pius cringed at the thought that he had actually granted Charlotte an audience, soon to take place. It was a meeting that he did not look forward to. What if she were really insane? But then, had he not already affirmed that in his letter to Emperor Franz Joseph?

"Why did I agree to see her? What was I thinking?" Pius said out loud as he cupped his chin in his hands.

All the while, his eyes were riveted on the damming letter from Napoleon.

Holiness, her attitude toward us was sarcastic and caustic.

The emperor's words struck the pope as exaggerated, and he cautioned himself to remember that Napoleon was a complainer, that his whining should not be taken too seriously. Yet, Pius reflected, there was the possibility that what he said might have some substance, and that more attention should be given to the letter.

Pius took it in his hands and held it close to his myopic eyes.

When I pointed out certain principles pertinent to the differences between men and women, she balked and even defied my position.

"What in the devil is the Frenchman talking about?" wondered Pius aloud, "What gibberish!" He went on reading and now found himself intrigued by what came next:

Her unfeminine attitude toward me expressed itself when she challenged my wisdom. She even accused me of being responsible for the collapse of the empire in Mexico.

"When will Napoleon ever cease being such an arrogant cretin?" Pius muttered as he let the letter slip from his fingers onto the desktop. He had enough for the moment.

"Besides, it's the truth. He *is* responsible for the collapse of that ill-fated empire. Any fool can see that much!"

Pius knew that eventually he had to analyze what Napoleon had to say about Charlotte, but not just then. He could not deal with more of the emperor's pompous words. He needed a respite. At that moment, a rapping on the door reminded him that it was time for his morning cup of chocolate.

"Éntrate, Umberto."

The valet entered, silver tray in hand, bowed respectfully and then placed it on a marble-topped table. On another table he spread out a crisp linen tablecloth, then the exquisite china, napkin, a fluted vase with a rosebud, silverware, and finally a tiny basket filled with freshly baked rolls, along with a pitcher of steaming chocolate. The aroma spiraling from that miniature banquet aroused the pope's appetite.

"Grazie, Umberto."

The valet smiled and silently backed away until he was out of the chamber. Barely had he disappeared when Pius sat at the table. He buttered a portion of a roll, popped it into his mouth and followed that with a sip of hot chocolate. He settled back into the armchair trying to enjoy the delicious tastes swirling on his tongue, but it was impossible. Thoughts of Charlotte stubbornly intruded. After polishing off the roll, Pius licked his fingers, wiped them on the napkin and got to his feet to take up Napoleon's letter once again.

Your Holiness, Charlotte Habsburg had the impudence to bring up my letters to Maximilian in which I promised to support the empire at all costs. She went so far as to state that she is disposed to circulate those letters abroad, and so expose me as a man who reneges on his word. This is blackmail, Your Holiness! Pure, indecent blackmail!

This time, Pius read those words with concern, wondering what Charlotte's intentions could have been in approaching Napoleon in the first place? Had coercion been on her mind? At first glance, that would not appear to be the strategy of an insane woman. Although Pius had already made the mistake of going along with the allegation of her lunacy, he was now experiencing second thoughts. He felt a headache coming on as he returned to the last part of Napoleon's letter, and rapidly scanned what he considered yet more whining.

She did not, to her convenience, mention the countless badger-ing letters with which she bombarded me in the hopes of breaking down my resolve to end France's futile involvement in Mexico. This item she conveniently failed to include in her tirade.

Pius was fed up with Napoleon and was about to put the letter aside when he noticed that there was another page that he had not yet read.

The empress betrayed disturbing signs of mental instability. Her hands trembled uncontrollably and her voice became shrill, then muffled and sometimes nearly inaudible. At other times she screamed. Her eyes wandered aimlessly, as if lost. However, the sign that left Her Majesty and me utterly disturbed and fearful for Charlotte's mental wellness was an incident regard-ing a simple glass of orangeade that she took freely and willingly. When she drained the glass, she suddenly raved and ranted accusations that we had poisoned her. She screamed that the tainted orangeade was proof of our criminal act. Needless to say, both Eugénie and I were completely shaken by this prepos-terous allegation.

There it was! The assertion of Charlotte's madness again emphasized by Napoleon. Pius put down the letter to ponder this point further; he wanted to come to the heart of the emperor's posi-tion on this matter. What did Napoleon stand to gain by Charlotte's lunacy? Why did he harp on it so much? After giving that query careful thought, Pius' mind pushed the issue. What did any of Europe's involved leaders have to gain by her supposed madness?

Of more importance to him was the impact of demands by Charlotte on Vatican policy. What embarrassments could she con-trive for his papacy? He told himself that he had to be prepared for her to accuse him of something or another regarding the fall of the Mexican Empire. If that were to be the case, then how could her assertions be discredited? Was that at the heart of Napoleon's insistence on her madness?

"That's it!" Pius hammered a closed fist on the open palm of his other hand. "If her madness was asserted by all concerned, then whatever came out of her mouth would be meaningless. Is the world ready to listen to the ravings of a mad empress? Of course not!"

Now his headache was full-blown. He turned from the desk and made his way through the double doors and headed for the private chapel, where he hoped to receive consolation from the Holy Spirit through prayer and meditation. Empress Charlotte was scheduled to meet with him within the week, and he intended to be prepared for whatever agenda she might have.

Most troubling to him was Charlotte's proposition to deprive the Church in Mexico of its holdings. This plan, of course, was impossible, even unspeakable, but if this were to be what was on her mind, then any meeting between him and her would prove to be fruitless, and she stood to be the loser. He would be prepared.

Chapter Twenty-Seven

September 1866

Rome

By the time Carlota awoke, the Chontal sisters had returned from the Corso with fruit, bread and a pitcher of water. When the women finished eating, the sisters set out Carlota's black dress, a simple string of pearls and a black mantilla. After they helped with the empress' toilette, they brushed and set her hair, then applied the usual cosmetics. After that ritual, they checked to see that Carlota's necessary accessories were also ready: gloves, handkerchief and a small purse.

When Carlota looked at herself in the mirror, she was satisfied that her appearance was as it should be. The sisters knew, however, that she was tense underneath that elegance and beauty. They asked themselves, who would not be nervous meeting the most important man in the world?

Lula, Tila and Chelo were excited to be included in the empress' company. In preparation, they had taken care the night before to stretch out the second rebozo and huipil they had brought from Mexico. As a last touch, they had twisted fresh crisp colored ribbons into their braids. When Carlota turned her gaze away from the mirror, she looked at her companions and smiled in approval.

A rap on the door announced that the carriage was ready to take them to the Vatican. They slipped out of the room, Carlota leading the way. She glided down the broad staircase, followed by the sisters and the rest of her entourage. As the small group wound its way down toward the lobby, hotel guests stopped to bow or curtsy, their eyes filled with admiration for Carlota's beauty, and curiosity for the colorful images of the three women that walked behind her. Waiting for them was a contingent of uniformed soldiers, sabers drawn in respect for the empress. The guards stood at stiff attention in dual columns facing one another all the way down the entrance steps, where the coach awaited and liveried valets stood on each side of the coach's door, ready to assist the empress as she stepped up to take her seat. They did the same with the Indian women, but not without exchanging significant glances under raised eyebrows. The rest of Carlota's retinue followed in separate coaches.

The drive from the hotel to the Vatican was not long but it was interesting, especially for Tila, Chelo and Lula, who listened to Carlota's descriptions as she pointed out fountains, palaces and churches. She explained that she knew her way around Rome because she had visited that city during her childhood when she had accompanied her father King Leopold.

The coach finally entered Saint Peter's Piazza and pulled up next to the colonnades adjacent to the papal offices. There, too, the empress was again greeted with pomp and reverence. When she and her companions stepped out of the coach, they found Swiss guards in colorful uniforms, several cardinals regaled impressively, as well as representatives of Rome's distinguished families.

In rhythm with the cadenced march of their escort, Carlota, the Chontal sisters and the rest of the Mexican legation ascended a wide marble staircase leading to the papal throne room where Pope Pius IX, seated under the official canopy and surrounded by more cardinals, waited for the empress of Mexico. There, she paid the pontiff homage. She kissed the ring on his gloved hand and murmured words of greeting. The other members of her entourage then took their turn to kiss the Pope's velvet slipper.

Immediately after the initial ritual, the Pope got to his feet and gestured for the empress to follow him into his study, where they were to meet in private. The rest of the retinue was instructed to wait in another chamber.

At that point, the ostentation ended. Once alone in the study, Pius wordlessly signaled Carlota to sit in an armchair placed beside his while they waited for tea to be served by the valet and his assistants. It was an impressive service of tea and delicate pastries that Pius relished, but he noticed that Carlota didn't take even a sip of the hot drink.

"Majesty, is the tea not to your liking? Perhaps you would prefer a cup of chocolate?"

"No, thank you, Your Holiness. Nothing for me at the moment."

He nodded, but his face did express uncertainty. Nonetheless, he smiled and, as protocol demanded, he took the lead in the conversation.

"Daughter, I hope you find yourself well?"

"Yes, Your Holiness."

"Your accommodations are satisfactory, I trust?"

"Beyond my expectations, Holy Father."

Pius went on with a list of the routine pleasantries, asking, wondering, smiling and gently prodding his guest. When he came to the end of those formalities, he cleared his throat and spoke with unexpected frankness. Even the tone of his voice changed when he got down to business.

"Tell me, daughter, why do you travel with those native women? Are the women of your own race and rank not adequate?"

Carlota knew from the beginning of her travels that the privileged place she had given her companions was bound to amaze and even scandalize her society. She knew its prejudices and notions thoroughly and thus the Pontiff's question did not take her off guard. However, she did find it out of place in what was meant to be a meeting to discuss matters of state. Nonetheless, she responded.

"Your Holiness, I've chosen the company of these three sisters because they have proven by their past service that they're dutiful and loyal. I ask for no more from my ladies, whatever their ancestry might be. Additionally, they are Mexicanas and I am, after all, empress of their land."

"On the other hand, daughter, I'm sure you've heard voices that imply that they are of a race that by nature is untamed and even prone to occult practices."

"Holy Father, there's good and bad in every race, wouldn't you agree?"

"I agree. Interestingly, I've read in certain chronicles that Captain General Hernán Cortés, when visiting his sovereign in Spain after his conquest of Mexico, similarly made it a point to always be accompanied by natives and other creatures, such as parrots and monkeys indigenous to that land. It seems he aimed at impressing those of the imperial court with proof of his exploits."

Carlota frowned because she caught the implication of Pius' words, yet she hesitated to respond harshly because she didn't want to annoy him. She kept silent for a few moments before speaking.

"Your Holiness, with all respect, my ladies are neither parrots nor monkeys, much less are they proof of my exploits. On the contrary, they have been my faithful companions through difficult times now that I'm in exile."

Pius bit his upper lip pensively while he absentmindedly twisted his gold chain. In a few moments, he got to his feet and walked over to the desk. Midday sounds from the piazza drifted upward into the studio through the open terrace doors. A clock on the mantelpiece ticked. When he turned to face Carlota, his expression was a mix, resolute yet uncertain.

"Daughter, what's on your mind? How may I be of help?"

Carlota could no longer bear to remain seated. She also got to her feet and went to stand by the pontiff. Her diminutive stature was emphasized by his height, and that difference between them seemed to make both of them uncomfortable, so Pius moved around to the other side of the desk to put some space between them.

"I have one desire, Your Holiness, and that is to understand why the Vatican has withdrawn its support of the Mexican Empire."

"Humm! I've been told of the direct manner in which you speak, and here I have an excellent sample of that frankness. I wonder how it is, daughter, that a woman of your intelligence has not discerned the response to that question on your own."

"Your Holiness, may I ask you to please speak directly and without subtlety. A simple response to my question will suffice." Carlota's voice was sharp, even forceful.

Taken aback by Carlota's audacious response, Pius raised his eyebrows to demonstrate his displeasure. Yet, there was something he saw in the young empress that urged him to put aside his irritation; instead, he would try to deal with her inquiry without compromising his position. He rubbed his chin while he reflected until he decided to answer with yet another question.

"Let me pose the following to you, Majesty: What if you were asked your opinion regarding the Church's holdings in Mexico? Is this question direct enough?"

"Yes, it's a good question, but it's still a question, not an answer. Your Holiness, I'll respond to it by stating what is already known about my position regarding the Church in Mexico. I believe that the Church owns a disproportionate share of that country's wealth and that it must share those assets with its people."

Pius felt the hair on the back of his neck bristle, but he ignored it and pushed on with another question. "And if you were asked to differentiate your position on the matter from that of Benito Juárez and his cohorts, what would be your answer?"

Carlota recognized that the pontiff had chosen to play a game of questions with her. It crossed her mind that it was just as it had been with Louie Napoleon, except that Pius was much more intelligent and astute, more indecipherable.

"I would say, Your Holiness, that on this one point, I have no differences with President Juárez because justice is justice. Yes, the Indian president is the enemy of the empire, but that does not mean that he is wrong on all issues."

Pius squared his shoulders and looked hard into Carlota's eyes. "Majesty, you astound me!"

"And you, Holiness, distress me beyond words. Am I to understand that because the empire aspired to dispossess the Church of some of its holdings, the Church withdrew its support, leaving Maximilian empty-handed? What did the Church expect in the first place? Surely, the Church must have been aware of our ideals and political position from the beginning."

By now Pius had turned his back on Carlota, pretending to look out onto the piazza, but her words compelled him to turn around to look at her, even if it was askance. Her words incensed and astounded him at the same time, and he wondered how it was that such a petite woman could be so forceful, even intimidating.

"What did the Church expect, you ask? How naïve you are, Madame! Surely, someone of your intelligence knows that what the Church expected, in exchange for its support, was respect and reverence. It did not expect the empire to embrace and perpetuate policies set up by that Indian bandit Juárez. Not one Mexican bishop, or monsignor, not even the humblest peasant priest would even think of surrendering the Church's holdings to a ragtag mob. That wealth belongs to God and must never be given over to a horde of brigands and thieves of which Benito Juárez is the leader."

By now Carlota was also angry, especially because Pius would not deviate from worn out platitudes and other nonsense about hordes and bandits and God.

"Before we end this interview," continued Pius, "I must ask one more question: What is your view regarding the United States' position on the fallacy of freedom of religion?"

Carlota understood that with that provocative question, the pontiff had abruptly ended the audience. She was insulted by his disrespect for her as empress of Mexico. Now she intensely desired to snub him in like manner. The only thing that came to her mind was to answer his question in as blunt a way as possible.

"I believe that country's policy regarding freedom of religion is correct. Freedom of religion is not a fallacy but a gift to which everyone is entitled. Yes! I believe in that freedom."

Carlota saw by the expression of shock on the Pope's face that she had hit the mark. He was quick to retort with a quivering voice.

"Oh, my child! You are so wrong! Don't you see that so-called freedom of religion is the road to damnation? Don't you understand that it leads to all sorts of heresy and other forms of profanation?"

This time the empress didn't respond, and Pius took the moment to gape at her with dilated eyes. He was struck hard by the potential danger posed by Charlotte Habsburg, a woman who had the influence, intelligence and heart to cause the Church serious problems. Perhaps, he thought, Napoleon as well as Emperor Franz Joseph had reason to fear her relentless meddling in their affairs. And perhaps it was at that moment that Pius made up his mind. The empress had to be discredited before she became a formidable enemy.

Shaken, he moved to the armchair and, once he was seated, he looked at Carlota. "Majesty, we're both exhausted, let us end our interview." He rang for his valet who appeared within seconds.

"Umberto, please show Her Majesty and her company to their coaches. When you've done that, please return. I wish to speak to you. You also have to clear away what's left of the tea you served."

Carlota, who had withdrawn into an exhausted silence, bowed to the pope in a deep curtsy. She then kissed his ring before leaving the chamber. When she was at the door, she turned and looked hard at him.

"Your Holiness, I thank you. You have given me what I expected. I wish you good health."

Still seated, an agitated Pius acknowledged her departure with a bow of the head. He felt a sudden pang of anxiety at her parting words, sensing they held a hidden meaning that he had missed. Was it a veiled threat? What were her intentions?

He got to his feet and went to the desk to again study Napoleon's letter, especially the parts that cast doubt on Carlota's sanity. Pius knew that she was far from being mad, but perhaps Almighty God was showing the way to disarm her. Her position on so many matters of importance was, after all, dangerous for the Church.

When the valet returned, Pius asked him to come nearer, that he wanted to have a word. The man reverentially approached with his head inclined. Pius spoke to him in a soft, subtle voice.

"Umberto, did you see that the empress was helped in every way possible?"

"To the best of our ability, Your Holiness."

"How did she look? Happy? Concerned? Did she demonstrate any particular emotion?"

"Well, she appeared sullen, Your Holiness, but I'm certain that it was because she was tired. Her face reflected much fatigue."

Having said that, Umberto turned to pick up the tea service. Just then, Pius cleared his throat to let the valet know he wanted his attention.

"By the way, Umberto, did you notice that Her Majesty didn't touch the tea you served?"

The pope's question caught the valet just as he picked up a cup and saucer, but stopped to reflect before responding.

"Yes, Your Holiness, I noticed but I have not given it further thought."

"Why would she abstain from taking even a sip?"

"I don't know, Your Holiness."

"Is there a possibility that she thought the tea was poisoned?"

The valet was shocked by Pius' words, and he swayed as if he had been pushed. The cup and saucer rattled precariously in his hand as he gawked open-mouthed at the pontiff.

"Poisoned? No, Your Holiness, that thought didn't enter my mind. What makes you ask?" By now thinking that somehow Pius was hinting that he was responsible for the empress' rejection of the tea, the valet became thoroughly alarmed.

"I cannot really say. It only now entered my mind."

"Your Holiness, do you think she fears being poisoned?"

"That's not for me to say, Umberto."

"Oh, Your Holiness! Poison! Who would poison such a lovely woman?"

"As I said, that's not for me to say."

"Regina Coeli! Why did I not see her turmoil?"

Umberto paled and his lips were a tight line that crossed his face from cheek to cheek. He rolled his eyes, inwardly searching for missed clues, anything that might explain the poor empress' fear of being poisoned. He stood in a stupor as if paralyzed, although he wanted to run, to get away from that place. Running away, however, was impossible because he was obliged to wait for the pontiff's instructions.

Umberto stood frozen, yearning to be released. Pius was no longer even looking at the valet but was gazing at a document on his desk. Finally, as if only then remembering that Umberto was still there, Pius looked up.

"Umberto, please bring me a cup of chocolate. I'm fatigued beyond words. And while you're out and about, please tell my secretary to come. Inform him that I need to send a telegram to Prince Philippe, brother of Empress Charlotte. Tell him the matter is urgent."

Now that Umberto had his instructions, he bowed low and withdrew as the tea service in his hands jiggled and clanged all the way out. By then, there was a ringing in his ears so loud that he could hardly hear himself think as he headed for the back stairway with the intention of rushing down to the kitchen. Wild thoughts swirled in his head. Why would the empress even think that the tea was poisoned? What kind of a person got such thoughts? Was she crazy?

Umberto halted abruptly. Before saying anything to anyone, he needed a few minutes to reflect. After a long pause, he saw that there was only one thing for him to do: Tell his fellow servants what had happened in the pope's chamber. They would make sense of it all.

Chapter Twenty-Eight

I f Pius had intended Umberto's cup of tea to become the germ of gossip, he succeeded. After the valet unloaded what the pope had implied on his fellow cooks, scullery maids and charcoal boys, gossip of Empress Carlota's unusual behavior took root, and it broke out in different varieties of rumor, insinuation and whisperings. What spilled from the sacred chambers of the Vatican, however, had already been preceded by a similar wave of talk that seeped out from as far away as the Schoenberg Palace in Vienna, Saint-Cloud in France and from distant Laeken Palace in Belgium, the ancestral home of Empress Carlota.

"The Empress of Mexico has gone mad!"

Those words were at the heart of the gossip that spread in epidemic proportions throughout Rome and other cities, ultimately crisscrossing not only from this palace to that castle, but from inns to bedrooms and from there all the way to marketplaces and street corners. Tabloids printed anecdotes and constantly updated juicy tidbits on Carlota's supposed condition. Cigar-smoking gentlemen in coffeehouses eagerly read the gossip, hardly waiting to run to their mistresses with the latest rumor regarding the mad empress.

The main culprits of those lies were Carlota's own entourage, jealous and outraged because they felt slighted by the empress' preference for Indians. It was those snubbed servants that fabricated tales of Carlota's so-called invasion of the Vatican, demanding to sleep where no other decent woman had ever dared. It was they who invented the lie that she and her Indian wenches kept live chickens in their hotel room, ready to be slaughtered and devoured.

The cruel gossip flew from lip to lip, each time expanding and spinning more detail, some of it believable, most of it vicious, much of it so exaggerated that thinking people laughed. Nonetheless, everyone was entertained, hearing and talking of poor Mamá Carlota's demise, so it went on and on.

Ordinary people, the downtrodden, kept the gossip on the move and alive because of the satisfaction they felt hearing of the fall of a member of the high and powerful who, after all, were made of mere clay just like everyone else. Insofar as certain key figures were concerned, that gossip suited them because Empress Carlota had become a liability. She was too strong, too influential and too outspoken. She would not keep silent about who had brought the Mexican Empire to its knees. She was, they all agreed, someone who had forgotten her place as a woman, and they did nothing to disarm the insidious gossip that she had gone mad, because it fit into their agenda to silence her.

Chapter Twenty-Nine

B y the time the pope's wire reached him at Laeken Palace, Prince Philippe had already heard the rumor of Carlota's madness from his valet. It happened one evening as the servant poured the prince a snifter of cognac. Carlota's brother calmly took in what his valet murmured, not believing the gossip as he was by nature a man unreceptive to such nonsense. Philippe was only three years older than his sister, and they had grown up close. No one knew her intelligence, precociousness and her impulsive hot temper better than he did.

Philippe sipped his cognac while he enjoyed a good chuckle, remembering their childish antics. It was a while before he remembered the telegram that had been left on the table next to his armchair. The prince took the envelope and held it close, while he examined its seals and official emblems. He turned it over several times, looking at both sides with curiosity, although he knew it came directly from the pope. Philippe had little desire to read its message.

"Pius can be dreary."

Philippe muttered under his breath as he returned the unopened telegram to the tabletop, deciding to put off opening it. Instead, still thinking of Charlotte, he savored another taste of the fine liqueur while reclining his head against the armchair. He then held the snifter up to the light to enjoy the colors escaping from its prisms. It was Philippe's favorite time of day, when important matters had come to a close, and he was alone and undisturbed. His way of enjoying those moments was just as he was now doing: a sip of cognac while he sat by a warm fire. Unfortunately, this evening his cherished time had been interrupted, and the intrusion was waiting on the table by his elbow. The prince sighed, knowing that he could no longer put off the inevitable. He picked up the envelope and opened it. The message was brief.

Serene Highness, your sister's mind is seriously troubled. I advise you to come to Rome posthaste. She needs assistance. Blessings. Pius IX.

Philippe let the telegram slide through his fingers onto his lap, unable to stop his sudden shock. He had not expected it, but the pope's words seriously disturbed him. He felt a quick rush of anxiety, and he tried to relax. No matter how much he concentrated on loosening the muscles in his back and neck, he tensed yet more and his breath quickened. Was it possible that the rumor about his sister was not just gossip, after all?

"Just a moment, Philippe. Think before you come to any conclusion!"

The prince often talked out loud to himself, given that his was the only voice he really listened to. He took another sip of cognac while he gazed at his surroundings, hoping to regain his normal calm. He looked at the blazing logs in the fireplace and then ordered his eyes to roam the walls, stopping to focus on the portraits of his and Carlota's ancestors. They were the German Saxe-Coburgs on their father's side and the Bourbons on their blessed mother's part, and not one of them, Philippe reminded himself, had ever suffered from even a drop of dementia. They were not like the Habsburgs that hatched one lunatic after the other over the centuries.

Philippe couldn't help himself. His thoughts returned to the telegram: *Your sister's mind is seriously troubled.* Impossible!

Philippe countered those words with thoughts and memories of his sister, of her talents, constant reading and how she loved to debate issues. He closed his eyes and recalled the time she actually stood up in front of their father's court to discuss one of the great philosophers whose name Philippe could not remember, and how everyone responded with complete silence as if struck by lightning. He thought of how he and Charlotte had later on laughed at the Wobbly Double Chins, as she called the old dukes and duchesses.

"Maybe that's when it started, darling Charlotte. People hated how you made them look like fools. They knew that you saw yourself as better than anyone else. That was it, sister! You flew too high."

The prince drained the snifter and licked his lips, but his mind was still focused on Carlota. He recognized that she had been highstrung as a child and that she easily sparked to a fight. She even threw things at whomever she felt was getting the upper hand of the argument, especially if it was Leopold, their older brother, because she considered him stupid.

"You were always clear thinking and never outside of reason. You were never crazy!"

This last word stuck in the prince's throat. He could not believe his sister had lost her reason, her beautiful mind. No!

Nighttime was falling and the library was growing dark. Philippe became aware of the valet's quiet steps as he went about lighting the smaller candles as well as the candelabra. When the man stoked the fire, the blaze leaped and sputtered with tiny sparks that filled the room with crackling, snapping sounds. Gradually the room became shrouded in moving shadows that reflected on crystal flower vases and cordovan leather upholstery. This was the prince's library. Here no one disturbed him, and he could be at peace, except for today, at this moment, when he was distressed.

"Highness, may I get you anything else?"

The valet unexpectedly pulled Philippe out of his thoughts. "Not right now, Rigo. I will, however, ask you to pack me a bag. I'll be traveling to Rome tomorrow. Alert our driver to have a coach ready at dawn, when we'll make our way to the train station."

"Yes, Highness. May I ask how long you'll be gone?"

"I'm not sure. Two weeks, I'd say."

"Would you say that I should pack cooler garments? Rome is usually warmer."

"Good thinking, Rigo. However, I'm not sure I'll stay in Rome, so pack some warmer things in case I head back north."

"Very well, Highness. Ring for me if you need me."

"Wait, Rigo! Inform my secretary of these plans and that he will be traveling with me. We'll need passage from Brussels to Rome. Yes! That should be enough."

"Highness, wouldn't it be good for me to go with you as well? Perhaps I may be of service."

The prince looked at his valet, grateful for his loyalty and willingness to serve. "Well, I had not thought of it, Rigo, but now that you have offered to come, yes, please do. It may take the three of us to attend to whatever is waiting in Rome."

When the valet left the room, Philippe's thoughts returned to the telegram, and he tasted bitterness coating his tongue. He poured another snifter of cognac, hoping to wash away the taste. He leaned back to reflect on the pope's words, but then he pushed them aside because he hated them and he didn't believe them. Instead, he gave himself over to thinking more of his sister and how much he had always loved her.

Charlotte had been a beautiful little girl, pampered by everyone, especially by their father. Philippe looked back on their days as children, when they ran through the corridors and chambers of this palace where he now lives, and he sighed because those had been the happiest times of his life. Again, his thoughts returned to her intelligence that had always been sharp, keen to the point that she ran circles around him and Leopold. Philippe's memory still rang with her laughter when she answered any question sooner than either of them.

The prince dropped his head into his hands because he could not help thinking that out there, along dirty streets, false vicious gossip was seeping through grimy teeth and that dimwitted bastards were saying that Charlotte had lost her mind. How dare they?

What did anybody know? She was a young woman with her life ahead of her. His hands fell to his lap to calculate her age on his fingers, remembering that he was three years older.

"She's only twenty-seven years old!"

Prince Philippe could not hold in the mounting turmoil that was assailing him at the thought that his sister had gone mad. He frowned and his lips twisted into an angry snarl, thinking that her mistake was having married that weak-willed, foppish, conceited Maximilian; but a yet greater mistake had been allowing herself to be seduced by the empty dream of building an empire in Mexico.

The prince left the library and headed for his bedroom. He would try in vain to sleep.

Chapter Thirty

OCTOBER 1866

Rome

P rince Philippe was nervous and worried as he made his way up the elegant staircase of Albergo di Roma. He was fatigued by the long train trip from Brussels to Rome, especially since he had not taken time to rest, much less refresh himself. His jaw was shadowed by a growth of dark stubble and his eyes were reddened by sleepless hours, but because he was anxious to see his sister, he had put aside everything else.

He rapped at the door of the suite, but when it opened, a sight appeared that took away the prince's breath. It was a woman so different, so foreign, that her appearance left him speechless. He could only gape at her. When Philippe glanced beyond her, he saw that she was not alone, that behind her were two other women who looked nearly identical. Their complexion was smooth and dark brown like chocolate and each one was dressed in a colorful skirt, blouse and shawl. Philippe was captivated by their hair that was braided high on their heads with wide intertwined ribbons, also of many colors, giving each woman a crown so intriguing that he stared unabashedly, not knowing what to make of the apparitions that stood looking at him. When the three women curtsied, he bowed low because he didn't know what else to do.

At that moment Carlota appeared. She emerged from behind the trio, and her presence helped Philippe snap out of his astonishment. Still not finding words to say anything, he moved into the room just to get close to his sister. As if it had been only a day since they last saw each other, brother and sister put their arms around each other in a long, quiet embrace.

Without a word, Carlota took her brother by the hand and led him to a small sitting area that was so quiet that Philippe was certain the women could hear the beating of his heart. He put his hand to his vest, thinking that if they didn't hear his heart, surely the thumping under his shirt would give him away.

One of the dark women took his hat, the other his coat and the third his walking stick. When that silent ritual was over, Carlota and Philippe sat down and faced one another. They were hard pressed for what to say. Some three years had passed since they had last met, so they relished that moment with a joy difficult for either one to describe. When they finally spoke, their voices were hushed.

"Brother, I was expecting you."

"Who told you?"

"My companions heard it on the Corso."

The prince's face snapped over to stare at the Indian women, and his eyes again filled with amazement. He tried not to look stupefied, but could not help himself. "Charlotte, who are these women?" he finally blurted out his confusion.

"I told you. They're my companions. They're also sisters and serve me faithfully."

"What about your ladies? Where are they?"

"They've disappeared, like all the rest. One by one my attendants have vanished, leaving the four of us here alone. Now Tila, Chelo and Lula are my ladies."

Philippe stared at the sisters. He had never before been so close to natives from that other world. The thought flashed through his mind that perhaps here was a reason why people thought his sister had lost her senses. Yet, when he narrowed his eyes to take a longer, more careful look at the women, he concluded they were beautiful, exotic and intelligent.

When the sisters left the room, Philippe turned back to take an even closer look at Carlota and realized that the period of their separation had not been kind to her. Those three years had smashed her cherished dream. She had been forced to accept the humiliation of banishment, and she had paid a steep price. She had changed. She was well-groomed and powdered, but her face had become angular, no longer round and soft as it used to be. Her lips were tight, as was her posture, which appeared to be rigid, as if on guard against something unexpected.

Philippe glanced at her hands and saw that her fingers twitched nervously. But it was her eyes that had undergone the greatest transformation. They were wider, as if startled or fearful, and, unlike before, they were deep-set. Although she had not lost the squinting that she had had since childhood, there was a strange glow in her eyes, an intensity that had not been there when they last met.

"You've suffered, Charlotte." Philippe furrowed his brow as he used to when they were children.

"Yes."

Her response saddened Philippe, but more than that, her truthfulness struck him because few people admitted to suffering, most pretending that it was something that never happened to them. Her admission had been so honest that he realized the depth of her distress was more than he could imagine. He wanted to get close to her and embrace her.

"I'm sorry, Charlotte; however, you will soon be home and all will be well. That's why I'm here. You'll see."

"It was Pius who sent for you, wasn't it?"

"Yes."

"He meddles in my life. They all do."

Her words made him feel uncomfortable. He looked at her imploringly and asked, "Who does, Charlotte?"

Carlota looked at her brother and smiled ironically, as if saying that he well knew who her enemies were, but that he was only testing her.

"Napoleon, Pius and Franz Joseph. They are my enemies, Philippe, and you know that I speak the truth. Who knows, perhaps even our brother Leopold fits into that circle of conspirators."

Philippe's face colored at the mention of those men, especially their brother. He shifted uneasily in his chair. As always his sister wasted no time in getting to the heart of any issue. The hair on the nape of his neck bristled, thinking that it was this sort of talk that was making it easy for people to think that she had gone mad.

"Charlotte, you shouldn't say such things."

"It's the truth."

"Perhaps. Still, it does you no good to say such things out loud."

"I see! I may believe what I want so long as I don't say so out loud. Is that it, Philippe?"

"Sister, you're making me feel very bad."

"I don't want to do that, but you know as well as I do that Napoleon is the Antichrist. He's Satan himself! I will say that out loud so long as my tongue can move in my head."

At this point the sisters again joined them with a tray of fruit, nuts and tea. Philippe, grateful for the interruption, smiled awkwardly at them. No one spoke; only the tinkling of china and silver filled a silence that was growing tenser with each second. Carlota took an orange, peeled it, separated it wedge by wedge and then gave each one portions, much as might be done with children. Although Philippe thought that what his sister was doing was unusual, he said nothing. Instead he gratefully savored the orange.

"Brother, I had a child while I lived in Mexico."

Carlota's matter-of-fact words crashed in on Philippe, who could not respond because of the half-chewed wedge stuck on his tongue. He forced the piece of fruit down, cleared his throat and finally managed to mutter a few nearly incoherent words.

"A child? You and Maximilian?"

When he mouthed those words, he nervously glanced toward the Indian women, obviously embarrassed that they were hearing his sister reveal such a private matter. He saw that the women went on munching and sipping tea, apparently unperturbed, so he assumed that it was because they didn't understand their language.

At least that was what he hoped, especially when Carlota became even more detailed.

"No! No! Not Maximilian! How in the world could you believe that? You, of all people! I took a lover, a Belgian officer. We made love every day in the cathedral."

Philippe leaned forward in the chair, frowning disapprovingly as his mind wrestled with what she was saying. Because her voice was so relaxed and uninhibited, the thought struck him that perhaps she had indeed gone mad. Or was she joking? On the other hand, what if what she was saying were true? If so, then she was not insane but shameless.

Philippe's intense turmoil reflected on his face. Carlota tried to calm him by caressing his hand. She even smiled at him as she used to when she was a girl, making him think that she was enjoying his discomfort.

"Holy Mary! Love making in the cathedral! And with a man not your husband! What are you talking about? Charlotte, if you're playing a game, I'll tell you that I'm losing patience. It's unkind of you to make fun of me."

"Forgive me, brother, but I'm not making fun of you. I did love a man, I still love him and always will, and I did have his child, but please don't ask me any questions about it."

Her apology changed nothing because Philippe resented Carlota's disregard for his feelings. It was she who first blurted out that she had taken a lover, that she had his child and now she was abruptly closing the door on the subject.

Averting his eyes from her, he leaned back in the chair and crossed his arms to show his irritation. He looked at her once again and saw a deep sadness in her face. He was moved by something urging him to help her.

Almost whispering, he said, "Charlotte, they say that you've gone mad."

"I know, Philippe, but it's groundless gossip. I don't give it thought nor do I worry about it."

"You should give it importance. Gossip can be destructive."

She looked at him. Now her expression had softened, but her eyes still burned with intensity.

"I know those tongues say that I and my companions do insane things, that we keep live chickens here in the hotel room, that they kill and cook them right here for my pleasure."

"Yes, I've heard that much."

"Philippe, how can anyone believe such an outrageous thing? Do you see chickens here? Feathers? Blood? A stove? The most ridiculous of all is the chatter that says I begged the pope to sleep with him at the Vatican. The very thought revolts me! Worst of all, there are dozens of variations of all this worthless nonsense. It depends on who's talking. Tell me, brother, would I not really go mad if I paid attention to such rubbish?"

"Of course, you're right, Charlotte, but you must know that people believe what they want to believe, and it breaks my heart to hear such things about you."

After this, Philippe fell silent. He felt hot tears burning behind his eyelids and he feared that they would leak out. He changed the subject.

"Charlotte, will you at least tell me why you left Mexico? It's rumored that you've come to beg help from the very men you've just accused of being conspirators."

"False! Lies! I did not come to beg them for anything!"

"Then why have you returned?"

Without answering her brother's question, Carlota unexpectedly cut off the conversation, got to her feet and headed for the bedroom. As she reached the double doors, she looked back.

"I'm fatigued, and I must rest. Ask my companions anything you want to know. They have been witnesses to my most beautiful encounters as well as the bleakest. They know why I've returned."

Carlota walked away, leaving behind a baffled and depressed Philippe with nothing more to do than to stare at the sisters, who were by now showing that they, too, were distressed. For the first time since his arrival, he turned to speak to them.

"Ladies, I speak Spanish. Is that your tongue?"

Lula was the first to answer, "It is one of the tongues we speak, Alteza."

"Very well. We'll speak in that language. Tell me if what my sister has just said is true. About the child, I mean."

All three sisters spoke up. "It's true."

Now it was Philippe who got to his feet to walk over to an open window overlooking the Corso. His eyes followed the majestic thoroughfare to its end at the steps of Saint Peter's Basilica, where the piazza opened round and wide like a voracious mouth ready to devour the entire city.

"God, how I hate this city!"

Philippe meant to keep his thoughts to himself, but because he spoke out loud, Lula, Chelo and Tila heard him. They agreed with him and nodded, letting him know that they, too, disliked the city.

Tila got on her feet to get closer to the prince. "Alteza, the empress has been very sad."

"What happened to the child?"

"She crossed to the other side of the volcanoes."

Philippe turned to stare at Tila. Even though he understood her words, their strange meaning slipped through his mind, like water through his fingers. He reflected for a few moments, and he finally realized that the child had died. He too was saddened.

"I'm so sorry! Was it a boy or a girl?"

"A girl."

"The father? Where is he?"

"He left our land and crossed the ocean to this world. He's somewhere in these parts."

"Does he know that he and my sister had a child?"

"We do not know."

"Did the child live at least for a time?"

"No. The empress was poisoned. We were able to cure her but the child had already swallowed the evil potion."

Philippe was appalled by what the sisters were saying. He had heard the wild rumors about Carlota's irrational fear of being poisoned, but here was something that was more real than contrived street gossip.

"Poisoned! Who did it?"

"Witches!"

Philippe was struck by the thought that no rumor or gossip regarding his sister, no matter how wild or unbelievable, had come close to what the sisters were revealing. Yet, when he turned to look hard into their eyes, he saw that what they were saying was true, and he believed them.

The prince tried to grasp the essence of the strange, perilous, magical world into which Carlota's dream of empire had thrust her. When he spoke, his voice was faint.

"Why did my sister leave Mexico?"

"She was cast out by her husband."

Philippe had turned away from the sisters but those words forced him to look at them once again. Why would Maximilian rid himself of the only strength on which his world was based? Without Charlotte, Maximilian was nothing.

"Why did he get rid of her?"

"Because he was jealous of her."

Philippe was by now so exhausted that he knew that he was no longer thinking clearly. Still, despite his fatigue, the notion of Maximilian's jealousy made sense to him when he remembered his brother-in-law's incompetence, his weak will and his exaggerated need to be loved and admired. On the other hand, if anyone thought it out, it could be said that Carlota was Maximilian's rival in every way and that it was likely that he saw her as a threat. Yes, that would make him jealous of her, but the fool had done away with the only real support he had.

"Ladies, you must follow my instructions, so listen carefully."

"We will do as you ask."

"Pack your mistress' things, every piece of clothing, all her jewels, shoes, hats, gloves, everything. Nothing can be left behind. Most important of all are her documents and papers. Pack your things as well and be ready tomorrow at sunrise. Will you do that?"

"We are going also?"

Tila stood facing the prince but at the same time glanced at her sisters to be assured that she was speaking for them. In an instant, she saw that they were willing to follow the empress.

"Yes. I have a feeling that she won't come without you. We're taking Charlotte to Miramar; her castle."

Chapter Thirty-One

1866

Miramar Castle

*M*y odyssey came full circle when our small party landed at Miramar Castle, the site where I first allowed myself to be seduced by the dream of an empire. As the boat neared its moorings and the castle's silhouette loomed out of the mist, I wondered if it was real or a flash of my imagination. I asked myself if people would one day come to those towers and terraces in search of the beginnings of Carlota's folly? I told myself that some people might say it was not a castle but a reverie, the place where I had dreamed the dream. Yet, the most discerning of those onlookers might say that this was the place from where I soared toward the sun.

I looked away from the castle, thinking that whatever the future might bring, the truth was that at that moment, on that day of my return to Miramar, my thoughts were floundering. They were without bearings, and I was afraid.

On that day the sea was serene, but as our small party drifted closer to the castle, my turmoil grew as I struggled with conflicting sentiments. Memories of Mexico and its people crowded my emotions. Recollections of that country's tropical coast reminded me that it had been I who abandoned its soil.

Adiós, Mamá Carlota. Adiós. Adiós. Adiós. Those words taunted me, repeating and rhyming. In truth, I longed to be in Mexico, but Mexico did not want me. I gazed up at the towers and gables of

Miramar Castle, but visions of that other castle, Chapultepec, got in the way.

As soon as we landed, Philippe and the sisters followed me into the chambers of the castle. As if my absence of a thousand days had not slipped by, I saw that the rooms and furnishings had remained intact. The same parquet floors echoed my footsteps, and the marbled walls reflected its vaulted ceilings, just as they had done when the ambassadors first came from Mexico.

Mirrors, crystal vases filled with brilliantly colored flowers, chandeliers, beveled glass, all combined to create a world of light and reflection, as well as deception. Outside, the same exquisite verandas and terraces overlooked the Mediterranean on one side of the castle and the Adriatic on the other. It was all unchanged.

I turned to look at my companions, expecting to see awe stamped on their brown faces but, instead, I saw expressions of discomfort. I turned to look again at the surrounding opulence, and I understood the sisters. I knew that although they stood in the midst of elegance, for eyes such as theirs that had beheld the majesty of volcanoes and pyramids, the castle was but an artificial thing, a museum.

Without a moment to refresh myself, I was asked to review the contingent of servants: butlers, valets, footmen, chambermaids, cooks and gardeners. As if they had been a small army, those men and women stood at attention under the Habsburg shield that Maximilian had devised and placed over the oversized fireplace in the audience chamber. The servants were dressed in their best uniforms. All smiled and, at a given signal, the women curtsied stiffly and the men bowed just as rigidly. What stood out were their eyes, fascinated as they were not by my brother or me but by my three Mexican companions.

Standing near the servants, and of an importance that I was later to understand, was Professor Reidel, the Viennese doctor of disorders of the mind. I should have known what was in store for me, but I didn't. I didn't know that my brother, Leopold, had ordered that man to present himself at Miramar to study me and to confirm my insanity. The eyes of that man also stood out, with the difference being that they were not staring at the sisters, but at me.

Chapter Thirty-Two

NOVEMBER 1866

Miramar Castle

The encounters between Professor Reidel and Carlota were destined to be short-lived and bitter. In the beginning, she submitted to just a few meetings, only because her brother Leopold had ordered them. Reidel asked questions, and she responded despite her growing doubts as to the man's ultimate purpose. She found most of his inquiries so silly that she often laughed in his face. When he persisted in passing insinuating references to her fear of poison and to what he called her wild behavior at the Vatican, she became uneasy and then testy. The breaking point happened when the alienist said, "Tell me why you keep those unsavory women by your side."

Carlota exploded, realizing Reidel's investigation was based only on what he had gathered from gossipmongers and from sordid whisperings spread by broadsheets. On that day, her temper flared. She got to her feet, stamped her foot and angrily walked away from the bespectacled man, leaving him with his mouth hanging open. As she hurried down the corridor, Carlota shouted, "He's the lunatic, not me."

That encounter with the alienist was her first and last. Carlota refused to meet with him again, no matter how much Philippe struggled to change her mind. He tried to persuade her every way he could think of, but mostly by sitting quietly next to her, hardly saying anything, simply letting her know that he was there to help. "Please reconsider, Charlotte." He said this over and again in a soft, yet coaxing tone.

Her only response was to keep quiet, now and then moving her head from side to side in silent refusal. Days passed while Professor Reidel gradually lost patience. He had been humiliated by Carlota's haughty disdain and disrespect. His dislike for her intensified day by day, and although he tried to keep a professional posture, his sentiments leaked out.

An incident occurred that convinced Philippe that his sister had indeed lost her bearings. It happened one evening at dinner, when they sat waiting to be served. As always, only the Mexican sisters were permitted to wait on her while the butler and the kitchen maid served the men. When she was given a plate of fruit and nuts, the doctor committed the mistake of passing what he perhaps meant to be a joking remark about how the empress disappointed the cook by not tasting her food.

"Majesty, is it because we're afraid of being poisoned?" His voice was a condescending, sarcastic purr.

Carlota became so incensed by the alienist's patronizing that she picked up an orange and flung it at him. The fruit spun through the air with such speed that, although he tried to duck, the missile struck Reidel on the forehead, cracking one of the lenses of his spectacles. The whole thing happened so fast that it took everyone, including the alienist, a few seconds to realize what had happened. By the time he recovered, Carlota was on her way out of the room, leaving behind only the reverberation of the slammed door and people aghast at her behavior.

This episode seriously unnerved Philippe. He wanted to help his sister through her ordeal, but her unshakable stubbornness, and now this latest display of bad behavior, wore him down and he found himself wanting to run away. Perhaps to alleviate his distress, he gradually allowed his thoughts to revert to how much he missed home and its library, where he enjoyed his cognac at day's end. He especially daydreamed of his pretty fiancé who was, at the moment, planning their wedding.

THE MADNESS OF *Mamá Carlota*   177

These feelings made Philippe yearn to end his stay at Miramar. There was little for him to do, and he had already conformed with his brother, Leopold's, instructions to settle Carlota's financial matters and see to it that power over her enviable inheritance was removed from her hands and transferred to Leopold.

Few people imagined that Carlota was one of the wealthiest women in Europe, but now the authority over her own money was solely in her brother's hands and, thanks to Philippe, she was dependent on the family. He had helped disinherit his sister and, no matter how much he searched, Philippe could not come up with a justifiable reason.

Shame quickly turned to guilt in the prince, and then resentment of Carlota. Why did she not cooperate? Why did she not simply agree with what Reidel said and get it over with? After that, they would be free to pack their bags, head for Belgium and the past would be behind them with a new life in store. The truth was that his sister stubbornly refused to hear one word from the doctor. Instead, she spent her time walking through the gardens or gazing out over the sea as if she were in a trance.

What was even more dangerous was that she persisted in writing letters to Queen Victoria, to the Tsarina, to Franz Joseph and to anyone else that came into her tormented mind. Each letter conveyed details of what had happened in Mexico, all of it as she saw it. She described how everyone shared in the responsibility for the downfall of that empire, especially Napoleon, whom she identified as Satan and the Antichrist. In her mind, even Pius IX was the French Emperor's fellow conspirator.

Unknown to Carlota, those letters were intercepted and made accessible to Reidel as well as to the prince. Philippe especially was shocked at the extent of Carlota's extreme efforts to bring attention to the failed Mexican enterprise.

"Her passion is boundless," Philippe murmured after reading one of the letters. Reidel responded, "Passion? You mean madness."

When Philippe discovered Carlota's letter-writing plan, he was near the end of his patience. So great was his anxiety, that he even considered turning to her Indian companions to assist in bringing

Carlota back to her senses. To turn to a trio of lowborn women for help would be too demeaning for someone of his rank. Nonetheless, after reading the most recent letters, he was so troubled that, contrary to what he had decided, he finally approached the sisters. He found them seated at a table, stitching Carlota's undergarments, seeming not to have noticed when the prince came into the room. When Philippe realized that he had not been seen, he lost courage and took the moment to change his mind. He quietly turned to leave the room.

"Alteza?" Chelo acknowledged.

Philippe returned to the table and sat down next to the sisters. It took a while before he spoke, but finally he found the words.

"I'm worried. My sister's not well. You must have noticed her condition."

The women stopped sewing and looked at the prince. They, too, appeared sick. In the short time of his encounters with the sisters, he had come to realize that there was a bond between them and Carlota, a tie so strong that their faces reflected her own inner condition. He marveled at that extraordinary occurrence.

Tila spoke up. "We know that her heart is sad."

The prince braced his elbows on the table and leaned forward to get closer to the sisters. He was thinking. At the same time, he took hold of an edge of the garment that was spread out so each of the women might continue stitching. He held the material between his thumb and index finger, and slowly caressed it in an absentminded way.

"It feels as soft as a butterfly's wing," he murmured, but his words were loud enough for the sisters to nod in agreement. Without looking up, Philippe asked, "What can I do for her?"

"Free her." The sisters spoke at once, in a single voice.

Still gazing at the fabric he held between his fingers, Philippe sighed. "People like us are not destined to be free. We're like birds that are kept in a cage from the beginning."

There was a pause of several moments before Lula murmured, "Even a bird must be freed from her cage so that she may fly away to wherever she desires."

The prince reflected on Lula's words. When he spoke, his voice was still subdued, but now he was looking into each sister's eyes.

"If freed, that bird will no doubt be destroyed by a predator. Or worse, the little thing will starve to death."

Philippe leaned back in the chair, eyes closed, and stayed that way for so long that it seemed he had dozed off, but he was awake and thinking of what he was about to say. When he spoke, his eyes remained shut.

"No, my sister must return to the castle from where she came and there she will remain for her own safety. And you, hermanas, should also return to your land. I promise to provide you a safe voyage."

When he opened his eyes, he saw that the sisters were on their feet and had moved to a window where, heads together, they huddled. The declining winter sun cast its long melancholy light on them. To his eyes, they became silhouettes, dark and foreign, like carved images on the temples of their ancient land. It was from there that Chelo answered Philippe.

"If the empress is to be sent away, then we will follow so that whenever she looks up, we will be there."

The prince got to his feet and left the room. From there, he went to speak to Professor Reidel, who was expecting him. When he knocked on his door, it opened on its own. The alienist was waiting for him, seated at his desk, but he didn't give Philippe time to speak.

"Her Majesty cannot be allowed to roam the castle and its grounds as she has been doing. She must be controlled. Of equal importance, she must also be separated permanently from the Indian women. In order to take these steps, however, I need your Highness' permission. After that, I guarantee that Her Majesty's problems will be resolved."

The alienist's words puzzled Philippe and evoked a swirl of questions in the prince, but he didn't ask anything. He nodded in affirmation and left the room.

The next day Carlota went missing. When the Chontal sisters awoke, they found her bed empty. Professor Reidel was notified, and he acted quickly and sent the men out to scour the grounds in search of the missing empress. The sisters and Philippe searched in separate directions, hoping to reach her before Reidel's men did.

The winter day was short, and darkness would cover the castle's forested slopes and gardens within a few hours, making the search even more difficult. Everywhere, voices called out Carlota's name, echoing throughout the day and into the late evening, but no sign of her was found. Finally, one of Reidel's men discovered her, scratched, disheveled and with her face dirt-splattered. She had been crouching under a tree trying to hide.

"Come with me, Majesty. This is no place for you."

When he reached out to take her hand, she sprang away from him with such speed that the man lost sight of her. She disappeared into the thick hedges, making it nearly impossible to find her in that labyrinth of bushes and trees. Soon she was discovered again, but this time there was no talk, only powerful hands and arms that took hold of her. Carlota resisted, pushing, pulling away, kicking and scratching, but she was overwhelmed by these burly men who pawed her as she had never before been handled, making her cry out in pain and outrage.

She screamed for the Chontal sisters and for her brother, but they were not near enough to hear her calls for help. At last, as the trio approached the castle, her shrieking became so desperate that the sisters and Philippe heard her. Horrified at her howling, they ran toward her, but it was Reidel who stopped them before they could reach the empress. He ordered them away.

"If you desire Her Majesty to be treated, you must keep out of the way."

Those words intimidated Philippe, and he froze, but the sisters defied the alienist and pushed their way toward Carlota. Other henchmen, now on the scene, intervened, but found that the Indian women fought with a ferocity that nearly overcame them. They were especially unnerved by the high-pitched shrieks the women let out. Their screams were filled with frightening words the men didn't understand, made worse by their scratching, kicking, and hands that pulled tufts of hair from their scalps.

Reidel's thugs fought back and eventually subdued the sisters. Once in control, the doctor gave orders for the savages to be driven from the grounds; they were not allowed to be anywhere near the empress. Following his commands, the sisters were chased into the forest and forced to disappear into the night.

Carlota's shrieks would not stop, unnerving her brother so grievously that the alienist implored him, for the love of his sister, to leave Miramar. At that point, the prince, already at the end of his courage, convinced himself that it was in Carlota's best interest that Professor Reidel be left alone to resume his treatments.

Had Philippe understood that those methods included forcing his sister into a straitjacket for days, confining her to a small cell without means to communicate and even subjecting her to submersion into icy water, then perhaps he might have objected, but he was incapable of imagining such tortuous treatment. He left Miramar for his castle in Belgium, but before leaving he telegraphed his brother Leopold.

Our sister is mad, but I believe that her husband's recognized and notorious impotence played a large role in her instability. It is said that Maximilian has never even touched her. He is the one to blame.

Although Philippe left Carlota, he did not abandon her. He would visit her during the long years of her confinement in Castle Bouchout. He came to her every year on her birthday until he died thirty-eight years later. It is unknown if the prince was ever informed of his sister's brutal treatment at the hands of Professor Reidel. More importantly, it is unknown if he regretted his role in the scheme that disinherited his sister, thus making her a dependent of the dynasty. He did not express remorse that it was with Carlota's pilfered money that their brother, Leopold, embarked on his inhumane and brutal colonization in the African Congo. In truth, nothing is known of Prince Philippe's sentiments on these matters. He neither spoke of this nor confided even a hint of it in the pages of his diaries.

Chapter Thirty-Three

There was a small building erected by Maximilian, meant to house workers while Miramar Castle was in construction. It was located away from the castle, yet close enough to reach quickly when necessary. The structure was small, functional and, what was most important, iron bars secured its windows, and it had only one entrance. Even in Maximilian's time, the tower was known as the Castelleto, the Little Castle. It was this place that Reidel chose for Carlota's treatments.

The professor's method of treatment was based on deprivation and physical stress meant to shake the mind back onto its moorings. He believed that Carlota, although an empress, was no exception to this basic rule. When Carlota was taken that evening, her trauma was so great that she lost consciousness. She was not aware of being dragged into the little castle, and, when she awoke, she found herself confined to a darkened room with barred windows and only one door. Completely disoriented, she sat up blinking in an effort to clear her vision, but all her dilated eyes made out was that she was on a narrow cot with a chamber pot by its side, and, in a corner, a stand with a basin alongside a water jug.

Words squeezed out of her lips but she hardly heard them, the throbbing of her heart and the ringing in her ears being so loud. Carlota searched, hoping to make out a table with writing paper, perhaps a few books, but there was nothing except a solitary lighted candle resting on a ledge next to the door.

"I'm alone." This time she heard her voice but it was so distressed that she barely recognized it. "Philippe, where are you? ¡Hermanas! Come this instant!"

She repeated her cries until they were no longer words, but croaks that bounced off the walls only to crash back on her. Carlota, a woman who rarely wept, felt hot tears burning behind her eyelids but she didn't permit them to flow. She pushed them back until they reversed and dripped down into her parched throat, smearing her palate with salty saliva. She hunched over on the cot until her forehead connected with her knees. There she finally surrendered and allowed bitter tears to escape out of her mouth, nose and eyes. Wrapped in darkness and fear, Carlota lost a sense of time, with no idea if hours were passing or merely minutes. She could only be sure of the silence that bore down on her with such force that she was incapable of sitting, so she laid prostrate, unmoving, with her eyes wide open and dilated. It was only when Carlota became aware of the sound of a key unlocking the door that she realized it was morning.

Without saying anything, Professor Reidel appeared with a tray that he placed by her side and murmured, "Majesty, your breakfast. Please nourish yourself."

Carlota looked at him and an incongruous flash of amusement hit her when she saw that his spectacles had been hastily put together, their cracked lens patched with glue, and the crooked rim held in place with string. But that absurd moment passed, and she returned to glare at Reidel, despising him almost as much as she hated Napoleon.

She looked down at the tray, and a wave of nausea washed over her, forcing her to concentrate on overcoming the reflex to vomit. Carlota pushed herself onto her feet to make her way to one of the windows, hoping to feel the sun, but its bars were so close to one another that only thin rays of light crept through them.

At last Carlota said in a quiet voice, "Reidel, how dare you?"

Intimidated by the aura she radiated, the alienist needed time to respond. Finally, he stammered out an answer.

"His Majesty, your brother has commissioned me . . . "

"Commissioned you to do what?"

"To cure you, Majesty."

Reidel's voice was shaky, but he was able to squeeze out those few words, his throat tightening more with each moment.

Carlota turned to face the alienist, and she glared at him for a long time. Her squinting eyes unnerved him in a way that he could not have imagined before that moment, but what shook him to his foundation was the ageless and deep-rooted awe felt by underlings when face-to-face with the majesty of royalty.

Reidel reminded himself that he was a recognized, even admired professor, and she but a fallen empress. Still, he could not help himself from experiencing that wave of dread, and it was undeniable that Carlota intimidated him without having to utter a word. Acknowledging that he didn't have the inner stamina to resist her, the alienist moved toward the door, but once there, he turned to look at the empress.

"Majesty, I'll leave you for now but I shall return, and next time you will follow my instructions. I'll begin my treatment regardless of your opposition."

She ordered, "Take this tray with you. Bring me unpeeled fruit."

Reidel obeyed her command and disappeared. When he was gone, Carlota looked at the chamber pot and at the jug of water on the stand. Then she murmured, "Very well. If this is the way it must be, it will be."

The treatments began in an adjacent room that was just as cramped as the one she occupied. This one had a table, two chairs and a contraption that looked like a bathing tub. When Reidel's assistants pulled a resisting Carlota into the chamber, Carlota struggled, pulled and kicked at her assailants until she was finally forced to sit down. Reidel was already at his chair with his head bent low over a document that he was reading, or pretending to read, with extreme attention.

The truth was that he was myopic, and everything he looked at seemed to take his attention, but it was only because he had diffi-culty making out anything at first glance. A result of his life-long nearsightedness was that his eyes had grown used to always being wide open, nearly unblinking and always focused, giving his face the startled look of a mannequin.

Carlota sat glaring at him, again taking satisfaction that he had been forced to patch his spectacles broken by her good aim. Her expression was cold and disdainful, making it clear to him that she was filled with contempt for him and his middle-class upbringing. Those looks let him know that she loathed even the ordinary cut of his cheap coat and battered shoes.

When the alienist looked up, he understood what was stamped on her face. Nonetheless, he cleared his throat, signaling his intention to return to the questioning segment of the treatment that previously had been interrupted. When he was about to speak, it was Carlota's voice that spoke.

"You have reptilian eyes."

In an effort to interpret her words, as well as to reclaim the offensive, he mumbled, "Reptilian eyes?"

"Yes! You have the look of a lizard sunning himself atop a rock. How can you explain that, Professor Reidel?"

Using every resource at his disposal, the alienist did all he could to still the blood pounding at his temples. He understood that the empress had jumped ahead and snatched the offensive, putting him in the position of having to defend himself, but in his effort to find a way to regain the lead, he lost valuable time. Carlota sensed his hesitation and used the opportunity to pursue her lead, and she again pressed him.

"I've asked you a question. How do you explain that lizard look in your eyes? Could it be because of their faded watery-blue color?"

Reidel's hatred for the empress overwhelmed him, and he could go no further for fear that he might physically attack her. Although his knees were shaking, he forced himself onto his feet, gathered his documents into a portfolio and made for the door. He turned to her and spoke, but only because he felt that he had regained control of his voice.

"Madame, this session is ended. We'll meet here tomorrow for the next level of your treatment."

Carlota was also on her feet with her chin arrogantly aimed at the little man. She blurted out one word: "Majesty!"

He blinked, trying to assimilate her meaning. He raised his eyebrows, questioning her remark.

Carlota's voice had grown husky, but she repeated what she had said. "To you, Reidel, I am Majesty! Not Madame!"

Finding her arrogance intolerable, the alienist turned his back on the empress, slipped out and slammed the door behind him. He neither cared what she thought nor what might come of his disrespectful behavior. All he knew was that he could not have withstood one more minute in her presence. Tomorrow would be another day.

As ordered by Reidel, the treatments followed. The alienist subjected the empress to icy baths followed by prolonged submersions in that same bathwater, making her believe that she was on the verge of drowning. He kept her on a diet of water only, without even a piece of fruit or a few nuts. And all along he kept her isolated.

He recorded each treatment under the guise of clinical privation intended to shock the patient into normality. He ordered her to be bound in a straitjacket for hours during the day and even some nights, when he had her chained to her bed for hours, he again noted the treatment as part of a routine intended to force her back to reality.

Professor Reidel used the most severe methods at the disposal of the science of his day. All of it, he claimed, was in keeping with the axiom that a subdued body ultimately houses a balanced mind. His staff followed his orders rigorously and without questions, believing that his expertise was indisputable. No one imagined that in his heart the alienist's treatments were imposed on Carlota, not for professional reasons but in revenge, for the humiliations and offensive behavior he had suffered at her hands.

On the other hand, Reidel had no real idea of the effect those treatments had on the empress who, because of the abuse, walked through purgatory each minute of each hour. He would have been elated had he known how much she suffered, but the truth was that he didn't have an inkling of the anguish he caused her. He would have rejoiced knowing that at nighttime she suffered most when she was not allowed even a candle to break the impenetrable blackness of her cell, when she was forced to grope the walls and floor until she found the chamberpot.

The professor would have been satisfied knowing that when pangs of thirst and hunger gnawed at her, she clamped her hands on her mouth, fearing that someone might hear her whimpering. He would have considered himself vindicated when, in her terror, she called out for her father, for her beloved grandmother and for her companions, whom she feared were injured or even killed. Reidel would have been gratified had he known that she suffered most of all when her cries were overheard and mocked with words that offended her deeply: "She has lost her mind."

The professor worked diligently until it was he who ultimately lost the will to go on. On that day, Carlota's month-long torment abruptly stopped. The alienist ended the treatment with a declaration that all science could do for the patient had been done. To continue any process, he later wrote in his formal report, would be inhumane and futile: the empress' insanity was untreatable. With Reidel's signature on the report, the book was officially closed. Unreported was his inability to overcome Carlota's unrelenting resistance and superior wit and intelligence.

Before leaving Miramar, Professor Reidel had to face the empress one last time. On that day, he came to her cell, but not before he arranged for her washing and grooming. That done, he approached her, and with his head bowed, forced out a few words.

"Majesty, my work's complete, and I've come to bid you goodbye."

He looked up and was met with the same disdainful eyes, the identical haughty chin pointed at him, the same erect and arrogant body. The ordeal she had endured had not taken anything out of her. She seemed even stronger and more disposed to crush him. Reidel feared her more, realizing that he had never known a woman such as Empress Carlota. He bowed, backed away and slipped out of the door. He never again saw her, but he reaped his reward upon hearing some time later that she was confined for life in the medieval castle known as Bouchout.

While he and his assistants waited for their train at the Trieste station, Reidel sent King Leopold his last communication.

Her Majesty, the Empress of Mexico, is indeed suffering from insanity, with a persecution complex produced by a mental disease more serious than we could at first believe. The prognosis is poor, due to her growing agitation. I also believe that her condition manifested itself due to the climate and conditions in Mexico and to the painful failure of her negotiations with Napoleon III. I advise her immediate return to Belgium.

Chapter Thirty-Four

The Chontal sisters were in distress. Reidel's henchmen had chased them with frightening ferocity, forcing them through the woods toward a fishing village. When villagers saw them emerge from the forest, they thought the sisters were forest spirits come to haunt them, and they drove back with a barrage of rocks.

The sisters huddled close together that night to keep warm and try to sleep, but by daybreak the cold and hunger compelled them to return to the castle for shelter. They made their way around the back of the castle to the kitchen, in hopes of finding food, but a footman caught them. When he saw them he hissed, "Hey, you! What are you doing here?"

Unafraid, Chelo responded, "¿Qué crees?"

The man didn't understand her words but felt her desperation. After a few moments of hesitation, he gestured for the women to follow him into the pantry, where he gave them a loaf of bread and cooked meat.

"Here's some water. I suppose that you heathens get thirsty, too. Don't you?"

Lula snatched the jug out of his hands. At the same time she pointed at her sisters and herself. "¡Tenemos nombres! Nos llamamos Tila y Chelo. Yo soy Lula."

The man appeared to understand her meaning and repeated their names. After thanking him, the sisters fled back to the safety of the forest, but the cold was too much for them, their clothing too thin and skimpy. Consequently, they stole their way back to the castle stables to find shelter in one of the horse stalls. There they finally felt warm and safe.

The sisters filled their days by scrounging for food and their nights sleeping with horses while they waited for something to happen that might liberate the empress. In the meantime, they suffered not only because of cold, hunger and fear, but because they often heard shrieks coming from the Castelleto. They recognized Carlota's cries, and her distress filled them with anxiety and frustration, but there was nothing they could do.

One day, the same servant who had been providing them with food came to them early. He found them huddled under a pile of hay and could not help but laugh at their disheveled and dirty appearance. Soon he became serious and announced, "Ladies, the little maggot has packed his things and left us. He's gone!"

The sisters sat up, squinting as if reading the footman's lips to understand his words. One of the sisters repeated the word *maggot*, and the footman realized he had to make them understand in some other way. He imitated Reidel's body movements and mocked the alienist's myopic blinking eyes. At last the sisters grasped what he was saying.

The women jumped to their feet and took the man's hands, "¡Gracias! ¡Gracias!" Their joy was so great that tears came into his eyes. He was surprised because the thought struck him that it should have been they who should cry, not him.

The sisters lost no time. They rushed through the main entrance of the castle as if nothing had happened to make them keep away. As always, they made their way arm-in-arm looking neither right nor left, only straight ahead.

Their presence caused a stir among the footmen, parlor maids, valets and other servants, but no one made a move to stop them. Everyone knew where they were headed. The servants were relieved to see the sisters. Professor Reidel's presence had created such a depressed atmosphere in the castle, that the sight of those beautiful brown women was like a gust of fresh air.

The sisters headed for Carlota's room and knocked at the door. They heard a familiar voice call out, "Adelante." The moment they found themselves face-to-face with the empress, they were taken aback. Staring back at them was an emaciated woman with hunched shoulders. Her eyes, always lustrous, were now dull, wide open and dilated. Her face was bony. Gone was her radiant complexion. The empress had aged. Carlota managed a faint smile, and that was all.

Without a word, the sisters took off their shawls and prepared to help the empress. Lula hurried to the kitchen to fetch tea and whatever she thought Carlota might eat. Chelo called for a chambermaid to bring enough hot water for a bath, as well as towels and soap. Tila set about taking off Carlota's clothes. All of this was done in the quiet of those morning hours.

Only once, when the bath was ready, did one of the sisters ask the empress, "Majestad, will it be as always?"

Carlota responded, "Sí."

Then as usual, her bath began. When the empress was submerged, Lula loosened her hair and allowed it to float. To the sisters' revulsion, the tangled mass showed that it was infested with vermin. Lula soaped, rinsed and picked at Carlota's hair until all trace of the infestation disappeared. Tila was even more shocked to discover raw bruises ringing Carlota's neck and wrists.

"How were these wounds inflicted, Alteza?"

Carlota, whose eyes were shut, opened them to look at one of her uplifted arms. She rubbed at the scar as if trying to remember, but it was not that she had forgotten. It was that she found it inconceivable.

"I was locked into a garment that kept my arms secured to my sides. I tried to free myself, but you see that instead of freeing myself, I only inflicted more pain."

"We have never seen such a garment. Is it like the harness put on oxen?"

"Yes, Tila, very much like that."

Distressed, the sisters stared at the wounds, but said no more. They helped the empress out of the tub, emptied it and filled it again with clean water. Carlota stepped into the bathwater again. It took nearly an hour to dig dirt from under each fingernail where heavy filth was packed from clawing at the walls of her cell.

The morning hours drifted by, until the short December day began to come to an end. At last satisfied that the empress was nearly herself again, Chelo set a fire to warm the room. Exhausted, hungry and thirsty, the Chontal sisters sat down by Carlota to sip tea and eat bread with marmalade as the room became shrouded in the long shadows of the declining sun.

"Alteza, you've suffered as never before." Tila voiced what her sisters were feeling.

"You and your sisters have also endured much for my sake."

Carlota's voice was subdued, filled with fatigue, and her body slumped lethargically against the chair. The four women sat side-by-side, silently listening to the crackling logs and thinking of the torment they had suffered. It was the empress who had endured the greatest nightmare, but the sisters, too, had suffered unspeakable fear and privation.

"Majestad, what were your thoughts when you were in captivity?"

Carlota looked at Lula, aware that no one else would have the audacity to ask such a question. She took no offense. This woman and her sisters were an exception to all the rules that governed her life.

"Terrifying thoughts came to me, especially in the blackness of those nights when I could see nothing. Yet, I heard even the tiniest of sounds: the scratching of rats, the hoot of the owl, a moan that came to me from I-knew-not-where. I screamed. I was afraid, and I howled just to hear my own voice, because it was my only companion. To escape my fears, I thought of my beloved daughter buried so far away from me. Hermanas, I wished that I could have gone with you to her burial. I longed to see her resting place, if only in my mind."

"Alteza, the place is covered with white flowers, but remember that even if her body is beneath those flowers, her spirit is free and walks with Tonantzín."

As Chelo spoke, Carlota closed her eyes and tried to imagine what that goddess might look like and why she was taking her place beside her daughter. But it was impossible. She could not envision her daughter, much less a goddess. Carlota sighed.

"I thought of Maximilian and also of Alfred van der Smissen. My mind lingered on thoughts of the empire."

Carlota felt free enough to speak of her thoughts of her husband and lover, as well as the empire, but she kept back the other part of how she had survived in the midst of torture and sleepless nights. She kept secret the experience of seeing herself as never before during her ordeal.

Chapter Thirty-Five

I kept secret how my mind forced me to cling to some kind of order, to not allow my nerves to shatter despite waves of doubt and anxiety. I didn't tell how, in an attempt to make sense of what was happening, I compelled myself to retrace the steps that had brought me to that dismal torture chamber.

During those bleak nights, I began with Reidel and his hatred of me. I then turned my thoughts back toward the beginning of my life. Step by step, I followed the events leading to my first recollections when as a child I sat by my grandmother, Queen Amélie, listening to her tales of princes and queens and empires.

In the darkness of the cell, I commanded my memory to conjure the people that had guided me. I focused on professors and governesses, trying to remember how they dressed, how they spoke, what they ate. I then brought out of my dim recollections the images of my brothers and cousins, of how we played, swam, rode, fought and envied one another.

When I exhausted those memories, I returned to my life as a grown woman, to the powerful impulses and desires that moved me. I focused on the Mexican officials who came with their offerings of an empire and how that temptation seduced me. My thoughts then left the ministers to move forward to revisit Chapultepec, where I embraced love encounters with Smissen and pleasures with him. At the same time, I was compelled to face my failures with Maximilian.

My mind also forced me to dwell on the enemies who poisoned me. I spent dark hours meditating on my unmitigated hatred of them, as well as my wish for their disastrous death. Those bleak nights told me that I should feel guilt for that loathing, but instead I wrestled with that impulse, all the time refusing to cease my hatred.

I revisited my confrontations with Napoleon and Pius with equal bitterness. Unrelenting, my mind forced me to move on until I agreed with Philippe to return to Miramar, to be imprisoned in the dark pit of solitude and anxiety in which I now found myself.

I repeated this painful ritual of survival over and again, backward and forward, each time rendering myself stronger, farther beyond the reach of Reidel, whom I knew wanted to shatter my mind. But if I emerged stronger, I had at the same time come out humiliated and ashamed and guilty. In revisiting my life, I had forced myself to come face to face with my sins, my weaknesses and inordinate ambitions.

I withheld all of this from the sisters, although I still cannot decipher why I shared some parts of my inner self with them, yet held others secret. It might have been that I left this part of my ordeal unspoken because it had been an encounter with myself, exposed and filled with doubt. Had I really gone mad?

Chapter Thirty-Six

Carlota remained deep in thought while the chamber grew dark. Before they set about lighting candles, the sisters also sat quiet and thoughtful in the dusk's long shadows. They stayed there until the empress emerged from her reverie.

"My brother Leopold's wife is coming to accompany me to Belgium. He thinks that it's the best place to wait for word from Maximilian. I have agreed with him."

Carlota hesitated, as if wanting to say something else, but something was holding her back. When she finally spoke, her voice was a thin murmur.

"Hermanas, will you come with me?" She paused again, but before anyone could answer she went on. "But if you do come, perhaps you may never return to your land."

The Chontal sisters exchanged an instantaneous glance filled with meaning. It said that the empress sensed what was to happen, that this could well be their last chance to venture out on their own. Carlota didn't give the sisters time to answer.

"Think about it. Tell me when you're ready."

Chapter Thirty-Seven

If the empress had aged during her tribulations, so had the Chontal sisters, whose ordeals mirrored those of the empress in a curious way. They too had experienced being pursued. They also had felt indescribable fear. Like the empress, they too had known hunger, cold nights and homelessness. They too had become haggard and had lost much of their vitality. They needed only to look at one another to see it, but they also realized that throughout Carlota's anguish, their closeness to her had grown deeper and stronger. Now that tie was again being tested by her wish that they follow her, this time with the certainty of never returning to their land.

Tila led her sisters out of the empress' chamber once they saw to it that she was in bed and asleep. They found a quiet corner where they sat for a long while, each one pondering Carlota's request to follow her to yet another unknown country.

Tila was the one to break that silence. "Hermanas, do you think that she believes what she is being told?"

"What part?" Lula was not certain what Tila was asking.

"The part that the emperor will communicate with her when he arrives."

"I think that she believes it. Don't you?"

Tila looked around to assure herself that there were no prying ears lurking close by. Although satisfied that they were alone, she went back to speaking in her native tongue.

"I heard chatter in the kitchen that makes me doubt it. People say that it's not true. That the emperor does not intend to see her again."

Chelo interrupted her sister. "Why would he not try to at least send her word?"

"How can you ask that? Were we not witnesses to the bitter scenes between the empress and her husband? Why should he want to renew those terrible feelings?"

"Well, if the long tongues in the kitchen know that much, they must have an explanation as to why the empress' brother intends to send her back to the land of her birth. Why not allow her to live as she chooses, wherever she wants?"

"Because it's a trap."

"A trap?" Lula pressed her sister.

"I heard that the professor who made the empress suffer so much, has convinced her brother that she has lost her mind and that she's to be imprisoned for the rest of her life in a castle. This is what I heard in the kitchen. It's not my invention."

Lula pursued the point. Her voice was so intense that it startled Tila. "We believe you, Tila, but what if what you heard are lies! Why should we believe ignorant kitchen maids in the first place? This is terrible! Think of it! She's a powerful woman, a queen! How is it possible that she will be made a prisoner?"

"Calm down! Yes, it might be a lie spread by lazy kitchen maids with nothing better to do, but remember how easy it was for the little man to imprison her for a month, right here under our noses. And what could we do about it?"

"That's different! We're different! We're nobody! We could not do anything! It would be another thing if the evil doctor tried it again with the empress' brother looking on. Remember, he's a king! And what about Prince Philippe who loves her?"

"Prince Philippe? Didn't he just slip away without helping her?"

Tila was quick to answer Lula, but then Chelo interrupted. It was obvious that she was deeply disturbed to think that Carlota might be imprisoned again.

"I think the two of you are forgetting something important about the prince. Wasn't it just a short time ago that he told us that his sister must be returned to the castle of her childhood and that she must stay there for her own safety? He didn't say anything about waiting for the emperor."

Her sisters stared at Chelo. They remembered that he had even offered to return them to Mexico, but they had decided to stay.

"And what did we say?" Chelo went on speaking. "I mean, what did *I* say? I said that if the empress were to be put in a cage, we would follow so that when she looked up, there we would be. Have you forgotten so quickly that we agreed to follow her?"

More silence wrapped itself around Tila, Lula and Chelo as they sat thinking that here again was a turning point on the path they traveled. Each one's thoughts raced in different directions. As if on a signal, the three women began to chatter at once, their words clashing, jumbling and making it difficult to know who was speaking.

"What if we returned to our land?"

"To what? Go back to a new patrón? Or to become maids to an arrogant woman who looks down her nose at indias like us?"

"But it would be someone that spoke like us. We would be among others like us."

"I don't like what you're saying. We would only face the same hunger and even live on the streets like so many other unfortunates."

"What about the Acuñas and their vicious dogs? Do you think they have forgotten us?"

"¡Ay, hermanas! I say that we not think of that cruel family."

"No? Then of what should we think?"

Suddenly the jabbering stopped. Their nervous questions and doubts had inexplicably brought them to the same conclusion, and it was Tila who put it into words.

"We cannot leave her now that she needs us most, and we must not be afraid. I want to be there when she looks up. For my part, I say that we follow her."

Lula and Chelo looked at one another, acknowledging that their sister had captured their own wish. Without speaking, they nodded in agreement. Lula muttered words that she meant to keep to herself but that her sisters overheard.

"She, too, has been violated."

Chapter Thirty-Eight

DECEMBER 1866

On Route

King Leopold provided the private train for his wife, Queen Marie Henriette. Her mission was to accompany his sister, Charlotte, on the return trip to Bouchout Castle, the ancient citadel located outside Brussels. Unknown to Carlota, the medieval fortress had been designated as the permanent place of her confinement.

Of the many family members, it was only Marie Henriette who volunteered to undertake the arduous journey to bring her sister-in-law back. She did it because she was overcome with pity for Charlotte's disastrous loss of sanity, as well as her future confinement. "Poor Charlotte!" This is what the queen said over and again whenever she felt overwhelmed by the hardships of the long trip.

When Marie Henriette stepped off the train at the Miramar station, she found Charlotte and her three unusual ladies waiting to greet her. In the queen's mind, that desolation was all too pathetic. She looked around, expecting dignitaries and other figures of distinction, but she found only a few disheveled footmen and the three strange-looking women. Marie Henriette found no trappings of royalty, only drab workers that seemed eager to obey the empress but who clearly had no notion of the pomp required for the rank of Empress Charlotte and Queen Marie Henriette.

When the queen looked at Charlotte, she was shocked by how much she had diminished in three years. Gone was the radiantly beautiful young woman renowned for her lustrous eyes and glorious hair. Vanished was the haughty posture and the inimitable poise. In the place of that beauty was a drawn face, dull eyes and stooped shoulders.

As the two women stood gazing at one another, unspoken but vivid memories returned. Marie Henriette remembered how Charlotte had disdained her for her plain looks and clumsy manner. She recalled how both Philippe and Charlotte had laughed at her ordinary appearance, and how they treated her as someone insignificant. Remembered also were the hurt feelings that filled her because of that rejection, but now standing face to face with her husband's sister, Marie Henriette could feel only sympathy for Charlotte's great downfall.

If her beauty had been erased by suffering, it was the loss of her intellect that was the greater tragedy, for it had been Charlotte's mind that defined her in the eyes of her world. Now it was the shame of lunacy that hovered over her like a dark cloud. Her insanity was a family disgrace that had to be hushed up at all costs and kept a secret behind thick walls.

As for Carlota, memories surrounding Marie Henriette also rushed to her. As she stood facing her sister-in-law, she too remembered how she had mocked and disdained her because she looked more like a peasant than an Austrian royal. Carlota, to her shame, remembered how she had detested Marie Henriette's humble manner.

Now as the women stared at one another, it was Carlota who held out her hands hoping to grasp those of Marie Henriette. Gone was the arrogance of the young Belgian princess. In its place was a fearful, fragile Carlota who knew that her future was no longer glorious but dimmed by Maximilian's and her own failure in Mexico. Yet she yearned for Marie Henriette's understanding.

After that first meeting, Marie Henriette needed only a few days to recuperate her strength to again resume the last part of her task. During that brief interim, the two queens spoke only when necessary, although with politeness. When all was ready, the travelers left Miramar Castle for its private rail spur.

The royal train was waiting. Its crew had precise instructions regarding the route they were to take to Brussels in the shortest amount of time. There would be no visitations or stopovers, no greeting committees or dignitaries to wish the two royals a good journey or to bid family members goodbye. The train was to make its way through Italy, Austria and Germany and head directly onto Belgian soil, where King Leopold had readied Castle Bouchout for Carlota's internment.

The entourage boarded the train at dawn on a wintry day. It was snowing heavily, but their coaches were fitted for the unrelenting cold. The travelers settled in for the long trip. Four ladies-in-waiting, a physician, a cook and footmen made up Queen Marie Henriette's company. Empress Carlota had only two chambermaids and her Mexican companions to attend to her needs.

The journey was long and tedious through bleak snowbound landscapes. Cities followed nameless villages, but because of the constant snowfall and drifts, none showed any differences except for a cathedral spire here or a castle turret there. Rivers and lakes were caked solid with ice. The speeding train transformed the people into blurs. They were faceless, without differences in dress, except that some were men and others women, all bundled against the bitter cold. Crossing the Alps did give the passengers a brief break from the monotony, and even some thrills as the train sped through tunnels, canyons and passes at frightening speed.

The travelers passed time in different ways. Marie Henriette embroidered some of the time. At other periods she read, but most of the time she sat up with eyes closed as if in meditation. Lula, Tila and Chelo, the only ones spellbound by what they were seeing, chattered almost constantly. No one understood their language, and their presence was soon overlooked.

As for Carlota, she stared out the window when there was daylight. She did the same even at night, when she seemed hypnotized by the impenetrable darkness that wrapped itself around the clattering train. Perhaps it was because she sensed that each moment and every kilometer was carrying her away from life as she knew it. Perhaps the disenchanted empress felt the rhythm and sway of the train deeper in her heart than in her body. Perhaps she understood that its movement was taking her closer to an unknown life for which she was unprepared.

She had not been given notice of what awaited her at Castle Bouchout. Neither did she know anything about Maximilian, except that he was leading the confrontation with Benito Juárez. So, for now, the empress had no other choice but to stare out at the fast-moving landscape.

When the train pulled into the Brussels station, its passengers were already on their feet with hats and coats on and gloves in hand. As protocol demanded, Queen Marie Henriette was designated as the first to descend from the train, and then Empress Carlota would follow. Behind the two monarchs, the entourage of ladies, maids and other staff emerged.

When Marie Henriette stepped onto the platform, a brass band broke out with the Belgian anthem, and a group of elegantly uniformed dignitaries, the feathers in their military caps waving in the breeze, moved forward to greet their queen. Marie Henriette was not known for gracefulness, but because she was kind, she was beloved. To show their loyalty, a large crowd had gathered at an appropriate distance. When she showed herself, loud cheers and applause broke out. She responded with her well-known toothy smile and a broad wave of her large, gloved hand.

Close behind her was Empress Carlota, who was elegantly dressed in black. Because her looks had changed so much, it was difficult for some of the dignitaries to recognize her. Those mustachioed dukes and colonels tried to suppress their astonishment at seeing the empress so transformed from the haughty young archduchess they had last seen three years earlier, but their shock leaked out and they stood gaping at her. It took a few moments before they recovered their poise and, as if on signal, those men snapped to attention to greet the empress, some by raising their hats in homage, others with a military salute. She responded with an appropriate bow of her head.

The distance from Brussels to Castle Bouchout by carriage was some three kilometers. Once the monarchs and their entourage were loaded onto carriages, the trip was brief. The road took them first to the village of Meise and then to its fringes, where the castle was located in a thick snowbound forest. By the time the travelers arrived, the day had nearly ended and the castle loomed in front of them ominously.

When the coaches halted, only Marie Henriette accompanied Carlota to the foot of the entrance. She explained that she was due to continue on to Laeken, so she brushed Carlota's cheek with a light kiss, curtsied and returned to the carriage to join her entourage. With a shrill whistle and a crack of the whip, Marie Henriette's carriage bolted out of sight, leaving Carlota and her companions. The Chontal sisters escorted Carlota up the imposing steps leading to the front doors that stood open for her arrival. There, footmen, butlers and maids lined up to greet her. All bowed and curtsied deeply, and Carlota responded with the usual bow of the head.

A butler escorted the empress and her companions to the wide staircase leading to the upper floor. Once upstairs, the women were led through the darkened corridor to the tower that would house them for the next sixty years. As they entered the audience chamber, Carlota abruptly stopped to stare at the imposing walls and vaulted ceiling.

Her eyes were vacant, but Tila, Chelo and Lula understood that the empress was in the grip of powerful thoughts. Carlota realized that she was not there to wait for word from Maximilian. It was a lie, a deception. She had agreed to her own captivity. The sisters also saw that Castle Bouchout was to be their only world. It was like a prison; the great stone asylum would shut them off from everything they had ever known.

Tila, Lula and Chelo looked at one another, aware that Carlota, better than anyone else, grasped that they were now the only ones in that dreary world and that she was to pay with her freedom for aspiring to reach the heights of power. Empress Carlota's dream of a Mexican empire had come full circle and vanished. Hers and the sisters' odyssey had ended.

BELGIUM

Sixty Years Later

Chapter Thirty-Nine

JANUARY 1927

Castle Bouchout

Winter descended on the medieval fortress. A thick fog shrouded its forest, and the castle's towers loomed dark against the steely sky. The lake surrounding the ancient walls was solid ice. Centuries ago, the castle's main tower had been a dungeon, but that prison was now empty, filled only with sighs and whispers.

There was a middle section that joined the dungeon to another tower and, as with other ancient fortresses, its corridors and staircases were inhabited by the ghosts of generations of men and women who had lived in the castle. Like dampness, memories clung to its walls and dark recesses. Echoes of passion and anguish, love and jealousy, despair, hope and fury, infiltrated the soul of that ancestral place. The castle groaned under the weight of so many centuries, retaining memories of those who had been born, grown old and died under its roof.

It was into this castle that Carlota, Empress of Mexico, was confined for sixty years, as it had been determined that she was insane. Surrounded by dusty medieval armor, faded tapestries and dim portraits of the many usurpers and scoundrels that once inhabited the citadel, the old woman wandered its creaky corridors that resonated with the click-click of her walking cane. Soon the memory of her life, her loves, passions and dreams would join the other faded memories destined to haunt the vast chambers of Castle Bouchout.

Chapter Forty

The Chontal sisters interrupted their prayers and listened. The tap-tap of the old empress' walking stick echoed through the dark corridor as she shuffled into the audience chamber. The cavernous room was nearly dark as the winter sky closed in on the disappearing daylight. There was silence except for the sighing wind that seeped through the dilapidated window frames.

Blinking against the gloom, the empress pulled a heavy shawl closer around her stooped shoulders until her eyes adjusted to the flicker of flames in the fireplace. Her dress was of a thin material cut in the style of the previous century. It was frayed at the hemline and dragged clumsily on the wood floor. Her thinning hair, pushed back into an old-fashioned bun at the nape of her neck, was mostly white with a few strands of faded brown. Her face, which had been a beautiful oval in the years of her prime, now was round, wrinkled and lumpy. Her eyes, however, retained their brilliance, despite their constant squinting.

At the entrance of the chamber, Carlota rotated her head to aim an ear toward the fireplace where she made out the sounds of prayer. Chelo, Tila and Lula prayed frequently to their goddess Tonantzín, but whenever they were aware of the old empress' presence, they switched their orations to those of her faith and chanted in her language.

Reina de los cielos, ruega por nosotros.
Reina de los ángeles, ruega por nosotros.
Reina de los apóstoles, ruega por nosotros.

Empress Carlota's ear followed the repetitious chant until she discerned the three silhouettes against the red-orange of the embers, where they were seated around the fire. The old woman was especially grumpy that evening because her bones ached as they always did before a winter storm. When she focused on the sisters, she let out a scornful croak.

"¡Hermanas! You think that I didn't hear you mumbling before I came in?"

The silhouettes interrupted their prayer. Unperturbed, they turned their craggy toothless faces toward the empress and then glanced at each other with an expression of patience. They knew that she was in pain. With the passage of so many years together, the women had grown to know each other's likes and dislikes, whether one was healthy or hurting, sad or joyful. Theirs was a closeness that was unspoken, unexplained one that came to them from living under the same roof for decades, from hearing the same sounds, breathing the same air, eating the same food and hearing each other's voices day in and day out. They knew each other as if they had been lovers; or husband and wife, with the difference that their intimacy came from the powerful bond of shared memories.

The Chontal sisters had not lost their Mexican ways even after all those years, and this was especially true when they spoke among themselves in their native tongue. Despite the decades of living in Bouchout Castle, the sisters still dressed in the same style they had worn in their native Mexico sixty years earlier: the multicolored huipil that covered their shoulders instead of a blouse and a skirt that reached to the floor.

They sewed their own clothes, insisting on using only cotton, and wore each garment until it was faded and threadbare. Because they found the cold Belgian winters nearly intolerable, they made sure to have their feet covered with thick woolen stockings, although they still wore huaraches, sandals that they crafted for themselves when the previous pair was too worn out to be useful. European shoes felt clumsy and painful to them; the sisters thought they were more suited for mules than for humans.

Still standing at the entrance of the chamber, the old empress waited for her eyes to adjust to the gloom. All the while she stared at the sisters and finally muttered in a more tolerant tone, "Leave me!" The sisters paid little attention to the grumbling of the old empress. They knew she didn't mean it. They had heard it all before. They merely huddled closer in an attempt to ward off the cutting chill of the castle's stone walls, a coldness they had never been able to get used to despite their long vigil in that desolate place.

Empress Carlota narrowed her eyes to make out the faces turned in her direction, but it was no use. Her dim eyesight simply would not help her. Anyway, she knew well what they now looked like: wrinkled brown skin, toothless mouths and craggy cheekbones that cast deep shadows beneath their slanted eyes. Only the broad graceful eyebrows that spanned their foreheads, like the wings of a black bird in flight, remained from their youthful beauty. Another remnant from the sisters' young years was the manner in which they wore their hair. They still braided it around their head, only now their hair was no longer thick and black, but thin and silvery.

The old empress moved closer to the sisters, supported on her walking stick, cautiously feeling out a path to the fireplace. She groped first one chair, then another, until she found the one she wanted and there slid her frail body into it. She massaged her knees for a while, trying to rub away the ache in her arthritic legs.

"Hermanas, when did we grow old? What hour? What year? When did my legs become brittle and my back hunched? When did my hands get wrinkled and spotted? Why did we not warn each other that getting old creeps up in the night silently, insidiously?"

It was Tila who responded. "Let's not speak of what we could not prevent."

"Oh? Then of what should we speak?"

"You know that it brings you calm to tell of what happened in our México."

The old empress leaned back against the armchair's dusty cushion. Yes, she was willing to tell the well-known story, the one she had repeated countless times over the decades, but as she mulled over those thoughts, minutes passed, and the silence in the chamber became heavy, broken only by the rattling of the dilapidated windowpanes. When she was ready, she spoke softly. "*Bien.* I'll tell the story again."

Chelo continued to press Carlota. "Will you tell the full story this time?"

The old empress snapped her head toward la india and for a long moment glared at her.

"¡Impertinente! I'll tell only what I want. What I tell will have to suit you because it is all that will pass my lips."

Undaunted by the old woman's displeasure, Chelo went on with what she was thinking.

"Alteza, we are not impertinent. It's just that we know you have a multitude of secrets that burden your heart. Wouldn't it be a relief if you shared them with us, your closest companions? Remember, mi Señora, that we are old now and that this might be our last opportunity to hear you relive your life's story. After all, we've grown old together. Why keep anything hidden?"

"But we have relived my story countless times. What is it that you have yet to hear?"

"The parts that you have left out."

"What parts?"

"The ones that matter. The ones that changed your life but that you have kept secret."

"Very well. I'll tell it all again. But this'll be the last time." Empress Carlota leaned her head against the chair and stared vacantly. "I was born Marie Charlotte Amélie Augustine Victoire Clementine Léopoldine of Saxe Coberg und Gotha on my father's side, and . . . "

Lula broke in. "¡Ay, no! Not that all over again. We know that your father was Leopold, the first king of Belgium. We know also that on your mother's side you descend from the royal house of Orléans, kings and queens of France and that you were born in a castle close to this one. We know all of that, everyone knows it, but now what you should tell is what you have left unsaid."

The old empress looked at Lula with a vague smile, thinking that there was little that the sisters didn't know about her. Yet, there were thoughts, those that had haunted her over the years, some bitter and others sweet. There were those that she had cradled in her breast, but now she was willing to share them with her companions.

"Tila, Chelo and Lula, you've been witnesses to the most important moments of my life, and you've heard me tell of even the most intimate experiences I have had, so there's nothing that you don't know except secret thoughts that come to me in the night. If I reveal those thoughts, you'll laugh."

"Why would we laugh?"

"Because I'm old and my body is decrepit and those thoughts are about my youth. Sometimes I even remember Alfred van der Smissen and weep when I remember that he took his own life. I fear that it was because of me."

"Alteza, he took his life because he had no reason to live after he abandoned you."

"Smissen had no choice but to leave me, just as I had no choice except to allow my enemies to bring me here to this forlorn prison. Alfred and I loved, but we lost. The story's a simple one."

The women fell into silence while they thought of what the empress had just murmured. Although unspoken, images of those last days in Mexico came back to them. Pictures of panic and disorder that gripped the court at Chapultepec Castle, the running back and forth, the hasty withdrawal, all of it loomed vividly in their recollections. Clearest of all were the memories of Carlota's near death caused by toloache, and the loss of her daughter.

"I have never told what I saw when I walked through the land of the dead."

When the old empress uttered those words, the faces of the Chontal sisters snapped in her direction. Here was something she had kept from them, but they wondered how that could be, since el yerbolero had assured them that Carlota would not remember walking among the dead when in Mictlan.

Chelo murmured, "You remember? You have never spoken of it."

"No, but the memory has not left me. I walked in a place covered with white flowers, where the path took me to my Grandmamá Amélie. She was young and vibrant and, although she said nothing, her eyes spoke of the joy seeing me gave her. She held flowers in one hand and the other held the hand of a beautiful young woman. Grandmamá said to me, 'Charlotte, this is your daughter Precious Flower,' and I saw that she was the most beautiful woman I had ever seen. She, too, smiled at me and took me in her arms. I don't remember if she spoke, but I felt her words."

The sisters kept silent. They were confounded and wanted to hear more because they had never before known anyone who had the memory of walking among the dead.

"The memory is with me always, reminding me that Precious Flower is not gone, that she's by my side always. It lessens my grief."

Carlota said nothing more. She seemed to be attentive to the crackling logs and soft murmur of the wind, but she was really in deep reflection.

"Such are my secret thoughts. They visit me often, especially at night when this old castle groans with its own memories. When I listen to the whispers of other captives like us, who lived here and had nothing more to do but to remember."

When the old empress stopped speaking, the sisters got to their feet to help Carlota to her bedchamber. They were surprised when she reached out a shaky hand to gesture them to return to their seats.

"You know everything important about my life and now even about my thoughts. What about you? I know that you've been my faithful companions and that you refused to abandon me even when you had the chance, but beyond that, I know nothing else. Tell me your secrets. After all, as you said, it's time, perhaps it's our last opportunity."

The sisters returned to their places and looked at the old empress with an intensity they had never before shown. After a few moments, they looked at one another as they often did when they were on the verge of an important decision. Tila spoke for her sisters.

"We were as young as you were on that day when we first met, which means that our lives up to then were brief. But yes, we already had a secret, one so great that if others had discovered it, we would surely have been executed."

The old empress stared into the burning logs as if she were alone, but the sisters knew that she was listening. As she often did for so many years now, she rubbed the knuckles of her arthritic hands for a while until she looked up and said, "I'm listening."

It was Tila who told of their childhood spent on La Perla in the sacred land of Cholula. They had no recollection of family, only that they were of the Chontal tribe and that their beginnings were spent on the hacienda where they grew to be young women.

"And that is all, Alteza. We were happy as we served the family of that hacienda."

With those words Tila leaned back in her place and stared into the sputtering fire. After a few moments, the empress looked at her with an unconvinced expression stamped on her face.

"Is that all? That's your secret?"

"No, Majestad, that alone is not our secret."

Lula could not keep silent. She described Arcides Acuña, telling in detail of the ordeal he had inflicted on her when he raped her. As if it had taken place the month or the day before, Lula recounted how she and her sisters planned their revenge afterwards. She told how they knifed the predator as he slept naked under the walnut trees in that faraway place called Los Nogales.

"We were able to escape only because your soldiers invaded those parts and el patrón of La Perla was not able to hunt us down. We fled, but we were almost killed when your soldiers battled our indios at Puebla. When the fighting was over, we made our way to the city where our path eventually led to your palace."

Lula stopped talking and lifted her hands to reach out to the old empress. "Now you know that we murdered a man, a secret we have kept to ourselves all these years."

Carlota looked into Lula's eyes and responded to her uplifted hands by taking them into hers. She didn't say anything, but her eyes filled with tears.

"Majestad, if you had known our secret when our paths crossed, would you have banished us?"

Lula's voice was husky and filled with emotion. Although it was she who asked the question, Carlota knew that it came from her sisters as well. She turned to face all three.

"No! I would not have sent you away. You didn't have a choice." A few moments later, she repeated softly, "You had no choice."

The old empress leaned back and closed her eyes. She held her fragile hands in her lap while their fingers clasped and unclasped as if tapping to a rhythm only she could hear. Outside the wind blew harder, dragging with it snowdrifts that would soon shroud the castle's towers and lake.

Chelo got up to stoke the fire and added logs to the embers. Strands of smoke curled out from the grate until the wood erupted into flame. After that, tones of orange and red tinged the women's faces as they sat thinking of Arcides Acuña.

Chapter Forty-One

"Each of us has caused grievous injury." The old empress slumped into the armchair as she spoke. "Arcides Acuña's path crossed yours, he abused you and you took his life. I took my destiny into my hands and I soared to forbidden heights, causing war and suffering. In the eyes of the world, we have transgressed, we have sinned, but we have atoned with a lifetime of confinement."

"¿Tiene arrepentimientos la emperatriz?"

"Yes, I have regrets, but not for everything that I've done. Like you, sometimes I had no choice and, if there's no choice, why should there be regret? Do you have regrets?"

The sisters pondered the old empress' words, remembering that Arcides Acuña violated Lula and, because she was part of the other sisters, the abuse was also theirs. If they had had a way to find justice, they would have followed that path, but there had been no such alternative. They were left without a choice.

"No, Majestad, we have no regret for what we did to Arcides Acuña. We also took our destiny into our hands when we chose to kill him."

"Yes, Tila, that's what you did."

"Gossipers often said that on the outside you were beautiful but on the inside you were ambitious. Alteza, is that one of your regrets?"

"Ah, Chelo! Those despicable gossipers that prowl in dark corners and never show their false faces! You must consider that my beauty was nothing more than a thin veil that covered my face and body. Never was it of great importance to me. Why should I regret something so fleeting and unimportant? On the other hand, ambition is different. It is deep and not merely a cover like beauty. Who in this world can change what's inside of her? I was born with my nature, and if I dreamed of being a great queen, it was because I sucked that desire from my mother's breast. You see, I had no choice. How then can my ambition be one of my regrets?"

The old empress stopped speaking. She was expecting one of the sisters to say something. The truth was that she would not have been displeased to hear a voice because, now that she was speaking openly, she longed to unburden herself even more. Carlota turned toward her companions. Her eyelids flickered, trying to clear her vision, and after a while she saw that the sisters had their eyes closed.

"Hermanas, are you asleep?"

"No. We're listening. And thinking."

"Thinking? Of what?"

It was Lula who was speaking and she did it slowly, evidently searching for the right words. For a moment she seemed to have changed her mind, but then she went ahead with her question.

"With respect, Alteza, why don't you just say that above all you desired to become the empress of Mexico?"

"Yes, that was my desire. Was it so wrong? I don't think so, nor do I regret wanting it. My only regret is that I chose to bury everything inside my soul. I decided that no one should ever know what was inside of me. As I grew in age, I became secretive and reclusive. I paid a price. By the time I was a grown woman, my solitary life led me to profound sadness, a melancholy that has never left me. But there was something more important that followed: My isolation created enemies that saw me as aloof and arrogant. For this, more than anything else, I'm regretful."

Expecting a response from at least one of the sisters, Carlota waited, but there was nothing. She again turned to look at them to see if they were asleep, but saw that all three had their eyes riveted on her. She raised her hands and shrugged, indicating with that gesture that she expected something from them.

It was Chelo who spoke. "We knew that you were lonely the first day we saw you. We understood that you were alone and could be hurt. That's why we have been your companions since that moment."

"Was that really your only reason?"

Chelo was taken aback by the empress' discernment, feeling somewhat embarrassed by the question; nonetheless, she answered it truthfully.

"No, Alteza, it was not our only reason. In the beginning, we clung to you because we feared being captured for killing Arcides Acuña and we knew that you would shield us. As time passed, we wanted to stay close to you, to be of help to you, and we grew to love you."

"Yes, I know. You loved me even to the point of saving my life at your own peril."

The sisters sat up straight and tense, as if they expected more to come from the empress now that she knew that in the beginning she had been used as a cover. But nothing happened. Suddenly, as if struck by a long forgotten question, Carlota looked at the sisters with raised eyebrows.

"Did you discover who it was that poisoned me?"

"Do you not have suspicions?" Lula responded with another question.

"Yes! I have always suspected that it was that Sedano woman."

"Your suspicions have told you the truth, but only part of it, because it was her entire tribe that had worked the evil. It was known that the Sedanos always concocted their poisons together, although it was only one of them that secretly slipped it into their victim's food."

Carlota shifted in the armchair so that she could watch the sisters. "I heard that she died alone when she was still young. Do you know the cause of her death?"

Grateful that the empress was not angry or offended, Lula gave the details. "We made a pact with the sorcerer in exchange for your cure. We agreed to put into his hands something that belonged to her, anything that had touched her body, a rebozo or a huarache. Eventually we found exactly what we needed."

Fascinated by what she was hearing for the first time, the old empress motioned Lula to go on, to tell the whole story. La india detailed the story of what happened six decades earlier, just as if it had happened that day.

"The same boy who helped us with your cure knew where the Sedano clan dwelled. At our bidding, as if he was invisible, the skinny boy slipped into the hovel inhabited by the Sedano woman and hastily stole the first thing he found. It was a comb clogged with her long black hairs. He brought it to us."

"Go on." Carlota clung to the words, all the time envisioning the hovel, the comb and the oily black strands of hair.

"As agreed, we went to the labyrinth called Tepito, where we put the concubine's comb into el yerbolero's hands."

"What did he say?"

"Nothing. We only saw that his serpent eyes gleamed as he passed the comb to his accomplice, a shriveled up toothless india that ran off with it. Because we had kept our side of the pact, there was nothing else for us to do but leave the sorcerer and his helper. A short time afterward, word spread that Concha Sedano died screaming and twisting in pain.

"It was said that before she died, her beauty disappeared and she was transformed into a monster. It was also whispered that her tribe howled like wounded dogs because she was their favorite."

The old empress sat back staring at the burning logs with wide-open eyes. It was a long time before she reacted.

"When did that happen?"

This time it was Chelo who spoke. "While you recuperated and we prepared for the journey to Vera Cruz to cross the ocean to these lands." She paused for a moment and then asked, "Are you displeased with us?"

"Hermanas, would you do it over again?"

Tila rushed to answer for her sisters. "¡Sí, Majestad! It was Concha Sedano's life or yours. We chose yours."

Chapter Forty-Two

On that last night the old empress massaged her wrinkled hands as she stared at the Chontal sisters and saw that they had retreated into their own thoughts. She looked away and tried to keep her mind on the present, but memories evoked by what they had just related about the death of Maximilian's lover haunted her.

Abandoning herself to the force of those images, long-forgotten visions of Mexico surfaced. Carlota shut her eyes to better conjure the vastness of the capital, its Zócalo, its cathedral and palace. Reflections of elegantly dressed men and woman floated behind her eyelids, and she even heard graceful music spilling from the upper lofts of the court residence. Couples danced under the glow of countless candles, while their rhythmic movements reflected on crystal vases and mirrors.

Those pictures melted away and others appeared, the ones the old empress remembered from long journeys through her empire. Her eyes still closed, Carlota revisited that landscape. She envisioned vast panoramas with an endless spread of volcanoes and maguey cactus, sharp black silhouettes that knifed upward from craggy horizons toward a blazing blue sky. She remembered the dense jungles of Yucatán and, as if she were there, she breathed in the heavy aroma of vanilla combined with the fragrance of orchids.

Mexico's striking landscape summoned more images for the old empress. She envisioned silhouettes of men hunched against mule-driven plows alongside figures of women and children stooped low over endless rows of maize. As they did in the past, those scenes of poverty and despair unsettled her. She turned an ear to listen to the soft strumming of a guitar. She was enjoying the memory of its plucked notes mingled with a voice that sang in the lilting language of that land. The ballad told of lost love and separation, of death and forgiveness, of hunger and war.

Still thinking of Mexico's people, whose devotion she desperately wanted but never gained, Empress Carlota sighed. Her thoughts filled with terrible recollections of disputes and clashes that took place when it became evident that the empire was crumbling, when she and the others pointed fingers of blame at each other.

Then Maximilian's image facing his executioners loomed, and she asked herself if it was she who was to blame for his death. Many voices said that she was the one responsible. The empress pondered this claim, just as she had done for years, turning the accusation over in her mind.

She sighed. So many recollections! Right there, in the gloom of the chamber, she again sensed the others, shadows that had kept her company for years. Her dim eyesight made out the return of the envoys from Mexico, small overly polite men that now glared at her with wide-open eyes. This time those officials said nothing except to bow low as they entered her presence and then evaporated into the cold, thin air. Their shadows were followed by the diminutive figure of the Indian president, Benito Juárez. He too bowed deeply, but she saw that when he lifted his face, it was stamped with an expression that warned that his people would, in the end, prevail over her flawed dream.

Transfixed, the old empress thought that she saw Louie Napoleon glide in behind Juárez's shadow. The French emperor teetered on small uncertain steps and, when he bowed, it was in a half-hearted, stilted gesture, while all the time his fingers nervously stroked his grayed goatee.

Pope Pius followed Napoleon. He cast a penetrating look at Carlota, reminding her that no one rattles the pillars of the Church. In the darkness, the old empress strained to stare at the pontiff's silhouette as he vanished into the gloom. As he moved out of sight, she thought that he imperceptibly shook his head as if to express pity for the folly of even thinking of chipping away at the Church's patrimony.

Then the images faded away, leaving the old empress expecting more memories to file past her, but there was nothing. It had all been a half dream from which she now awakened to wonder why she was the last of all those people left behind to bear witness. For the first time, Carlota questioned the destiny that had condemned her to a prolonged lifetime, to years of confinement and solitude.

Words spilled from the old empress' lips as she shook her head, trying to chase away so many memories and images, but it was no use because they were deeply rooted and, like tarnished, faded pictures, they taunted her.

To push away those impressions she looked at the flickering fire, then she stared at her old woman's trembling fingers. She no longer wore rings because of her swollen knuckles; she had long since accepted her hands just as they were, covered with wrinkles and lumpy blue veins. Looking at them, however, was not enough to distract her. The memories were stubborn.

She turned to gaze at her companions. Carlota's thoughts transported her to the first time she looked upon the sisters, her first day as empress of Mexico. She puzzled over the circumstances that had brought them into her life to embark on an unlikely journey together. New doubts crept into the old woman's soul: Were the sisters real or were they a creation, an illusion of her imagination? Were they a vision that she conjured in moments of loneliness and need? Yet whenever she looked up, there they were. She saw that they were real, that they now sat by her side just as they had always done.

"¿En qué piensa la emperatriz?"

Lula had roused and interrupted the faraway thoughts of the old empress, who was now weary and saddened from thinking of the past. The fire was nearly extinguished, and Carlota was so cold that her feet hurt more than usual. She was happy to hear Lula's voice to distract her from her pain.

"What am I thinking? I'm thinking of the many people and places that have filled our lives."

"Pero la emperatriz está triste."

"India, why do you say that I'm sad?"

"Because I feel it. Mi Señora, beautiful memories should not sadden anyone."

"But what if they are not beautiful?"

"There should be at least some memories that are beautiful."

The old empress gazed at Lula. "Yes. There should be at least some beautiful memories at the end of one's lifetime."

And then there was stillness. It was the quiet that often overcomes companions who do not need words to understand one another's thoughts. The castle was now wrapped in winter's night. The ancient fortress' echoes faded into the sighing wind. In that profound silence, the old empress and her companions felt the thickness of time and memory wrapping around their thin hunched shoulders like a shroud.

On this night, quiet surrounded them. There was nothing more to be said. Their story was complete. Its every detail was filled in, and silence was the only thing left for those women who had traveled from one world to another, from one century to another, and through it all, kings, queens, emperors, despots and dictators, presidents, even monarchies and governments, had collapsed and perished.

"Come, hermanas, help me to bed. I'm tired and I need to sleep."

The old empress held up her arms in a gesture that was answered by the sisters, just as they had done for years. Once on her feet Empress Carlota linked arms with her companions, and then arm-in-arm the old women slowly made their way toward the darkened bedchamber.

Chapter Forty-Three

The eighty-seven-year-old empress of Mexico passed away at dawn. Her body was carried in full cortege to the place of her birth, where she was buried at the Church of Our Lady of Laeken. The roads and highways between the towns of Meise and Laeken were lined with people who wanted to pay their last respects to the legendary empress. Some of the bystanders were old enough to know who she was. Most were too young to remember, but her legend had drawn them to the site. It is told that her companions, the Chontal sisters, died shortly afterward. No one knows where they passed their last hours, but most people believe that their remains rest in the dense forest that surrounds Castle Bouchout.